PANORAMICA

a novel by
HANK PINE

Panoramica
Copyright © 2021 by Hank Pine

Cover Illustration by Hank Pine.

All rights reserved. No part of this publication may be reproduced, distributed, or transmitted in any form or by any means, including photocopying, recording, or other electronic or mechanical methods, without the prior written permission of the author, except in the case of brief quotations embodied in critical reviews and certain other non-commercial uses permitted by copyright law.

Tellwell Talent
www.tellwell.ca

ISBN
978-0-2288-3874-6 (Paperback)
978-0-2288-3875-3 (eBook)

Special thanks to the beautiful women I have known and loved who together made Nara:

Tuula, Carolyn, Miranda, Tove, Ruby, Jordana, Julie, Galilah, Layla, Katrina, Kimberly, Astrid, Sarah, Autumn, Heidi, Carolina, Rachel, Kara, Lily Fawn, Amy, Mysha, Aubrey, Meghan, Emily, Sarah P, Jodie, Betty-Ann, and my mom.

And to the fellas:

David P. Smith, Ryan Totten, Pops, Anthony Hepburn, Evan Pine, Jason Job, Dave Wanger, Dylan Davis, Shaw Elliott Smith, Paul Woodward, Dean and Gene Ween, Ilijc Albanese, Curt Waller, Jeremy White, Alistair Lornie, J. Carr, Clay George, Johnny Pollard, John Carlin, Rob Bucci, Clayton Dach, Paul Oppers, Jimbo, and my Pops.

Apeirophobia:
A Fear of the Infinite

The wind whips with a whole lotta gusto around my sneakers, causing the shoelaces, frayed and missing their aglets, to smack me in the ankle.

In case you were unaware, aglets are those things at the ends of shoelaces that keep them sheathed.

I shift for a second, with my eyes fixed on the water, far, far below. After another moment of shoe-shuffling, I will fly up into the air and then plummet down like a misguided sausage javelin. Here we go! One, one thousand, two, one thousand, three . . . just long enough to realize the folly of my decision and open my mouth to scream in terror, but not long enough to do anything about it.

And I'm dead. Again.

Okay, Let's rewind that and play it again, this time from below, looking up. There I am, pleasantly plump and poised to plummet. I grew quite wide at the end of my days. I blame the medication and potato chips.

Here I come, like a cannonball wrapped in gray sweatpants and sweatshirt, mouth open, thin hair whirling on my skull. Whoooosh!

Boom.

Rinse, die, repeat. At least I was clean when I died. I was a fetid, sweaty mess in the moments before my passing.

It takes a lot of effort to rewind and start time like this. I was on a roll for a second there, like the perfect amount of drunk to be a darts champion, but I can feel my grasp and aim slipping. Before I metaphorically peg a bar patron in the temple with a dart, let's try one more rewind and view from above the bridge—

From this angle, I can see my feet flailing like they're going to propel me upwards and away, but they don't. I am kicking my way down through the air like a deep-sea diver.

Annnnd, Bam!

Same old, same old: man jumps off bridge, hits the icy water, neck snaps around, dead. This takes focus, like a kind of meditation. And meditation, as the better among us know, can be exhausting. So let's do the easy thing: Let's start time and let it roll, have another drink or twelve, and let the metaphorical darts fall where they may.

At twelve tonight I will jump off the bridge on Interstate 12-A, falling thirty feet into the icy waters below. My neck will snap around at the instant I hit the water, causing my quick demise.

But not yet. For the moment I'm quite content. I'm eating an ice cream cone and sitting at a picnic table near a roadside ice cream stand, one leg crossed over the other. Truly, the picturesque epitome of a contented man. My thoughts are languid and meandering like a big fat fish, slooshing against my big fat forehead with a lazy buoyancy. I'm thinking right now how delightful the afternoon sun looks on the bleached grain of this picnic table. And how remarkable it looks on the sparse leg hair near my exposed lower calf, turning each one to a shimmering gold.

This is rare. As we all know, these moments of calm and fortitude are fleeting at best. In this case, I happen to be lactose intolerant, and very soon the dairy from the ice cream I've ingested will cause an uncomfortable burning and nauseous pain to rip through my big fat intolerant belly. Is that why I jump off the bridge on Interstate 12-A? Is it because of the excruciating and unbearable agony of that one simple ice cream cone? In short, no.

But let's pretend you never asked about my death. Let's pretend you asked me why in the Sam Hell was I eating ice cream in the first place, if I knew that its consumption and beleaguered digestion would only end in pain? And to that perfectly fair and logical enquiry I would say . . . "Because, I like ice cream."

Questions and Answers:

I know a lot of things, now that I am dead and talking to you, things I certainly didn't know while I was alive. For example, I know that those things at the end of shoelaces are called aglets, I also know that I now have chocolate ice cream smeared all over my face, and that on a portly middle-aged gentleman with thinning hair like myself, this must look . . . intense. I apologize. At the time, I rarely gave a second thought to how I looked. Some would say this makes me mentally ill, while I could argue that it makes me healthily unselfconscious—a proud strutter of life's promenade.

Alas, it was the former. I'll mention now that I was most definitely mentally ill. In the eyes of the law, that is. No one knows what I'm going to say or do next, not even me. I shouldn't say no one—you do, because you saw it already, three times. I'm going to jump off a bridge and die.

There was this guy named Carl in my therapy group who claimed he always knew what I was going to do. But he's nuts. In all honesty, I think I'm a whole lot easier to figure out than most people you'll meet in your day-to-day activities. You can usually guess what my reaction will be: fear.

I am afraid of most things. When you are greeted by say, a deranged yellow-toothed clown, or a Volkswagen van, or a moustache, or the nozzle on the end of a gas pump, you could have any one of seventeen reactions, or a muddy combination of several of them. I, on the other hand, greet each of these things in much the same way: with abject and unadulterated terror.

I have a nametag—the sticky-on-one-side kind—stuck to a gray sweatshirt with an airbrushed picture of a wolf on it. The wolf has green eyes. I have green eyes. So if you saw me, you'd see two sets of beady green eyes narrowing in on you. The nametag says "HANK" in big tight letters. I went over it several times very slowly when I wrote it down, so it's extremely—almost aggressively—legible. I had been hoping to avoid any confusion at the meeting, as there was often confusion. I tried to be funny once, a harkening back to my earlier carefree and jovial days. I wrote "Carl." No one thought it was funny though. They thought that I thought that I *was* Carl.

Before finding this roadside ice-cream stand, I had been in a big smelly room with a bunch of other crazy people, trying not to listen to their crazy talk too closely. Whoever thought it would be a good idea for the mentally ill to listen to the conspirational ramblings of other mentally ill people in a confined space, was a few bricks shy of a load. After I left, it was a short yet harrowing walk from the outpatient wing of the hospital to this stand in the blazing sun, and the sweet cold comfort of ice cream.

I wasn't always this way—I used to do things all the time; things a lot more complicated than ordering ice cream, which took a solid twenty minutes to work up the gumption to do. In my final days on the planet, my energy was focused on this one simple goal: trying not to be afraid. Of course, I had help: a clinical cocktail of anti-depressants, anti-anxiety, mood stabilizers, and focus enhancers. All these things gave me a unique tunnel vision that seems even more tunneled now that I am outside looking in.

A word about mental illness: Obviously this is not a sensitive and compassionate discourse on the nature of such things and how best to handle the reality of this steeplechase existence for those that live in it. This is a story of a man with a bunch of anxieties, some relatable, some not; and it is through facing these seemingly unfathomable fears that we hope to garner some understanding of those who hold beliefs we cannot share. A shaky and fleeting form of empathy.

    I can see the chocolate ice cream hardening on my skin like a sugary mask. It is hard to have empathy with a man whose face looks like this, but we can try. I look at the little window where the nice bespectacled girl that gave me the ice cream is seated. She is looking down, and can't be a day over twenty-two. I was twenty-two once. I think we all agree that twenty-two is not a bad place to be, if you had to choose. I was thirty-seven when I jumped off the bridge on Interstate 12-A.

    I wanted to get up and walk over to that window and ask her for a napkin, but I was paralyzed by fear. Not *The* Fear, which we will get to soon enough, just *a* fear. I was afraid that if I got up and walked over there, I would have to walk down a thin path of white-painted gravel, then under a brightly colored umbrella to get to that little window. I was terrified that the umbrella would close as I passed under it and suffocate me.

    Not that I was terribly afraid of dying at the time, I just didn't want to be suffocated by an umbrella. I mean, who would? Maybe you are afraid of umbrellas too, next time you walk past one, you can look up into its spokes and let me know.

    Since I jumped off that bridge and died, I have made a most miraculous discovery. I didn't die. Not really, definitely not in the way that they always told us. What happened was that I sort of oozed out of my body, thinner and thinner, like butter spread on bread. Now imagine a piece of bread the size of the universe. Now multiply that by a really big number. What do you have? Besides a headache you have an infinite number of universes, some touching each other, some not, stretching on and on and on and on and on and . . . you have what I have come to call an Omniverse: the whole tapestry of the multiverses. You have me spread pretty darn thin. An infinitesimal butter layer, so thin as to be almost completely unsatisfying. But not so thin that I can't feel and see and taste and wonder about everything that goes on.

The downside of being a part of everything is that I see everything. I *am* everything. And let me tell you, humans are some nasty creatures. But not the nastiest, not by far. The nastiest, most loathsome creatures, are most definitely the fkfkkfk. And what do the fkfkkfk do that is so completely horrid? Do you really want to know? Trust me you don't. It's awful. No one should have to see that.

Despite being a part of everything that ever is and was I am still very much as I was in life. That is, unbearably and metaphysically lonely. Near as I can tell, I am the only butter layer going. This is hard to explain, but I really thought there would be more of us dead folk, some kind of party where I could see them, or feel them, or talk to them and trade recipes for tapioca pudding. It had been my hope that I would get to hang out with some truly fascinating people once I died, celebrities and revolutionaries, that sort of thing. I kinda do, as I am a part of them now, but it is a rather one-sided conversation.

What I get instead is a vague feeling of the rest of us, kind of like when you are sitting across from someone on the bus, but not really looking at them; in fact, you are taking every precaution you can to *not* look at them, just short of turning around or closing your eyes. While I lived and rode buses, I made sure to give an occasional sweeping glance to my fellow busmates, just to be polite. And that is very much what I do now, I give a broad sweeping glance to every atom that makes up every creature in the Omniverse, but something is most definitely missing.

What is missing is this: communication. Without communication an entity like myself can get very lonely, and it was partly because of my lack of communication skills that I jumped off that bridge. Being certifiably mentally unstable with a whirlwind of rampant, flailing fear tends to make daily conversations awkward. It was loneliness that got me in the end. And then got me again, this time for a whole lot longer than thirty-seven little years. Because . . .

Here I am.

But that's where you come in. If I wanted to, I could go on about the sickening habits of the fkfkkfk, and a whole slew of other atrocities, but I wouldn't do that to you. I see you. And, if you're reading this, you see me too. I mean, you have your faults, don't get me wrong, but from my new perspective I can't help but see them as hilariously beautiful. It's kind of like watching someone pee their pants. You may laugh at first, but at a certain point, your empathy takes over, and you want to help. It would be hard to convince you of your beauty, I know, so I will simply say this. You are nicer, and better looking than a fkfkkfk.

Positive attributes of my current situation: For one, I have access to a great deal of background information, including new words in all languages, of everything there was to be said on that dirt ball that we called Earth.

The next positive attribute is a little harder to explain. Being a devoutly paranoid, almost-schizophrenic hypochondriac during my life, I often had the feeling I was being watched. By people on the street, on the bus, by various governments, aliens, ghosts, demons, stuffed animals, even some plants. Now, for the first time, I feel as if I am watching the world, and the world *isn't* watching me.

And yes, it may seem rather narcissistic to focus on myself when I could be showing you countless other things, but focus is hard. We could take a moment to go watch Saturn's rings spin for a while if you want to do that later. Tell you what, if it ever gets too much, I will take us there. It's very relaxing.

The final attribute to my being a part of everything is that I have a limited and clumsy control over time as well. This we witnessed already, it's hopelessly intertwined in a co-dependent relationship with space, and thus when I flex the space around certain moments, I can alter how I see time, more than when I was alive surely, but not so much as I would like.

A note about past and present tense: This day here is my past, and yet, here we are experiencing it again in all its awkward glory together. To pick just one tense would seem to negate the other, and so we shall do our best to tango flirtatiously with both of them, in an attempt to please both parties, which most likely leaves everyone slightly miffed. It helps that time doesn't really exist the way we often think about it. The past and the present are one, and the future is tickling the back of your neck as you stumble backwards.

All this aside, when you're sitting there under the sweltering afternoon sun with ice cream drying on your face staring at a little window and a big menacing umbrella, time can seem very real. It can drag, it can hang like viscous slug-slime off the underside of a leaf.

Using my limited control of time, I have landed myself on the afternoon of the day I died, a bit before I jumped off that bridge on Interstate 12-A.

The plan goes as follows:

If I can see and live those moments right before I jumped off that bridge, maybe I can figure out just what happened to me, how did I get separated from the dead and left behind as a silent omniscient observer? It won't be particularly easy, what with the mental illness and all, as the more I focus on that one day, the more I get distracted by my lightning-in-a-bottle little mind as it functioned then. One second I'm staring at my leg hairs contentedly, the next I'm terrified of a giant umbrella. In all honesty, I've given this situation a whole lot of thought, and while I have my theories on the how and the why, I can't seem to find a way out of it, so I'm hoping that you'll have some ideas. It's like a choose-your-own-adventure tale, except that (so far) every ending is my horrific bridge-jumping demise. No pressure, it's just eternity after all.

CHAPTER TWO

Fantastic Piggery
and the
Sweet Scratchy Song of the Common Cricket.

Before this fateful day, I was trying to cram as much of myself as I could into breasts. Not just Earth-woman breasts either. No, breasts across the Omniverse have housed me. I have felt the jiggle, the cajoling, and the bounce! It is something to do because I never had breasts. Well, that's not entirely true, I had those saggy titties that come from eating too much dairy and french fries. I was a pig of a thing. Having said that, I feel the necessity to defend the creature known as the pig. Due in part to their appearance and unfortunate deliciousness, the pig got a raw deal on Earth at the hands of humans. Pigs are clever and funny. And while the pigs rule Earth's comedy club, the smartest cookies in the jar are definitely not the humans, and not the dolphins and octopuses—though they run a close second. The undefeated champions are the insects. There are the bees, who use elaborate choreographed dance moves to communicate where the best flowers are; the cunning and resilience of the common cockroach; the spider's web, with its two types of silk; and the superorganism that is a colony of ants. It is with a great deal of pride that I can announce that the planet Earth has some of the most astute bugs going.

In fact, on that very same day that I jumped off the bridge on Interstate 12-A, a large—yet proportionally small—colony of crickets was working on a quick and easy way to save the planet from its inevitable destruction at the hands and feet of humankind. Didn't you ever wonder what those crickets were talking about every night? It's not just sex and movie stars.

Of course, not all crickets are benevolent towards humans. In fact, their close cousin, the grasshopper, can mutate into a creature very similar in destructive power and mindset to humans. Oddly enough, this only happens when there is an overpopulation in one area. Once a grasshopper has a dwindling food supply, and continues to come in contact with other grasshoppers, a tiny chemical spark goes off, and that grasshopper, if it is a female, has larger, darker-colored babies. These babies grow into a creature whose sole function in life is to eat and conquer, and when the food runs out in one area, they form large swarms that block out the sun. I am speaking of course about the locust.

It doesn't take a huge leap in logic to see a parallel between the actions of humankind during this period of time and those of the locust.

Question: What can be done about this seemingly one-way ticket to worldwide desolation?

Answer: A complete rewiring and recalibration of modern society in such a way as to go against our very genetic code.

Follow-up question: How is this accomplished?

Answer: See Chapter Nineteen.

One more question before we careen back to the high drama of Man vs. Ice Cream Cone: Can humans recognize this dastardly part of their genetic code, this spark that makes them act like a locust, this "locust seed," and extinguish it in time to save the planet from their collective swarming and devouring?

Answer: Chapter Nineteen, again. A lot goes on there I guess.

CHAPTER THREE

Acid Rain
and
The High-Heeled Metaphysicist

So here I am, a large part of me lodged in the breasts of a twenty-two-year-old woman named Penny, part of me in my robust chocolate-ice-cream-coated human skin and bones, and part of me crawling along the Astroturf and picnic tables in the form of benevolent crickets. My bag of flesh and neuroses decides to stand. He stares for a moment at Penny in the window, and then at the umbrella, and then turns around and starts to walk away, foregoing any napkin-getting to avoid the umbrella.

What he sees when he turns around is a highway, not the fateful Interstate 12-A, but one with a much more pleasant-sounding name. This one is called the Oceanview Highway, recently renamed from the earlier Interstate 11. So now there is no Interstate 11. Which means that technically, I jumped off a bridge on Interstate 11-A, but let's not get didactic.

And just beyond that highway is a sprawling ocean, shimmering in the bright sun and blue sky, full of little fish, big fat fish, phytoplankton, whales, and yes, sea serpents! But by far the most incredible thing, more so than the whales, was floating up to shore just three miles down the Oceanview Highway. It was a large battered wooden crate—about the dimension of ten breadboxes, adrift in the ocean. Perched nervously inside this soggy crate as it grew increasingly more rollicking near the shore were thirty-three tokay geckos, so named for their distinctive noisy call, which sounds like "To-ka-toka." These geckos were under the tenuous leadership of one large female gecko named Zulaikha, and were from the village of Kudat, near Mt. Kinabalu. The crate had been sitting idle for months during confusion over whose legal responsibility it was to ship hundreds of unwanted staplers back to the US, and during this time Zulaikha had decided it was a good place to avoid the sweltering heat of the midday. Within days the rest of the geckos had joined her, as she was clearly the matriarch. The crate had come to be a source of resentment among the humans involved until finally the day arrived when it, and the other more intact and gecko-less crates, were hastily loaded onto a boat and shipped away. The crate resentment had grown until it was decided that quite simply, fuck it, why should we freight these fucking staplers when we could just dump them overboard. It was noted by a deckhand, Rayyan with the sparkling eyes, that this one crate did not sink like the rest, but he decided not to mention it to anyone. Frustrations were high.

The geckos drifted north for weeks, their numbers dwindling due to having to eat each other. Tokay geckos are normally solitary, nocturnal creatures, yet they all listened when Zulaikha barked her booming orders, because she had charisma. Plus, they were afraid she'd eat them. It was a potent and deadly combination that resulted in the mass exodus of thirty-three, make that thirty-two, geckos from Kudat.

At the moment that Zulaikha is warning a few of the more zealous ones that they were still too far away from the shore to disembark, my body walks up to the edge of the highway and stops. There are no cars on it, and in fact, no other visible humans except for Penny and myself. There are empty cars here and there, but in general this highway appears empty, the ocean appears empty, the entire seaside town, and thus, the entire world, seems empty. I did not know then about the crickets and the geckos. I was of course, petrified of most bugs, but mainly those little gray armadillo-looking ones that curl up, which my mother referred to as "woodbugs."

When I reached the highway, I was again paralyzed by fear. Not of the highway, I mean, really, it's just concrete and yellow paint; what froze me in place now was the darkening clouds on the horizon. Literally. The darkening clouds were rolling and collapsing and coming straight for me. I had lived in and around quiet seaside towns enough in my thirty-seven years to know that the weather could change inside of a minute, and the rains were coming fast.

In those same seaside towns, and more specifically, in the mental hospitals and shared outpatient facilities near those towns, I had watched a revolting amount of television. After card games were disallowed, and the jigsaw puzzles all got mixed together, which they always did, making the patients feel even crazier, television was the only thing going. There was this one TV-news-magazine-report-show I had seen about acid rain. It gave you cancer, acid rain did, and a whole slew of other bad things. Since that show, I had spent a lot of time indoors, nurturing my pluvio-carcinophobia, or cancer-causing rain psychoses. See, in my only slightly informed understanding, acid rain meant that the second a droplet hit you, your flesh would start to melt like ice cream under the hot sun. Before you knew it, you would be scarred for life, which relates to dysmorphobia, or a fear of being deformed. When you're deformed, people would stare at you, and I really hated it when people stared at me, but more on that later.

I looked frantically up and down the highway, then back at Penny, back to the clouds, and then back up and down the highway. I did this several times and was even considering making peace with the umbrella gods, when I finally decided to just run. Didn't you ever wonder why crazy people always wear running shoes? There's a heck of a lot to be afraid of when you're loony, so there is very often a need to run at top speeds. And, while I've seen it done with great proficiency in stiletto heels by an old oriental man who frequents the harbourside, I always opt for a good pair of new sneakers. My current pair was a week old, yet slightly scuffed from avoiding a puppy, and the laces were frayed, poofy, and missing their aglets from my incessant fiddling and retying.

About that Asian old man. I can explain it to you while my body, pumped full of the mighty endorphins fear provides, runs fat and free down the highway. I heard that he was once a professor at the local university. He taught physics, though his focus was in something called metaphysics—a quite different faculty altogether. The story goes that he was fine and coherent to a point, and then his wife killed herself and he had a very hard time processing this particular life event. He started wearing her heels to classes, which the students kept mentioning to the higher ups in a way that seemed largely uncompassionate, so he was asked to not teach there anymore, like a forced vacation. They called it a sabbatical.

I would like very much to find out just what was going on in there, but he died long before I died, and I haven't been able to get to that point in time yet. I keep missing him altogether and ending up inside a woolly mammoth tusk, at which point I forget about the old man entirely.

Question: Where do people go when they die?

Answer: To break it into largely unscientific terms, they get recycled, reused, and reduced into small little bits of matter and energy in our universe. Most people and scientists end up as dark matter, which is a type of matter in space that scientists didn't even think was there until rather recently.

It is my hypothesis, or theory, that the old man died of loneliness kind of like I did; that living without his wife, and then the subsequent closure of the two mental hospitals in this area left no one to take care of him. He wandered and wandered, got dirtier and dirtier, and then gave up and died. I'm not saying it is impossible to survive loneliness. I'm sure you've met a few lonely old survivors. In fact, I'm sure most of the old folk you've met are more on the lonely side than not. What I'm saying is that it can happen. If you're not ready, it can happen. Make some friends. Do all the insufferable things like listen to them talk about their crummy jobs and home renovations and help them move (again), because the alternative is the state I am in right now. It used to be the word alone was spelled *all-one*. As in, to be alone meant you were a part of everything. I am so alone.

So there I was, and here I am, trying to outrun the rain. I still have chocolate ice cream all over my face. I run until my slooshy, jiggly frame can do no more, then I hunch over and sputter, letting loose a high-pitched wheezing noise. After that, I look over my shoulder, see the acid rain hitting the water behind me, gasp a girlish, timorous wheeze, and start running again, as of yet free of acid rain and all it entails.

Pulling back a bit, like we are in a Hollywood crane shot, my fleeing takes on a more heroic tone. That is one determined individual. Everyone looks better from a distance.

CHAPTER FOUR

True Love,
the Twelve-Headed Chicken,
and
Why I Hate to Be Stared at.

It was at this point that I saw a gas station ahead. I have a clearly defined fear of gas stations, not just because Ford Mustangs might be found there, but because I am afraid the gas stored in those huge underground tanks will catch fire while I am standing over them, forming a giant orange fireball that engulfs me and everything in a one-mile radius. I will then be horribly disfigured and people will probably stare at me, and I hate it when people stare at me.

I know that quite often you have the uneasy feeling of being watched, especially if you are as paranoid an individual such as I. It's because you are.

There is a breed of creatures known in some circles as the Suth, who exist on a plane imperceptible to all creatures on Earth. I can see them though, and they look pretty frightening. Basically, what you'd see, if you could, is a convoluted web of matter and space, a warping of reality, all clustered around one orb which houses the eye. These things are not harmful, as they can't really affect our reality in any way, shape, or form, they're just kinda scary looking. They feed off of everything by simply watching.

I can see one now, on the side of the highway just before the gas station next to sandwich board that used to say, "COOL DRINKS," but was altered by an unpopular teen named Terry to now read "COOL D INKS." It sits and waits with its glowing red eye, not doing a heck of a lot.

I did briefly consider truckin' on past the gas station to avoid disfigurement and the horrors of fluorescent lighting, but after taking one more glance behind me, I saw that the rain was in fact hitting the highway, and that within seconds all of my running would be pointless. I hadn't spent the past five years watching the weather channel and covering myself in cellophane under my clothes to throw in the towel now. I didn't cover myself in cellophane anymore—I had heard that the chemical they use to make plastic soft also makes it ooze bad things—but I did it for years, sweating, suffering, making odd squeaking noises when I walked . . . all out of grim determination (which could be an attribute in someone). What it meant for me is constantly having to choose between two or more hellish options with no real way to back down. So, I decided that my years invested in avoiding rain were worth more than my years spent in avoidance of gas stations, and I made a sprint for cover.

Slap! Slap! Slap! Slap! go my sneakered feet on the still-dry pavement, working their way towards a spaceship-looking gas station, or what I thought spaceships looked like before I jumped off a bridge, died, and became part of the Omniverse. It had a large white tubular overhanging, to protect people from (acid) rain, and another large white tube where they sold almost unperishable food items.

Ooch. It's farther away than it looks, and my tiny heart muscle is straining in the effort to pump blood to all that mass. My heart thundered in my chest with the jungle rhythm of a tiny hummingbird in the throes of Tourette's syndrome—which is a mental illness I definitely did not have.

There are times when I could very well speed this up, but that would defeat the point of the exercise, and so, we wait. We wait for my stop/start journey from the side of the road all the way to the door of the gas station and we hope for the best. In the meantime, let's open up the floor to some questions, you can mentally insert your question here . . .

Question:

Answer: I wouldn't worry too much about that, it's all relative. The closeness to the subject matter truly blinds us, looking from wayyyy back you get to see how these things that seem so big are blips of light and bouncing atoms. Bounce bounce.

I'm so informative now that I'm dead. Just don't ask me for love advice. I've never been too good at that, and now, having seen love expressed in so many different ways across the Omniverse, it hasn't helped to solve the mystery. If anything, it's made my understanding much worse. Know these two things though: Love is a survival mechanism, and despite what popular songs on Earth say, you can make anyone you want love you, if you try hard enough.

This was shown quite well by a creature with a hard-to-pronounce name on the faraway moon of Renesgnon, who was quite ingenious in his pursuit of the beautiful Ghlsdfkhuwkdnlk. For years she spurned his many advances, so he sealed her in a clangdooron mine (clangdooron is a moon mineral that tastes really good on what is the Renesgnon version of chicken. The Renesgnon version of chicken has twelve heads). Once he had safely stored her in the deepest bowels of the clangdooron mine, he proceeded to destroy every other living creature on the moon by squeezing a deadly flower. This deadly flower emits a nasty gas, and when this nasty gas hits the limited atmosphere of the moon, the very air catches fire. Within seconds, everyone except for our suitor and his captive had been incinerated. The flower was not rare, it grew everywhere, but the people of Renesgnon knew instinctively not to squeeze it as it let loose a horrific shriek every time anything moved near it.

The rationale of the homicidal young suitor was that with no one and nothing else to love on the entire face of the moon, Ghlsdfkhuwkdnlk would have no choice but to love him, and only him. Well, it didn't quite work out like that, not at first anyway, she would run as far away as she could whenever she saw him. She was still angry about being locked in a mine, understandably. But once she found out what he had done to win her affections, it was hard not to admire his level of commitment. Commitment is a big deal on Renesgnon.

The first and only time I ever experienced love was when my soggy-armpitted, soppy-under-the-tits and ice-cream-laden face burst into that gas station, looking akin to a bloated fish long out of water. Behind the counter was the woman who would change me inside forever. She would look at my madness and fear and say, "You are not alone, I can take away the existential dread choking your heart with nothing more than a kind look." All that, and much more that can't be put into words. But not yet.

At the moment of me blasting into that gas station convenience store, all I noticed was that she had long dark brown hair with bright red streaks of color in it, and was wearing a lot of lipstick. Her skin was the color which used to be referred to by Caucasians as olive, but was more of a tanned-brown hue, due to her diverse and rich mixed heritage. She had full, gorgeous lips—another benefit of exceptional breeding—and a look on her face of barely masked indifference.

Her hair and lips reminded me of a clown, albeit a sexy clown. To no one's surprise, I was horrified and repulsed by clowns—coulrophobia. A lot of humans are, so it's not necessarily a symptom of my rampant hysteria and has more to do with my ninth birthday party at McDonald's, when Ronald McDonald got drunk and "accidentally" punched my friend Duncan in the head. My other thought, besides the clown-fear, was that the fluorescent lights were humming at such a twitch-inducing volume and that she must be a special person, perhaps a robot, not to be driven insane by the noise. With my standard razor-sharp wit, I blurted out as loud as I could, in between wheezy gasps for air, "Do you have a bathroom?"

Unfortunately, as loud as I could was not nearly loud enough for the sound to travel out of my mouth, through the many molecules between me and her ear, through her inner ear, and then her tympani and eardrum. Watching the soundwaves travel as I can now, I see it got as far as the candy bars just before her. She was surrounded by what seemed like a shrine of candy bars and brightly colored crapola. It was like she was some goddess of crapola.

When there was no response from the goddess, I took another breath and said, "Doyouhaveabathroom?" only a little bit louder and more urgent.

The problem being, I had always hated my voice, which came across as a mix of inexplicably foreign, hollow-sounding, and undeniably high and reedy. Similar to fingernails on a chalkboard or two pieces of Styrofoam rubbing together as method of communication. The sound of my own voice was so ghastly and uncomfortable that I would endure the awkwardness of complicated and not-at-all universal hand gestures in order to avoid using it. As a consequence of my laliophobia, I tended to mumble until my words were almost unintelligible, as if I had so little interest in what I was saying that I simply couldn't be bothered to properly pronounce words. On the contrary, as I only spoke when it was absolutely necessary, a desperate urgency was encased in each syllable I managed to choke out.

I use the past tense here because I'm dead and will most likely never have to speak again. So dying is not without perks. Huzzah! When met with my mumbling, most humans, and some dogs, respond in much the same way that this young woman did now.

"What?" she said, looking me up and down with undisguised disgust and mild frustration.

"DOYOUhaveaBATHROOM?" I shrieked, approaching hysterics. There was someone else in the gas station, standing near the Slurpee machine. I could feel him looking at me out of the corner of his eye. I maintained focus on the woman though, as I knew she could help me escape this watchful man.

There are beautifully delicate snowflake-like creatures living on an ice planet much like our Pluto, that excrete an acid that renders their icy environment into a substance much like a Slurpee. They then consume this half-frozen material and absorb what little nutrients the ice planet has to offer, leaving brightly colored fluorescent leftovers. Every few hundred years, the ice planet passes in front of their sun and the rainbow-colored excrement reflects off their delicate greenish-gray snowflake bodies in a truly breathtaking display.

The woman behind the counter stared at me with eyes of a greenish gray, and knowing what I know now, I would say that her eyes are very similar in colour to those achingly beautiful ice bugs. At the time though, I merely wished she would take her piercing ice planet eyes and look at something else. When she did speak to me, she decided to be mildly sarcastic and a little bit funny, as the situation before her seemed somewhat comical.

I was that situation. She found me comical, repugnant, and sad, all at the same time. "The bathroom is for customers. Can I interest you in a Slurpee?" She said this in a gloriously husky voice for someone so young, as if she had the vocal cords of an eighty-year-old who had smoked two packs of the most tar-drenched cigarettes she could find every day for sixty years. In truth, she did not smoke, had never smoked, but enjoyed heartily watching other people smoke. She would go to bars, clubs, patios, all those places that people go to socialize, and sit by herself watching others smoke and dressing them up in animal costumes in her head. Of course, while she sat there, being a stunningd young woman of well-proportioned bosom, many people would come up and attempt to initiate conversation. These attempts would usually die fast in the face of her obvious lack of interest. Her solitary nature had given her a clear reputation as a cold-hearted bitch, which was very, very, far from the truth. For her own part, she made no efforts to dispel this illusion, and actually enjoyed the feeling of strength and free time it provided her.

Moments before any customers had come into the gas station, she had been exploring the notion—in a pragmatic and almost scientific manner—of whether it was possible to actually die of boredom. What would that look like, feel like? She pictured cobwebs forming around her body as she stood at her till, slack-jawed and gazing forward. It was not a calming thought.

Her ulterior motive in mentioning the Slurpees—which she did without even glancing over in the direction of the whirling machines—was to draw attention to the man standing beside them, as he definitely had an odd air about him. He wasn't buying anything, which is unusual in a place of merchandise. I replied to this very subtle attempt at camaraderie and support regarding this man with one of my favored responses: a blank look.

She sighed and reached beside her for the bathroom key. It was attached to a cumbersome metal disc the size of a Frisbee. She made a small grunting noise as she moved the key from its position under the countertop. The small and—I can admit now—definitely sexy grunt noise was a result of the weight of the metal disc attached to the key. It was deceptively heavy, about the weight of a small human child, and on it the word "MEN" was etched into the metal. The disc was standard issue at all the gas stations this company owned, the idea being it was so unquestionably awkward that no one would lose it or bother to steal it. What the company people didn't consider was the laziness of their customers. The tiny key and the large metal disc were constantly being left behind in the bathroom, as the thing was too damned heavy to lug all the way back to the counter. Keys were required because crazy people did crazy things in gas station bathrooms. The gas station attendant was supposed to carefully examine each person, then decide upon their eligibility before dragging the key out. Either I passed the screening process, or she just didn't care. Knowing what I know now, with a part of me in her head at that moment, and spread throughout the cells of her body, I know the truth: She didn't care.

Grabbing the key in my sweaty palms, I mumble a vague response at her. In return, she gave me a slight, forced smile. Despite the forcedness, the left half of her generous lips showed something far more enchanting and beguiling than ordinary good manners. The left side was smiling for real. It was as if we shared some private joke, her and I. This corner of her mouth rose up, the corresponding eye squinting slightly, as if she was suddenly overcome with pride at the sight of me clutching that washroom key so desperately.

What she was actually thinking was, *This guy is going to shit his pants*. The thought of that gave her a wry smile, as most humans that wear pants can relate to the dire situations impending bowel movements can create. So it was indeed an understanding smile, one that congenially acknowledged the potential debasement.

I opened my mouth as if to speak when I saw the smile, knowing that I wasn't going to, and then quickly shut it again when I noticed that the watchful man near the Slurpee machine was now most definitely staring at me. Not just glancing, this man had both of his eyes fixed on me, with the rest of his slender body turned slightly away. There was no love, pride, or understanding in those eyes.

You will learn a whole lot more about this slender man soon enough, but for now I will tell you that he wore a jean jacket, dirty

pastel blue t-shirt, and was exactly twenty years and fifty-seven days old. His parents were from the Philippines, so he had skin of a rich brown color and hair that was shiny black. He was nervous, but trying to act like he wasn't. He had to urinate, but he wasn't going to. His name: Isadore Valencia.
I turned away hurriedly and could feel a chill on my back. In the reflection of the glass door I saw that he was still staring, and with great intent. It startled me so badly that I had trouble opening the door, fumbling for an excruciating five seconds before realizing that I had to push it open before I could shove my body through.

I will tell you part of how I acquired my opthalmophobia and scoptophobia—a fear of being stared at. It is partly because of how I was received by these two people. One with mild disgust, and one with hate; two emotional states I encountered often, being the unsettling person that I was. But the largest part of it is the eyes themselves. The eye, while supposedly capable of portraying fear, hate, revulsion, and many more complicated emotions, actually does nothing of the sort. They just sit there, eyes do, like two glass orbs sliding around in a nest of flesh. It is in fact the skin and muscles around the eye that portray these feelings. If you really think about it, the eyes just stare and stare and stare. I remember when this horrifying realization first dawned on me, which I can tell you while we watch myself waddle out the glass door and towards the bathroom around the corner . . .

It was one sunny day, but far from the vitamin-rich rays of sunshine, inside a small stuffy room under fluorescent lights, deep in the bowels of a bank, there were clean white walls up tight either side of me, some aggressively nondescript bland pastel art, and a tidy young man seated at a big brown desk.

The desk was bare and clean, the young man's skin was bare and clean. He spoke with a voice as devoid of emotion as he could manage. I was a young man myself at the time, and not yet riddled by my cornucopia of fears which grew like vines of ivy throughout every facet of my life over a relatively short period of time.

    I was in that bank trying to get a loan, because I was going to use the money to buy a great deal of sheet metal and tinfoil to cover everything I owned, but I didn't tell them that. I told them that I needed twenty-thousand dollars to go to school. I hadn't even bothered to think of what school I was supposedly attending as I was in such a hurry to purchase all that metal and tinfoil, get home, and cover every inch of my domicile. I was well on my way to my present state of "paranoia" and "irrational behaviour." I sat there with my hands carefully under my ass cheeks to prevent any revealing flailing, not entirely convinced that I was in the company of a flesh and blood human, as the young man before me seemed more like a money-guarding robot.

    And just as we would all like to believe, there actually is a solar system of all robots, living in harmony. They don't really look human, and, being machines, lack genitals. Having no means of reproduction, just extensive repairs, there simply are no new robots, which makes for a very boring, stagnant solar system all in all. Each one was only programmed with so many songs, dances, or speeches, and after countless centuries, it is no wonder that they get bored easily. And every time one of them gets bored enough to disconnect, or off themselves, they simply reboot the unit and start again. I mention it now to save you the trouble of ever visiting there, I wouldn't recommend it. However, keep these hapless robots stored somewhere in your memory banks, because something quite extraordinary occurs to them later today.

    The young man moved in a way that seemed predetermined. It was as if the two of us were performing a simple one-act play, and I guess in many ways we were. I was pretending to be an eager student, and he was pretending to be my congenial host or friend, who just happened to have thousands of dollars lying around that he wasn't using. The most troubling part of the entire performance was that this eager, young and wealthy robotic friend of mine insisted on direct eye contact from the moment I walked into the room all the way until that relief-filled moment when I left. The bank people had programmed him that way: To maintain eye contact, even when rearranging the pen on his desk so that its point faced neither me, nor him, but lay sideways, neutral. I wanted to look at the pen when he did that. I could see him move it out of the corner of my eye, but I dared not look away.

As I sat ensnared by his pale blue robot eyes, I came to the startling and maddening realization they were just hovering orbs, little planets of no emotion, in a sea of curling flesh. His face all but disappeared, leaving me with only those cold cold eyes, that stared, and stared, and stared, and stared. Under those searing alien orbs, I had to fight from crying out, sweat streaming unchecked down the middle of my back. I was afraid to blink; tears welled up and started to fall from my eyes in a mix of utter panic and fatigue. Instead, I just stared at those horrific glass balls and let out a myriad of small whimpering noises.

I didn't get the loan. My dream of coating my smelly apartment in sheet metal and tinfoil would have to wait another couple of years until completion.

It was similarly cold, unfeeling orbs I saw housed in that slender man in the gas station. Within seconds of our eye contact his face had dropped away and I had been left with tiny brown glass planets. If you ever want to feel crazy, look into the eyes of someone you love and hold dear, and really look at those creepy orbs, watch the face fall away and the grotesque reality set in. Conversely, you can just take my word for it and stay in love until you are both old and even more wrinkled.

CHAPTER FIVE

Philip's Beaver Problem,
and
The Hell from the Bathroom.

The washroom was on the far side of the gas station, meaning that I had to press my body against the side of the building and inch slowly along so as to avoid any of the now-drizzling acid rain. It was a nerve-racking experience, as I knew that at any moment a gust of wind could propel the toxic droplets at me. When I finally arrived at the door I saw that it was inexplicably filthy.

I can explain it now of course. Philip Coover, the septic tank man, had a very unfortunate incident with his hose two days earlier. Philip has been cleaning septic tanks for seventeen years with very little incident, and was so mortified by the explosion of the hose and the shitstorm that followed that he'd sped away from the gas station without ever mentioning what had occurred to anyone, or stopping to clean it up.

And what happened to that hose was the fault of one very unusual beaver. You see, Philip lived in a trailer park about two miles out of town, a nice spot, complete with Astroturf and patio lanterns. Beside it was a sparse collection of stunted trees with a little creek flowing between them, and living in and around that creek was one very lonely beaver.

Most of the beavers in Philip's part of the world had been killed because of their soft, water-repellent fur. Apparently, the fur looks great as a hat. People liked this fur so much that they killed and killed, and then sent boats, and built towns, so that they could kill some more. These towns became cities, and Canada was born! Which is partly why I never felt I belonged or related to being a Canadian. I think those beaver hats look goofy, not to mention horrifying. This fear is called doraphobia, and yes it has been noted in psych-wards often enough to warrant a name for it. Although, I think beavers look sort of goofy too, like big hamsters with tails that have been run over by a dump truck.

This particular giant hamster with a flattened tail thought the hose on Philip's septic tank would make a fine addition to his new house. Beavers build amazing dome-shaped houses with underwater entrances and cozy sleeping quarters, and this beaver was no different. Due to his paranoiac nature, his dome was surrounded on all sides by thick thorn bushes, and the hose was going to be used as an extra security device by placing it over the underwater entrance to trip up anything that came through the hole. Of course, it was highly unlikely that something would, as this was why beavers built their houses that way in the first place: nearly impenetrable security. But this was a very nervous beaver. So much so that when Philip came out of his trailer that night to stare forlorn at the stars, the beaver gave up a quarter of the way through his hose mission and scuttled as fast as he could back to the creek. He was so scared that he crapped inside his dome that night, too afraid to leave.

But it was not beaver poopies on that gas station door, it was the far more caustic collection of human feces and corrosive disinfectant, something most humans—myself included—are very reluctant to touch. I just stood in front of the shitty door, thinking. Then, despite my better judgement, I leaned forward and sniffed the door: It smelled awful. I usually carried moist towelettes in a fanny pack wherever I went, to wipe my hands and face every time I touched anything potentially hazardous. As bad luck would have it, there'd been an unfortunate incident with a squirrel yesterday, and my supply had run out.

Without my towelettes, I was reduced to using my gray sweatshirt sleeve to ease open the utterly disgusting door and deftly slip inside, like a ninja but with wild, terrified eyes revealing his apprehension.

Unfortunately, I sealed myself in before I remembered to locate and use the light switch. The weight of the heavy door slammed shut, and I was left with only the small crack of light which came from under the door. It was then that the smell hit me: The distinct potpourri of urinal cakes and fecal matter, combined with what could only be curried vomit. I inhaled deeply, letting the smell waft up my nostrils, even though I didn't really want to.

Potpourri is a blend of dried flowers used to scent a room, to make it smell like dried flowers. Popular with old ladies, it is said to disguise the clinging scent of mortality, but of course it has the opposite effect, as nothing smells more like death than dead flowers.

Urinal cakes are scented discs used to mask the potpourri of piss that collects in the trough at the bottom of a urinal. The cake part of the name has long haunted me in mid-stream, as I couldn't help but look down at the little blue discs and imagine scooping one out of the trough and lifting it up to my lips to take a hearty bite of its acidic, soapy essence, which always made me gag.

I didn't use urinals in my last few years, as it was inconceivable that I was going to stand in the most vulnerable of vulnerable positions, where anyone or anything could sneak up behind me and do whatever horrible thing they pleased. The very idea of urinals is an elaborate trust game, and for trust games to work, there has to be some measurable level of trust. I had envisioned in my head how I would respond, spinning around and spraying my assailant in the eyes with hot urine, then a few quick kicks to his or her groin area, but the scenario was never satisfactory. As a result, the few times I had attempted to use one, I was constantly spinning my head over my shoulder, spittling pee this way and that.

I realized then that I didn't even have to use the bathroom, that it had all been my clever ploy to mask my hiding from the rain. And now that I was sealed there, in the dark, my deception had come back to haunt me tenfold. There was of course a moment of panic. By now it shouldn't surprise you that I am afraid of the dark. Most human children are afraid of the dark. Me, I was deathly afraid that if something crawled out of the toilet, I wouldn't be able to see it. Or that I would stumble in the blackness, slip on the scuzzy floor and hit my head, falling into a pool of bacteria under the sink. There were a million and one horrors that could befall me in the dark, as opposed to the simple million that could happen during the light of day.

I am not a big fan of bacteria (bacteriophobia, coupled with a widespread bacillophobia, or fear of microbes). Rather, I didn't used to be. Having had my very essence saddled up right next to them, I can see that they're not so bad. There was/is a particular culture of bacteria under that scuzzy gas station sink commonly known as the water bear bacteria. Aside from dancing a mean flagellate jig, the water bear bacteria can be frozen, shipped out into space with zero oxygen, thawed out, and still dance with equal fervor. And this is how some people (namely NASA), get their kicks, torturing water bear bacteria! They are undeniably adorable when you see them close up; they look like teddy bears.

I may have this fond attachment to bacteria now, but at the time of my being trapped in the dark in a gas station bathroom straight from the lower pits of Hell, touching anything would be enough for me to spend the next four days scrubbing my blotchy skin raw. This was also part of my blennophobia: fear of slime.

So I fumbled around on the wall with my fingers safely curled inside the folds of my sweatshirt. As I neared the wall's surface my nostrils were coated with the sickly smell, and once again I had the compulsion to sniff deeply. I gagged slightly, which was enough to derail my attempts to find the light switch, forcing me to turn my focus towards locating the door handle. I groped and slid my hands around, all the while making small whimpering noises, until finally, success! Unfortunately, with my hands tucked in my sleeves, I had no traction to hold on to the slippery knob, and it was gone. It was at this point that the toilet let loose an ominous gurgling noise. I leapt away from the noise, pinning myself against the slimy wall behind me.

I can tell you now that the gurgling noise was in fact caused by Mrs. Emilia Knudson, who was busy watering her lawn two blocks away, even though rain was moments away from drenching both her and her most precious nasturtiums.

Mrs. Emilia Knudson had very bad posture. So bad that as she was hunched over watering her flowerbed, she had no idea there were thick, black, acid-rain-spewing clouds forming just behind her. The neighbors, had they looked out the window and seen her, would have thought she was off her rocker, which is the kind of crazy you get from being too old. The snails in her flowerbed already thought she was off her rocker, they'd just had a long, slow talk earlier that morning about how most humans seemed like homicidal irrational baby snails. The snails and the nasturtiums got along quite well though, as snails don't like to eat nasturtiums, which suits the little flowers just fine. So, Mrs. Knudson happily watered, humming absently an old song that her husband Earl used to sing. She was hunched over, and tone deaf, but not yet completely off her rocker.

At the time, I didn't consider a complication with water pressure as the source of the gurgling noise from the toilet. In my state of panic, with only my assaulted nose to guide me, all I could picture was a giant, obscenely toothed serpent working its way up the pipe, and then leering over the edge of the bowl. My therapist says this is a new fear for the annals of science, and he calls it herpe-bogy-rhypophobia, or fear of boogey-snake-shit-demons. As this was a fear I'd nurtured since childbirth, I had for many years taken to placing both feet on the toilet seat and squatting over the bowl when I needed to defecate. This way I could see if anything wicked and wrong was coming up the pipe. It had other advantages as well, which I would use as an excuse if anyone ever caught me doing it. The first and most obvious reason could be hygiene, especially in public bathrooms. The next is the fact that the human body shits best in a squatting position, with gravity and all the muscles working together. The final, and less obvious excuse was that I was making sure that my stool was the right color and consistency; that I was monitoring my diet very, very closely. All this bathroom anxiety, and the prescribed drugs coursing through me generally made me very constipated. My body had also just released another fresh supply of fear-induced endorphins into my blood, so any bodily functions that were not immediately mandatory were cleverly curtailed.

 So, defecation was the last thing on my mind, even though I was in a room of defecation and not much else. All I wanted now was to find the door handle, open the door, and get the hell out. I had already given up on my usual ritual, which was washing my hands, then my face, then my hands again. The chocolate ice cream was mostly dissolved anyway, having been sweated off. For the second time my sleeved hands locked onto either side of the smooth doorknob. Using great pressure and twisting my entire body, I slowly pulled it open towards me.

 Unfortunately, my misplaced foot stopped this blessed offering of light and clean air, yanking the door from my tenuous grip and sending it slamming shut in front of me. Most male North Americans of my age group would curse aloud when something like that happened. Me, I let out a small, squeaky scream of sudden panic as the toilet made another small bubbling sound.

Glurp! Glop!

There is nothing to fear in the face of knowledge; it was not a shit demon, it was Mrs. Knudson's nasturtiums that caused that sound. It is ignorance that breeds terror. Unless of course, the truth is far more terrifying than anything you could ever imagine in your most paranoid fantasies.

Heavy hangs the hapless head that holds hundreds of horrors, he (meaning me) harangued.

CHAPTER SIX

Guns are Fun
or
Set a Course for the Sun.

I don't mean that chapter title. Maybe fun isn't the right word. I don't even know anymore. I mean, as long as you have what you think is a good reason. Nature is full of murder and taking what you need when you want it. So I guess that answers the question of what happens to your morality and spirituality once you become part of everything. In short, not a whole bunch. Sorry.

Guns are exciting, this is true. Thrilling, dramatic, and loaded with terrible potential.

Let's take a break from me and my procrastinated ablutions, my phony potty emergency. Right about now you're probably wondering what's going on in the other parts of that gas station, and rightly so, as this is where the exciting part of the story happens. Here comes the high drama, the hallowed Hollywood moment is nigh.

Just outside that grim bathroom door the rain has abruptly ceased, it's common in that seaside town for a torrential downpour to whorl in, and then be buffeted away moments later. The sun is working its way out from behind the clouds, hitting the gasoline-soaked ground around the gas station and glancing off in shimmering pools of rainbows. It's a magical moment pregnant with burgeoning wonder.

And suddenly, *BAM!* those shimmering kaleidoscope patterns of rainbows became flying rainbow splatters as hundreds of crickets hop and chirp their way across the gas station parking lot and into the underbrush on the other side. They're not swarming like locusts or humans, more like your typical brownish field crickets, with an occasional mole cricket in there too.

The reason for the mass movement was a meeting down the road, just past the ice cream stand and its menacing umbrellas, in a huge open gravel pit. There, the United Cricket and Insect Coalition to Protect the Planet was having its first-ever meeting. Any cricket or creature that could understand cricket-speak and could make it within their life span had to attend. What was being discussed amidst the chirps and sweetly strange and scratching sounds was how best to deal with the Biped Menace, which is the technical cricket name for humans. The group of crickets that was at this moment coating the gas station in writhing masses was from very far away. These North Carolina crickets wanted a peaceful approach to the problem, they wanted to bury all the humans deep underground.

They moved exceptionally fast for their numbers, keeping tight ranks by listening to their platoon leader's instructions with the hearing equipment located in their knees, while the mothers kept tabs on their youngsters with long, sweeping strokes of their whiplash antennae. The meeting wasn't until tomorrow, but punctuality was of the essence, so when a few got caught in the oily rainbow deathtrap, they had to be left behind. The entire crossing took just over forty-five seconds, without a single Biped Menace noticing their existence. Isn't that exciting? I think so. But the high drama excitement I was referring to earlier was happening *inside* the gas station.

The young watchful man wearing the jean jacket—Isadore Valencia—had his nervous, twitchy hands on the trigger of .22 Magnum.

Guns.

Guns instill in every modern story an inescapable drama and existential peril. No longer is this the story of a big hypochondriac dingus in a quiet seaside town. Nope, now it is the tale of a desperate man, thigh-deep in some fuzzy moral territory, never knowing which second will be the last, and exploding with lust and hate from every pore. All that and some fancy shootin' too!

The strange thing about guns was this simple fact: They were very, very, common. Police officers had them, hunters had them, homeowners had them, park rangers, gun collectors, even Isadore had one.

This particular gun had been his unmarried uncle's. That's what unmarried uncles were always good for, owning odd things like collections of classic pornography, mugs with dirty sayings on them, and guns. His uncle didn't know Isadore had the gun, because he took it one night when his uncle was out watching a movie.

Isadore is now strolling up to the candy shrine that surrounds the beautiful and disenfranchised young woman. He is pretending to look at the chocolate bars, just like he was pretending to look at the Slurpee machine. He doesn't actually want to buy anything, he wants to pull out his gun, point it at her, and tell her to give him all the money in the cash register plus whatever is kept in the back. And now, living in his head and his bowels, I see that Isadore is a very simple, yet very mixed-up and hopelessly complicated young man, like IKEA instructions personified. He really thinks that by doing this, all his problems will be solved. He is not simple in the stupid way, he is quite brilliant when it comes to mathematics. Alas, Isadore learned that robbing gas stations was a quick and easy way to make some fast cash by watching a whole lot of cable television. Just like I learned about the acid rain. How informative TV can be! But in truth, lazy television programming was not entirely to blame. Isadore had fallen prey to the second-best form of entertainment going in North America: joining a cult.

The cult called themselves the Children of the Second Sun, and they desperately needed Sister Isadore to get them some money. All sorts of humans needed money around this moment in space and time, and would do all sorts of things to get it, but the gas station had been Isadore's idea, as he had to stop anyway to get gas for his Volkswagen van. The Children needed to buy a whole lot of expensive equipment, as well as pay some even more expensive scientists, and then there was all the dynamite! This cult, of which Isadore had recently been inducted in part due to his math skills, had but one purpose: to build a rocket, fill it with explosives, climb aboard, and then fly it straight into the center of the sun.

The cult leader's name was Ryan Totten. He made the girls swoon, the guys swell, and was outwardly benevolent with the children. He had blue eyes with a ring of orange near the pupil, and could hold anyone's gaze for as long as he desired. Other stats: thirty-four years old; five foot six; short, cropped hair with elaborately crafted sideburns. Despite all these obvious markings, he had not always wanted to be a cult leader. It was something he'd stumbled into after a particularly debaucherous weekend. I was there that sinful weekend, and part of me still is, hiding out in a pair of false eyelashes, lingering in the smoky air, and bobbing in the beverage that Totten pours into his gullet.

It may surprise you that I am also a part of false eyelashes. Though I prefer not to think about it too often, I am in the abundant supply of plastics and synthetic chemical compounds on the planet Earth as much as I am the gecko lizards of the world. And let me tell you, it really is a mess in there. Plastic, like a great many things we know and love, was an accident that might be better undone. Staring at the mountains of plastic trash piled high and filling the seas in lifeless islands, I am filled with the same feeling I got when I was mid-air during my descent from the bridge, the feeling being a sphincter-tightening. "Whoopsie!"

Ryan Totten, soon-to-be-cult leader, was seated in the corner booth of a greasy diner at seven o'clock in the morning, having been up all night ingesting drugs. It was about five past seven in the morning when, looking for a way to amuse himself, Ryan Totten suddenly started addressing those gathered in a loud, clear voice. It boomed, it echoed, it reverberated. He soon found that he rather liked the sound of this, and even more pleasing was the fact that everyone seated at that table, and the waitress, suddenly turned and looked, listening attentively to every word he uttered. So he started preaching. All manner of things at first, but taking careful attention to enunciate each diminutive nuance of every particular word. And, when he raised his fist high up in front of them, the people at the table could feel their will surrendering to his. Those hung-over club-kids became Totten's first followers. Their response to his resonating speech was so genuine and amusing, that he soon found he could not stop himself, even if he tried, from unleashing more and more ridiculous claims. One of these was that there were coded instructions on all the cereal boxes of the world, instructions on how to build a rocket. Which is something I suspected for a long time, but I was crazy for a long time.

Totten wasn't crazy—he didn't believe a word of it. The thing is, if you repeat your own bullshit often enough, you will eventually start to accept it as a viable narrative. His new, clear voice said to those people:

"I know these things, I know the truth. I am telling you now, as someone who has cracked open the universe and pissed through the hole, TRUST IN ME."

And they did!

Question: What does this say about the human condition?

Answer: We want to believe.

The only way I know about his whopper of deceit, his full-tilt carnival of lies lies lies, is because I've been a piece of dandruff on his scalp, a couple of pieces actually, I was sliding across the surface of his face as waves of refracted light, and snapping back and forth in the axons, dendrites and synapses in his head.

Being in someone's head is a whole lot like riding a lightning storm. It's exhilarating at first, but exhausting, and before long you wish you could just pull out and do something else. Alas, I can never fully pull out, but I can try to ignore it. It's as if I had a quadrillion mosquito bites on every part of my body. That sounds bad. It's not as bad as I make it sound, it's oh so much worse, and better at the same time. I mean, it's everything isn't it? *Bbbphhhffftttbrapbbbuhbuybibblebubyawwabbb!* If you ever want to express what it's like to know everything and nothing, and you're trapped in a human body, try that. Take your index finger and move it up and down very fast over your upper and lower lips while making an "ooh" sound.

Totten was not a con artist exactly, though he demanded very large monetary donations to keep himself in a constant drug-fueled state in order to feed the rampant hallucinations that were at the root of his "religion." He was careful that the visions fluctuate from grandiose and beautiful, to horrible and terrifying. He called these his "orders," though he never clearly said just who was giving them. And while he may have been high as a kite on every element that mankind has discovered and slapped together to inebriate, his formula to keep his subjects in line relied on the five classic S's of cult formation and maintenance. These were: Sleep deprivation; Starvation; Separation from family and friends; Sex rituals; and finally, Soothing, hypnotic music.

From the beginning he had told everyone that once they had built the rocket, and hopped aboard, leaving their lousy jobs and pointless lives behind, they would hit the sun and make it explode in this great big way with their great big bomb. The explosion was supposed to be like nothing anybody had ever seen, one with mushroom clouds shooting off in every direction; it would rip a hole in the space-time continuum, as they called it, tearing their souls from their bodies and setting them free in the cosmos, making them a part of everything.

A mushroom cloud is a big cloud of gas and smoke and dirt that occurs over a very large explosion. It is called that because it looks like a mushroom. The first human not in the army to use that expression for a big, nasty explosion, was Tom Street of Spring Mountain, on July 17th, 1944, in what came to be known as the Port Chicago Explosion. It occurred when the army boys of America bombed their own country with what was called the first atom bomb. In actuality, every ordinary TNT-type bomb involves atomic reactions, so what we are witnessing is really one of the first nuclear bombs.

So, Isadore was holding up this gas station because he wanted to be a part of everything, and in the process, he ended up indirectly making me a part of everything instead.

The fact that their plan could never work was of little importance to Ryan Totten. He knew that the craft would burn up long before it ever reached the sun, and more importantly, he knew that a bunch of horny, hungry, sleep-deprived, cereal-box-watching deadbeats could never find the materials to build a rocket, let alone launch it into space. Does that make him evil, leading these people on?

Question: Does evil exist? Or is it just broken humans reacting hopelessly to their brokenness?

Answer: See Chapter Nineteen, again. It's not like that's only part where things happen, but a lot happens.

When I need to add spice to my new confusing existence, I pretend I am something like that epitome of evil, the Devil; a fallen angel, or second-hand-man gone awry, where I have absolutely no cares, no knowledge of the master plan, just a big wide playground to run around and cause havoc in. I know I am deluding myself, in my present state my havoc-causing abilities are pretty limited. The best I can do in most cases is watch havoc happen.

Right now, besides remembering watching the atomic, I mean, nuclear bomb go off, I am watching Isadore pull a gun from under his jacket and point it at the face of that girl behind the counter whom I would love to call my own. She looks up at him, and her beautiful green-gray eyes grow wide. Her full, gorgeous lips part in an expression of surprise. He pauses for a minute, and despite the inappropriateness of the situation, he feels his penis start to swell.

A penis. Well, a penis is a penis. The name of penis-fear, which I have a mild case of, is ithyphallophobia—something for your Scrabble game. The penis is in fact alien in origin. We inherited it from the furry snake people, the Ezzzz folk. They came here a for a while and had some orgies in the ocean, that mixed their ugly DNA with the primordial soup that made all the creatures of the earth. Alas, the Ezzzz folk die very easily. Their blood slows down each time they orgasm, and they orgasm each time they open their mouths. It is a wonder they made it here at all, really. There were a lot of tight lips on that phallic spaceship.

Following the rules of good cult leading, Totten made very sure that he was the only one that ever experienced a full, messy orgasm. He would bring his followers to the edge of eruption with a variety of rituals and devices and then stop before they could release. His most frequent method was to have one of the followers dressed up completely in bubble wrap lick the anus of the one he was trying to brainwash.

Bubble wrap is another form of packing material, different than Styrofoam in that it is made up of tiny air-filled sacs. The bubbles come in a variety of sizes. It is great fun to pop those little bubbles, especially the big ones, and especially if you are sexually frustrated.

Totten told his followers that if they popped so much as one bubble, he would ensure they never had their anus licked again, and then they would be whipped with noodles soaked in hydrochloric acid. So when Isadore got that unsettling and unwanted erection, it was because he hadn't had an orgasm in one year and thirty-seven days, and thus, was constantly riled up. He was so sexually frustrated his hands shook. Which was what Totten wanted, he wanted Isadore loopy enough to perform whatever bizarre act he could dream up. Little did he know, Isadore was horny enough to hold up a gas station.

Pointing that gun at the Goddess of Snacks, and feeling the horniness swell up in him, Isadore was suddenly at a loss for words. He had the hormone-riddled notion of asking the girl to go watch a movie with him, but knew that he had most likely ruined that plan. Guns have a way of ruining a lot of plans. His second thought was that now he had the gun, he could order her to come to a movie with him. He thought this over for a second or two, and then his brainwashing hit him. He heard Totten's voice in his head saying, "Two Iguanas. Too Maracas. Two Chewbaccas," words Totten had made him recite over and over as he had his anus licked by someone in bubble wrap. They made no sense, not to Isadore, though he pretended they did, and certainly not to Totten, who didn't remember uttering them let alone making Isadore repeat them thousands of times in a row. Totten had just taken three doses of a designer chemical compound whose name was comprised of many, many letters. Its awkward street name was M-X-Y-D-N-L-S-P-D-C-A-B.

Isadore had spent so long staring at her, the barrel of a gun pointed at her face, without saying a word besides the odd stammering, that she went from being startled, to panicked, to mildly irritated. Every time Isadore looked like he was about to say something, she'd lean forward to hear it, then lean back when he continued to be all loosey-goosey and just vibrate the end of the gun at her with his horny hands. Finally, she could take it no more.

"What?" she said, with a slight air of exasperation.

CHAPTER SEVEN

Soggy Sweatpants
and
Love at Gunpoint

She had already reached under the counter and hit the alarm button. Within seconds the police would come and shoot Isadore to death. At least, that's what she thought. Alas, no one had ever bothered to test the button. It had been installed long ago and was older than some of the Twinkies (a Twinkie is a packaged pastry that never goes bad; it is a miracle and polyp of modern science; people have been making pastries for centuries, but nothing like these).

So when she pressed that button, nothing happened. She gave three good pushes, and then just stared back at Isadore, knowing that this sketchy, horny young man had her life in his hands. Looking into his wide brown eyes, she knew she should feel panic, but thought she could see by looking in Isadore's eyes that he wasn't going to kill her purposefully. It was a concern that Isadore could very easily shoot her accidentally. Guns are always going off in unfortunate ways. Of course, his eyes were just small, unfeeling glass balls, so it was more the creasing of the flesh around his eyes that gave her this reassurance.

Isadore finally managed to choke out the word "Money," in a flighty, nervous voice.

She sighed lightly and hit the "no sale" button on the cash register to her right. She had decided to make this moment last by taking each bill out of the register one at a time, in an effort to cherish the excitement of being held up. This was definitely the most exciting thing to ever happen to her while at the gas station. Had she seen Philip the septic tank guy's shit storm, it might have been a close second.

Isadore was busy staring out the doors, where his Volkswagen van was still running, so he didn't see how slowly she was counting out the money. When he finally did look back at her, he grew angry. Showy angry. He shifted his grip on the handle of the gun and said, "Faster!"

He was starting to get the hang of being an armed robber, and was mentally congratulating himself on this when I burst in the door holding the washroom key and that big metal disc in both hands. Had I any heroic blood or bones in me, I most likely would have hurled that metal disc at Isadore's head or arm, then dashed up and beat him silly. Instead, I stood there and pissed my pants.

There was a big moment then, when my goddess stopped counting the money and just stared. Isadore turned and pointed the gun at me as a big wet patch formed on my gray jogging pants. Everyone was silent until you could hear was the sound of piss dribbling off my shoe and onto the floor over the buzzing of the fluorescent lights.

The silence was only broken when the most beautiful girl in the world let out a sudden, short and raucous outburst. "Ha!" It was a very infectious laugh. Had I not been the object of that laughter, I most likely would have joined her. She tried to shake it off, but looking down and away from both of us just amplified the image in her head of me holding the disk and the wet spot forming on my pants.

I didn't piss my pants because I was afraid. I had been far more terrified in the dark pits of that bathroom than I was now. It was just that they were both staring at me, and at that moment I looked at the girl, and didn't see just a pair of empty glass balls looking back.

I am now surrounding the air around her, and let me tell you, it's glorious. The afternoon sunlight was suddenly coming through a window behind her, and there she was, standing bravely in front of a loaded gun, the candy shrine, shimmering sage eyes, streaked hair glinting like smoldering flames, and those full, pouty lips! I felt as if I was staring into a star from two feet away. Like my whole life had been a dream until that moment. Like I was strapped to a meteor hurtling into a black hole.

About black holes. There are actually only a few in our entire universe. I know, you probably thought there were hundreds upon thousands of them, but no, just a few. A strange thing happens to me when my parts touch them. They slow . . . right . . . down. It's very uncomfortable, so I generally do as much as I can to ooze around them. I tried once to squeeze into one, but it felt like I was holding my hand on the end of a vacuum and slowly turning up the suck—very uncomfortable.

As opposed to exploding into fits of laughter at the sight of me, Isadore panicked. This was not part of his "plan". He ordered me to stand over by the potato chips and I eventually complied, waddling over with the metal disc and key in the air with warm piss making my pants stick to my legs. I really wished then that I had used the bathroom when I'd had the chance. Isadore turned again to the girl.

"Faster bitch," he said in his non-threatening voice, almost instantly regretting it. He sounded like what a poodle would sound like if they could speak English. But he was a big, bad man now, a man with a gun. She kept her head down and started pulling the money out faster.

"Don't call me that," she said evenly without looking up.

"Sorry," Isadore replied automatically. He did feel genuinely sorry. He again had visions of himself and the girl, running down a beach naked, or huddled in the darkness of a movie theater, naked. She looked up when he apologized, and smiled an odd smile of amusement and compassion. She knew that Isadore wasn't really an asshole; he was just an asshole because he had a gun. She had a lot of questions she wanted to ask him; Where did he get the gun? Who told him that robbing gas stations was a good way to make a living? What was he going to spend the money on? Did he really think he could make a getaway in a Volkswagen van? For the moment, she kept these questions to herself and put all the bills in a nice tidy pile to her left.

I started to lower my hands as my arms were getting sore from holding the metal disc above my head. Isadore saw this and pointed the gun back at me. It was a shiny gun, as his uncle had spent many hours polishing it. Even I don't know why he did that. I don't think his uncle knew really, it sure didn't relax him while he did it, as I know from being a part of his squirrelly heart. His unmarried uncle was not suicidal, so it wasn't preparation. Guns are odd.

It was at this moment that all hell came bubbling forth, the havoc was unleashed and Pandora's box cracked its mighty lid in the form of a beige minivan pulling into the gas station.

CHAPTER EIGHT

Minivans
and
The Mania of the Misdiagnosed

The chaos—in what was an otherwise seamless armed robbery—came in the form of Murray MacDonald and his family of three, riding in their beige—or babyshit-brown—minivan.

A minivan is an automobile that has no inherent aesthetic value. It is cheaper on gas than a real van, yet big enough to haul around small families. Built with families of four or six in mind, it was unleashed on the world in 1983, but was in development since 1977.

The year 1977 was when everyone thought Elvis died. And technically he did, except that his DNA was harvested by a group of aliens and Elvis the clone with meticulously reprogrammed memories had a third comeback on a planet near the Andromeda galaxy. One late hour, Elvis was wallowing in his deep-fried destitution and praying over and over—as only Elvis could—that aliens would come down and take him away. Little did he know that his prayers would be answered years later when a cloaked mothership hovering just behind Saturn sent a tiny robotic probe to sample his Deoxyribonucleic acid from a dirty fork. Thus, Elvis was soon back in his hip-swinging glory and playing six nights a week as the King of Earth. New Elvis never bothered to tell the people of the planet that he was not actually the king of the planet, and when they asked him after many years if he wanted to return to his subjects, he politely declined. He was a clone that had spent his life in space, what did he know of Hawaii and hula girls?

Was this new Elvis as good as the old Elvis? Not even close, but I wouldn't tell those aliens that. They spent years attempting to recreate memories from old press footage and movies; sometimes you just have to be supportive of a creative endeavor for the sake of politeness, like when you attend a friend's art show.

Murray Macdonald and his family had an Elvis compact disc of music in their minivan. It was *Elvis sings Christmas Songs*, and they had been listening to it about an hour ago, even though it was the summertime. They were that kind of people.

You would think that I could not hate them now as I am a part of them, part of their shit-brown minivan, part of the french fries they gobbled for lunch, and the resulting litter that they tossed out their window. I am part of their shitty workplaces and their blaring television set, part of the boy's whiny voice and the full bladder that prompted it. But let me tell you, I hate them like an ingrown toenail, like a zit on my forehead the night of the prom. I hate them like I hate having piss-soaked pants sticking to my thighs.

I have something to tell you. We are all related. Now, what I mean is that we are all *actually* related. Through the mysteries of DNA testing you'll find this out soon enough, but I'll tell you now and spoil the surprise. We—humans that is—are all descended from Ablaya Mookdi of Africa. She was no one special, but she was healthy. And while the rest of her friends died off, Ablaya hung on. She had kids, who had kids, who had more kids. So, we're all inbred brothers and sisters! Wahooo! And how will this knowledge affect the course of history? Does this mean that once this fact is common knowledge there will be no more need for war, for race crimes? For hate?

Tell me, do you have any immediate siblings? I hate Murray like a brother, a zit, and an ingrown toenail, all at the same time.

Isadore looked out the glass door, and he freaked right out. He convulsively shook the gun in the direction of the glass door, the approaching minivan, and the people in it, as if this very action could halt them in their approach. When it did not, he sprung into a variety of seemingly unrelated actions. Running left, then right, then up to the counter, where he grabbed the money as fast as he could, causing some of it to spill over the counter-top and down onto the floor, like a small money explosion. The woman that most people would hope to marry one fine summer day did not immediately move to pick it up for him.

"Where's the rest?" he howled, watching with horror as the sliding door of the minivan opened and Murray Macdonald and his clan started to ooze out.

"I'm sorry?" she replied.

"The money from the back! I want that too!"

"The safe is locked. I don't know the combination, okay?"

Isadore was so angry when he heard this that he pulled his gun away from the Macdonald clan and pointed it back at her. She just shrugged her shoulders slightly and moved her hands in the gesture commonly used to illustrate helplessness in a situation beyond one's control. My fascination with her nonchalance was slowly unlocking a part of me that I didn't know existed. How could she, how could anyone be so calm when faced with very real and very obvious dangers? I was so hypnotized by her I felt oblivious to the pain in my right arm from holding the stupid metal disc high up in the air.

About intelligence in inanimate objects: It's real. Some things really are dumb. It has a lot to do with the molecules involved, the electromagnetic imprint humans leave behind, and let me tell you, that was one stupid metal disc.

"You two! In the back!" he said, waving the gun at us wildly, so that she cringed. I gave him my patented blank look. "Now!" he screeched in his poodle voice. I snapped alert, coming out of my own dream involving the beautiful woman. Mine did not involve movie theaters or beaches; it was all about tapioca pudding. I was slowly feeding her tapioca, and after every bite she'd coo, "mmm..." or, "yeah..."—something like that. I waddled toward Isadore and watched as She-with-a-capital-S climbed down from her throne and walked towards a white door on the back wall. She was losing a bit of her calm now, worried that Isadore was in fact crazy enough to shoot her.

Finally, she looked into my eyes in earnest, in a far different way that was not akin to pity and disgust, but with a silent plea and a glimmer of hope. I felt like I was going to positively explode with excitement just then, and my hummingbird heart started to thump even faster. I swelled up my chest and tried to give her what I perceived as a sense of manly reassurance. Unfortunately, just then I tripped on the shoelace of my left running shoe and stumbled forward, clonking her on the head with the giant metal disc.

"Ow," she said, reaching up to hold her bashed head. She looked at me in surprise, and then down at my soggy pants and untied shoelaces. The disappointment on her face made me want to do the opposite of explode; I wanted to implode. Isadore was backing up towards us, stuffing money into his pockets and pointing the gun at the glass door. He was backing up so fast he didn't notice that we hadn't moved yet, so he stepped onto my toe, hard. I felt the impulse to push him off, but didn't as he was holding a gun. Guns sometimes make people unnecessarily polite. He spun on us and rammed the gun tip right up against my forehead.

"Move!" he poodle-barked. She opened the door to the back of the gas station and we all filed in. It was a small room, so we had to huddle together like coworkers near a watercooler. Isadore slammed the door shut and ordered us up against the wall, which was a dumb thing to say, because we had nowhere else to be.

In the room were many shelves containing cleaning supplies; some uniforms; a desk cluttered with paper; and tucked under one of the shelves, a small metal safe.

"Where's the safe?" Isadore demanded, sounding very greedy. He adjusted the grip on his gun, using it to distance us from him.

"I told you, I don't know the combination," she replied.

"Where is it?"

She raised her eyebrows as high as she could, in the expression used for simultaneous disbelief and acceptance, and then pulled back a box, revealing the safe. We all stared at it in dumb wonder. Isadore had absolutely no idea where to go from here. We were rescued from standing there for eternity by a nasal, southern twang from outside the door, which hooted, "Hellooooooooooooo. . ."

This was of course Murray Macdonald and his brat devil-spawn of a child. Murray had one arm on the child's shoulder, but not in an affectionate way. It was to keep him in line; Julian was a kleptomaniac.

Kleptomania is yet another mental illness. The victim suffers from an uncontrollable urge to steal. They will steal anything, most often things they don't want and don't need but simply must have. They are now using drugs, fluoxetine and paroxetine, to stop people from doing this. They gave out drugs for everything then, in the hopes they could change a person by pumping a potpourri of chemicals into the bloodstream. And let me tell you, living now in the bloodstream of every person and creature that ever was, they're right!

Question: What does this say about free will if our actions are little else than the result of our chemical cocktails?

Answer: Free will is a very simplistic idea which does not factor in the many facets and factors of the universe that lead us to our decisions.

Question: If there is no free will then what does that say about a consciousness? A soul? Are well all just murderous puppets strapped to a Ferris wheel whirling around and around?

Answer: Some of us, yes. More on that later.

They gave me many drugs to stop me from getting distracted all the time by blind, naked fear. Some of these drugs included serotonin specific reuptake inhibitors, or SSRIs, which regulated my serotonin levels. Serotonin is a chemical made in the body which makes you happy, among other things. People were always screwing around with their serotonin levels in efforts to be happier.
What does this say about my decisions on this day?
Was every choice I made merely a result of a doctor's scrawled and barely legible handwriting?

Question: If free will is tied to a soul, does this make me a soulless automaton parading around in a human-shaped husk following a synthesized destiny?

Answer: The drugs were largely ineffective against my fears, as you may have noticed. I certainly did not seem outwardly joyous. Let me answer this one with a question, because everyone loves that: Could there be other effects, besides constipation, that these drugs were having on my role in the physical and cosmic realm? I believe so.

Murray Macdonald was unhappy quite often. He had misdiagnosed anger issues and was on a cocktail of his own to level out his moods. Julian, Murray's klepto-son, was too busy eating or stealing to be truly happy. At the moment he was eyeing the potato chips, not because of his disorder, but because he was very hungry. Julian was/is a gluttonous little troll of a human; an insatiable machine that manipulated, connived and pleaded his parents into feeding him every waking second. Murray sensed his son's gaze and tightened his grip on the boy's shoulder.

"Helloooooo. . ." he called again, this time very irritated. Inside the crowded back room Isadore turned the gun on the goddess. "Go out there. Get rid of him. And don't try anything."

I have seen Isadore as a child. I am in the orange carpet under his belly as a colony of dust mites, while he sits watching a bad cop show on the TV. The criminal is a seedy-looking guy with bags under his eyes who holds his pistol up high close to his face. He sneers and says in a weasel-voice, "You. Out there. Get ridda tha' guy, 'n' no monkey bizness, seee?" I wish that Isadore had said that thing now about the monkey business, but you can't change the past, unfortunately.

She nods and gives him a funny sort of smile. She will go out there, she will do as he says. She is so brave. She opens the door and slides out of it like an elegant jellyfish. Isadore leaves the door open a crack and watches her closely as she glides up to Murray and his son. I crowd up behind him, not because I'm curious about what's going to happen, but because I desperately need to continue looking at her.

Her mother was Mexican, so she has the most beautiful skin and proud lips. Of course I couldn't know that or see that then, as I was staring at her back, but now, as I form the gaudy red gas-station-uniform t-shirt that clings to her lithe frame and the tiny mites that live in her eyebrows, I know. Knowledge isn't always power. Can you imagine what it's like to feel every inane thought and impulse of every creature in the Omniverse? Some things are unbearably annoying to have knowledge of, like having accidentally memorized the words to a bad song. Strike that, to every bad song. In this case though, knowledge is definitely power.

From our stuffy hiding place, our flesh bubbles saw a heated exchange between Murray and that ephemeral beauty. She was saying that unfortunately the washrooms were closed. She had contemplated using an elaborate series of hand signals and coded words to let Murray know something was up, but after a quick, calculated assessment had decided that Murray was not her savior. She thought that the best thing now would be to just get rid of him before Isadore, or the soon-to-arrive police cavalcade, shot him in a flurry of chaos and bullets. But like I said before, the cops were not coming.

Oh, but in fact, there was one cop who was coming. Not in the traditional sense . . . No, I mean this more in the crass, pun-riddled sense that he was in the throes of experiencing an orgasm at the moment that Murray and the elegant human jellyfish were having their heated debate. His name was Officer Brent Cohen. A forty-one-year-old with a full, brown moustache, he'd been divorced for two months. He was very much alone, seated in his patrol car, during that pun-riddled orgasm. Being a police officer is a lonely job, so you will have to find it in your heart to forgive him for masturbating and then ejaculating from the tip of his hairless-snake-descended-from-race-of–hairy-alien-snakes (penis), while on duty.

You don't have to forgive him for his odd sexual quirks, such as removing his gun from its holster and running it up and down his thigh, while moaning "You like that?" and "Tongue me," or the fact that he owns a little terrier dog, whom he calls "snookieface" and "teddieweddybear" and other sickeningly cloying things as it licks his face. His wife got repulsed by this act, but that's not why she left him. It was because he worked too much.

All these children of Ablaya Mookdi and their lives!

I mention Officer Cohen now because we will see him later in the day, and luckily will have no knowledge that the small crusty stain on his police trousers is actually his own semen.

Meanwhile Murray was not buying the story about the washroom being closed. For one, he was just as stubborn as stubborn could be! Also, he actually had the smarts to realize something was up. This was because the supreme mistress of the gas station on Oceanview is quite the phenomenally crappy liar. She lies in the way where she wants to be caught, where if you can't tell that she is lying, then you deserved to be lied to. This technique has only ever come across as confusing when she does it, but she hasn't abandoned it yet as a way to assuage her own guilt.

The truth was, I was holding that stupid metal disc and key in my sweaty hands. Despite its ludicrous weight I'd forgotten I was holding it. So, there was no opening of any bathrooms while I was around.

Murray thought that she was just being lazy, and didn't feel like opening the bathroom. His sudden suspicion gave her a glimmer of hope that he might uncover the fact that she was being held up by a twenty-year-old with a gun. She told Murray that she had just remembered she'd left the key in the back, because they were having *security issues* and that *people* were *crazy* right now and *stealing everything*. She also asked Murray if he had a phone. Phones were like guns then; they were almost everywhere on Earth. Sometimes people would walk down the street with their phone in one hand, and holding the gun with the other, so they can tell someone about the other someone they are about to shoot.

Murray did not get the obvious plea for help, the sledgehammer of a hint she'd just clumsily smacked him upside the head with. He just looked at her like she was trying to make fun of him, sort of hurt and angry. He said that no, he did not have a phone, and then had to turn his attention back to his gluttonous son who was now inches away from the potato chips. He hauled back on his son's shoulder, hard, so that the boy spun around.

My sweaty fleshbag only then realized that I was holding the key. I looked down at it, Isadore did too. We exchanged a glance which conveyed this uncomplicated and immediate message, *Oh shit.*

As Murray, his son, and the goddess started to walk towards where we were huddled, Isadore began to hop back and forth from his left to right foot. I thought that he was trying to think of what to do. What he was actually thinking was how badly he himself needed to use the bathroom, how if he didn't piss soon, he would end up like me—sodden and soiled, clutching a useless bathroom key.

All over the Omniverse, at that moment, from the smallest cell to the great Plyynworths of the ocean planet Xueb, things were caught up in the act of defecation. But not Isadore, no, he had to hold it for a while longer.

His bladder made him even more impatient and nervous than he already was. He exploded out of the door, pointing the gun at the girl with crystal eyes and Murray Macdonald. Julian had used this opportunity to slip away and was about to snatch a bag of potato chips, when he noticed a can of condensed milk to his left, which due to his kleptomania, he had to have.

As far as the clever ruse that everything was hunky-dory, business as usual at that gas station, the gig was up. Murray threw up his hands, having been trained well by TV and movies. The beautiful gas station attendant froze in place. Julian paused with his hand just above the condenses milk, waiting. Isadore said nothing to his captives, and really, what needed to be said? He turned to me and barked, "You! Grab the safe!"

"What?" I replied.

"Grab the fucking safe," he yelped with his poodle-voice.

I turned and looked back at the safe. It was not big, but it looked heavy; it was a safe after all, designed much like the bathroom key—too cumbersome to steal. I looked back at him dubiously. He waved the gun at me in a move-along-little-doggy gesture. My sorry soup of sodden self shuffled toward the safe, hunched over, and gripping it by the bottom, lifted it half an inch off the floor. I tried not to think about the germs that would be on the safe as I touched it. It smelled like nothing in particular, but I sniffed it just the same.

I proceeded to drag it very slowly across the room towards the front door with Isadore hovering over me, gun in sweaty hand. He did not offer to help, he was busy holding the gun, so let it be said that guns make people lazy.

In an act of sublime universal love, that young woman walked over to the other side of the safe and helped me to drag it. She did not look at me as she did this; she was looking at Isadore.

"Just what the Sam Hell is your plan here anyway?" she said. Love, or admiration, or a feeling of belonging, something shot through me just then. Isadore did not respond. He turned to Murray, his eyes wild, big and brown. "Where's the kid?" he said. We all looked around, but Julian was nowhere to be seen.

I see him now! At this moment he's hunched beside the hygiene counter, busily shoplifting moist towelettes. Unlike me he had no use for them, but he needed them like he needed the can of condensed milk stashed in his pants pocket. Isadore was worried that the kid had run off and gone to call the cops. Murray was fairly certain that was not the case. He was pretty sure that his son was hiding somewhere nearby, stealing things he didn't need or want. At this point, in the midst of an armed robbery, Murray didn't really care.

"Kid!" Isadore yelled.

"Julian!" Murray called. He paused then, looking sideways at Isadore's sweaty squirrely face, "Run and get help!"

Isadore stared at Murray.

Murray stared at Isadore.

"Stay where you are kid!" Isadore warned, "and I won't kill your dad here. . ."

Murray glowered at Isadore. He wanted to grab that gun and shoot him with it. He felt that would be the best way out of this situation and could see Isadore's shaky grip on the shiny pistol. There was a carousel of lightning in his head as he debated whether or not he would die trying to snatch it from him.

"This thing is too heavy," she said, trying to draw attention away from what could be a bloodbath between Murray and Isadore. We had stopped moving the safe and were just standing around, although slightly hunched over. Isadore had his wide brown eyes locked on Murray's dull blue ones, but tore them away for one second to look at us.

"You two, move that thing out to the van! You," he said to Murray, "you lie down on the ground over there by the counter." We all complied. I was not as scared as I should have been, as I was currently engrossed in staring at the long red strands of hair against the silver of the safe, and smelling the sweet smell of this girl's head so next to mine. It was sort of spicy, and delicate, but definitely intoxicating.

What I was smelling was Herbal Essences' Tangerine Curry shampoo. She did not smell like gasoline, as all the pumps were automated self-serve pumps. She had not once smelled of gasoline in the six months she'd worked there. I smelled of pee.

We hunched over and began to waddle our way towards the door. It was slow going and I had enough sense despite myself to try and act like I didn't mind moving the safe, that it was no big deal. That I was strong, manly yet graceful, and could waddle with the best of them. She would notice the ease with which I maneuvered my body and feel instantly better about the whole desperate situation. I was just beginning to notice a small bead of delicious sweat on the brow of the beautiful woman before me, when a shot was fired from the end of the pistol.

CHAPTER NINE

The Not-So-Great Escape
and
Machine-Gun Hands

It was unbelievably loud.
We spun around to see Murray lying in a pool of blood. He had tried to resist Isadore as he was being ordered onto the floor, and made a clumsy grab for the gun. Isadore had avoided this by stepping slightly backwards. Isadore had then fired a warning shot just next to him, to show that he meant business.

At least, he had intended it to be a warning blast, but Isadore was an amazingly bad shot, having never actually fired a gun before, so the reaction that occurred when he pressed that trigger surprised even him. He was momentarily paralyzed by the noise, and the sordid sight before him. The bullet had ripped through the air, pausing slightly as it tore through Murray's right arm and then embedded itself in the linoleum floor. Murray had fallen to his knees soon after and cradled his wounded arm.

We all stared at him as he stared down at his forearm in disbelief. Rather quickly there was a whole lot of blood pouring and gushing out of both sides. He was not screaming aloud yet; he was in shock. Murray looked up at Isadore and displayed his very shocked face.

Isadore wanted to apologize. Even then I could tell he wanted to apologize. He looked over at us and gave us a silent apology for shooting Murray, like he was going to start crying. Soon we'd have a blubbering man with a gun before us, which is always a bad thing, blubbering can quickly turn into irrational, homicidal rage in situations like these.

"Holy fuck," she said, and this seemed to awaken Isadore. He shifted his weight from leg to leg and gave Murray a suave sideways glance.

"If you want to die, try that again," Isadore said, sounding very unlike a poodle. He sounded like a character from a movie; a gravelly-voiced, bitter man who is not surprised by anything.

Knowing Isadore as I do now (I live in-between his toes, among other places), I can tell you that line is from a movie he had seen once called *The Last One in the Pool*, starring a bunch of unknown actors. These actors are unknown to you, but many a frustrated actor I am and have been, many a wastebasket full of shoddy scripts, or cup of coffee sipped tentatively before another brutal and cheapening audition. I won't bore you with the career highs and lows of the people that starred in *The Last One in the Pool*, but let me tell you, the highs were sporadic and tentative like an old leaky faucet. The scene Isadore was quoting is a good one though, so I'll tell you about it. It involves a burly cop and a greasy gangster. The gangster makes a grab for the cop's gun, and the cop kicks him with his big cop boots right in the nads. As the gangster is lying there, choking and gagging, the cops says that line to him.

Had Murray's bladder been bursting like Isadore's, he probably would have pissed his pants right then. Instead he was hunched over holding his mangled arm to his chest and staring down at the ground, whimpering and moaning. All that courage and rage he'd been stockpiling before had started running the second the gun had gone off. Now he was very apologetic, and had begun pleading with Isadore to spare his life. Isadore felt a grim smile of satisfaction, which seemed locked on his sweaty face. The little bastard was starting to enjoy himself. He'd been just as startled as any of us when he'd fired the gun, but now! Now he could feel it in his hand: the power of death. It felt heavy, solid. He felt like a god.

There is in fact one race of creatures that live on a rocky planet with a very high level of gravity. They have no predators, mostly because the fingers on their long bony hands are fully functioning weapons capable of releasing hard, bone-like pellets. These pellets come out in great abundance very fast and very hard, like a Gatling gun. And as a direct result of this they quickly gained ultimate control over their hostile little world. It wasn't long before they instructed the rest of the inhabitants, mainly soft, worm-like behemoths, to erect elaborate shrines in their honor. There is a great deal of bowing and praising at one end of a pointed finger on that planet. In many ways, they are gods.

"Kid, get your ass out here and lie down!" the poodle voice called out, even more annoying in its sudden smugness. Julian appeared timidly from behind the aisle. Tears were streaming down his face. He had thought that his dad had died. Poor kid. Poor little Christmas-music-in-the-middle-of-summer troll. I feel for him now of course. Almost as much as those behemoth worm creatures. Is that Universal Love? The fact that now I can't help but feel pity for every creature in existence?

"You two," he said to the two of us frozen by the safe, "hurry up."

With one last glance at Murray, we dragged it through the door as the Goddess of Snacks used her tight bottom against the glass to hold it open. The van was a long ten feet away from the door. It was still whirring and clicking in that noisy way that idling Volkswagen vans do.

"Maybe you should pull the van around," she said coolly, having quickly regained some semblance of serenity when the afternoon breeze hit her face.

Murray's wife, Irene, sat in the passenger seat of the minivan and picked her nose with long, scooping passes of her lacquered nails, and let me tell you, she was really in there; scraping deep into the recesses of her nostril. She had not heard the gunshot, despite its volume, as she was partly deaf in one ear due to standing too close to a jet engine during their vacation in Maui.

She could still see though, and she suddenly froze in mid-scoop as we came dragging the safe out the door with Isadore close behind holding a gun. She dropped her hand and shrieked as loud as she could. Isadore pointed the gun at her. Her shrieking reached a new pitch.

In the surrounding area, five dogs (one very old), four cats, eighteen birds, thousands of insects (including that colony of crickets from North Carolina), and Emilia Knudson (the old woman in her garden), snapped to attention momentarily. The very atoms in the air at that gas station shifted and whirled as the sound waves buffeted them around.

Again, we stopped in our tracks towards the van, and again, Isadore hollered at us to continue. She turned to me and I froze under the beam of her gray/green eyes. She said, "Let's do this and get him out of here." I was so spellbound that I did not move. She began to waddle forward with the safe again, but I did not, and it came down on my foot. I let out a short bark of surprise. "Sorry," she said automatically, "are you alright?"

I just smiled back at her stupidly, not saying anything. I began to notice every curve of her face. While staring I saw one eyebrow raise as if in slow motion. She was starting to get an inkling of my dubious sanity. It was a familiar look to me and I put my head down, attempting to lift the safe once more.

At the time, and even now, I am amazed that she was not wondering aloud about our fate, asking me if I think that Isadore is going to kill us, or wondering where the cops are. She was just moving the safe from her workplace, into the sputtering Volkswagen van of a criminal she just met. She was not even complaining about the weight of the safe. She exists in this moment a bastion of calm and glory in an Omniverse rife with chaos and smell.

We finally get the thing to the van. Once there we stop and look behind us to see Isadore ushering Mrs. Macdonald facedown onto the greasy ground next to their babyshit-brown minivan. She was no longer shrieking but emitting a series of sporadic moans, squeaks and titters. Once she's mostly on the ground, Isadore starts running backwards towards us, his bad aim swinging back and forth menacingly. He runs up to the van to find us coated in the rank blue smoke of the van's exhaust. The girl waves her hand in front of her face in a useless gesture of relieving herself from the toxic fumes. I start to cough and move away from the van, but Isadore will have none of this. He moves in, cutting off my escape route and yanking on the sliding door of the van with his free hand. It whirls open, smacks the end of its track, and then starts to close again. Isadore sticks out his foot to stop it.

"Load it up there," he says, pointing with the muzzle.

Looking inside, we can see the carcass of the van is covered wall-to-wall in garbage: Potato chip packages, pop cans, those weird triangle sandwich holders . . . it is a sea of crumpled cellophane and gleaming aluminum. Mounted low on the wall, directly facing the open sliding door, is a large bust of a head covered in bubble wrap. It is surrounded by pictures of someone in what appears to be a variety of costumes. One could assume it is the same person that the bust was molded after, as all the pictures feature only this individual. Ringed around the head, scattered on the floor, and all over the vicinity of the makeshift shrine, is an assortment of red and yellow flowers. The goddess takes a long look at this and is transfixed momentarily.

The bust is molded after Ryan Totten of course. The pictures are of him in a variety of period costumes; in some he is in a Victorian breasted jacket, smiling at the camera; in others he is a cowboy staring wistfully away, one hand on his chin, pondering.

In all of them he looks like a real dandy. The idea was that it showed how Totten was eternal and had lived many lives on this planet, readying himself for his triumphant journey into the center of the sun. The shrine was also Totten's idea. He had told Isadore that with himself as the vicarious copilot, Isadore could never go wrong. Totten was so high all the time he didn't even think twice about sending an armed robber under his control to the scene of the crime with a bust of his own head in the getaway vehicle.

At the moment, Totten was/is busy having sex with one of his more attractive followers. He had no idea that Isadore was on this mission in the first place. One thing is for sure, high as he was, Totten would never have told Isadore to rob a gas station. A bank, maybe, but not a gas station.

My mass of flesh looked at the head and had no reaction whatsoever. At the time I thought Totten might be a pop star, and while I was well-versed on various contagious diseases, I was not up on my pop stars.

I bend over and start to lift, but the safe is way too heavy for me to hoist. Gas Station Goddess hunches over, and she too tries to lift it up. We lift it a full two inches before my fingers slip off and it falls noisily to the ground. Unfortunately for Isadore, his left shoe happens to be under the safe when it falls. This safe really has it out for feet. He quickly yanks it out, but his face is contorted in rage and pain.

"Ffffuck!" he bellows.

I think for a second that my girl is going to start laughing her quick infectious laugh again, but she does not. She looks at Isadore quietly, reveling in his current state of discombobulation. While she had instantly disliked Murray Macdonald the Second, he'd opened his mouth in the gas station, she was still angry that Isadore had shot him. She thought the safe falling on his toe was totally cool.

Isadore watched us attempt to lift the safe up and into the van two more times. After our second attempt, there is a flash of pink motion and he notices Mrs. Macdonald pulling herself up from the ground. He raised the gun straight into the sky, and closing his eyes, fires it.

"Motherfucker!" the Gas Station Goddess yells.

I'm sorry everyone curses so much. A sign of the times I guess. I was never one for expletives while I was alive, even though I would have found an abundance of occasions for them. They relieve stress; one thing I knew a lot about.

Our ears are ringing and a chunk of plastic falls at our feet as some white plastic dust wafts down like a nasty veil on a light summer breeze. Isadore has shot a hole in the overhanging, a crack has formed, and big plastic splinters are raining down onto the ground and the roof of the idling van. The result he desired has been achieved though: Mrs. Macdonald is now flattening her pastel-pink self against the oily ground like a perfumed pancake.

The Goddess was now highly irritated with Isadore. She had one finger in her ear in a belated attempt to stop the noise from entering. She stood back and cocked her curvaceous hips, making no effort to bend over and hoist the safe. Isadore looked at her once more, his desperation plainly showing.

And at this moment, this horrible moment, I can see the idea forming. Ideas are dangerous things. Isadore's eyes widen slightly, white and gleaming, his mouth hangs open, and then . . . and then . . . closes.

He has made a decision. He will take her hostage. She will grow to love him and worship him. He will never frighten her again. One day soon they will ride a spaceship into the center of the sun. He bends over and nods at me that we should lift the safe together. I follow his orders, and as we crouch down I notice that the piss is starting to dry. It is still unpleasant, but less so than before.

Isadore and I shove the safe into the van amidst all the garbage and the flowers. It won't budge, so he makes me crawl into the van and start to pull it in while he pushes it. Finally, the booty has been stowed and I move to make my exit.

It was at this moment that Officer Cohen drove past in his patrol car.

"Get in the back of the van!" Isadore snapped, his voice raised to a chihuahua pitch. I am reluctant, due to my amaxophobia, or fear of riding in cars. I actually preferred the bus, if you can believe it, and had been riding buses since I was sixteen. Isadore conquered my fears by forcefully shoving me into the van so that I fell hard just to the left of the safe. He then moved to grab the goddess by the arm, but she yanked it away defiantly. He held the gun up to her stomach

"Please," he says. He looked like a scared little boy.

Another remarkably viscous moment: She turned away from him and with a forlorn longing noticed that the police car was not flashing its lights, was not screeching into the gas station with guns ablaze in the afternoon sun. It was just driving slowly past and away.

From where Officer Cohen was sitting in his car, he could not see Mrs. Macdonald lying on the ground, or Murray bleeding on the linoleum, or Julian stuffing moist towelettes into his underpants, or even Isadore holding the gun against that beautiful young woman's stomach. All he could see were some gas pumps and some people standing next to a green Volkswagen van. He was humming a little song to himself as he drove, and shifted slightly in his seat, to let his freshly flogged penis rest more comfortably.

We all watched as the police car continued on its plodding, leisurely course. It was almost at the edge of the last pull-in when a bloody Murray Macdonald burst out of the glass door, smearing crimson handprints all over it while hollering,

"HELLLLLP!" and "OVERERE!"

Isadore pointed the gun at Murray, hesitating. The Goddess of Calm and Poise put her hand on Isadore's shoulder, who returned her gaze, and it was like cooling gel spread from her touch and went straight to his heart, where it soothed his very being. He lowered the gun.

Just then the police car stopped. Isadore watched as the red brake lights flashed like big radiant eyes.

"Shit!" he said. "Get in!"

She looked at my wide-eyed fearful expression, my utter helplessness in the present situation, and made her decision. She climbed in next to me. Why? Besides the young man pointing a gun at her, there was another reason, and there is only one way to show you that. We have to go into her head. Are you ready?

And here we go! Snapping and zapping through the axons and myelin sheaths of her brain in a dizzying zigzag pattern. I'm looking for the memory area, but the brain is such a cramped, twisting little mass of meat.

Well, here she is getting potty-trained. Her little brown legs and hair crouched over a bright yellow potty while her mother stands watching. And while it has been said over and over how the acquisition of this one act can form one's entire psyche, I am looking for something a little less obvious.

Aha.

When she was thirteen years and fifty-one days old, she was listlessly swinging on the big metal swingset in the school behind her house. Her long thin legs dangling below in pink socks and blue sneakers, tracing idle patterns in the dirt. I have spent a great deal of time visiting different parts of her existence, and this is one of my favorites.

It was late afternoon, and she had ditched the other kids attempts at a game of "capture the fag," a truly barbaric and outdated display where the older kids pick one of the younger, more effeminate males to go hide, and then chase after and beat the snot out of him. She had played this game only twice, which was enough times to start feeling bad for Morris Tataryn, as he always ended up being the one being chased. She was also slowly losing any sort of competitive urge whatsoever. Having faked it throughout numerous matches of volleyball, baseball and basketball, she recently had reached a zenith in her lust for competitive sports.

It was as she was swinging back and forth on the swing, her hair in tight ponytails, one foot dragging through the light gray dust beneath her, that the strongest, strangest feeling overcame her.

I'd say it's weird to feel someone's feelings, but I've gotten pretty used to it. It washes through me like waves of color and hormones. Emotions are a whole lot more physical than you'd think. This is a complex emotion though, a whole swirling color wheel of competing feelings.

She looked around at the huge open field, then behind her at her street, with her little nondescript house, and finally, the big open sky. The houses looked small and fragile, and oddly thrown together. She started to feel apart, as if she were floating in a bubble separate from the universe and didn't belong anywhere in particular. There was no real connection with her playmates running in the trees beyond the field, or with the field itself; with her house, with her school, even with her own mother. Everything felt random and misplaced.

This is commonly classified as another mental illness, dubbed ever-so vaguely as dissociative disorder. Pretty much the opposite of whatever it is that I have. While I am constantly paranoid and jerking my head around like a fat furious chipmunk, her psyche resembles a glazed and somewhat jaded cow, listlessly chewing on cud.

And instead of being rendered insane by the fear this would bring, like myself, she felt an eerie sense of calm. The overwhelming confidence that comes from the nagging feeling that no matter what she did, none of this really mattered. She didn't belong here, she was just an observer. Add to that the confidence that comes from being extremely good-looking and she couldn't help but feel more and more invincible with each day she added onto her life. Her first experience with this feeling was so great, powerful and shattering that she leapt off the swing almost instantly. Once her sneakered feet hit the dusty ground, the feeling started to fade. I say started to, because it never really went away, not ever.

As a result of this experience, this young woman generally accepts everything that happens to her with a truckload of salt. And if she is startled, say, by a young man bursting into her place of employment and shooting one of the customers, she recovers a lot quicker than most. What seems like bravery to us, I know to be a slight lack of interest. It takes a hell of a lot to faze her—even what's about to happen to her once she gets into that Volkswagen van won't throw her for long.

Isadore slammed the sliding door shut. It didn't close all the way, but he was too rushed to fix it and ran around to the other side and hopped onto the driver's seat. After some frantic shifting and grinding of gears, the van screeched away, narrowly missing the gas pumps.

Officer Cohen stepped out of his car as Murray rounded the minivan, clutching his bloody arm. The officer heard the van squeal and whir its way onto the highway, so he looked after it, then back at Murray for an explanation.

Huddled in the dark recesses of the clanging van all was jangling noisy chaos. The whole floor lurched upwards when we hit a bump merging onto the highway and debris flew into the air. She started to fall, and put her hand on my knee for balance.

a female Sadeekaninian.

HRINE
2021

CHAPTER TEN

The Queen of the Universe Uncoiled
and
More Pissing of Pants

The van sputtered and careened its way down the winding Oceanview Highway with Isadore hunched over the dash, not looking around and not saying much. He still had the gun in one hand, pressed against the steering wheel.

The two of us sat huddled in the back of the Volkswagen tomb with its painted over windows. I could see that the girl was scheming. She looked at the Totten shrine, then at Isadore's back, then at the side door, which was open a crack, and then out the back window. There were no police cars following us. It dawned on me that we could fling the door open and leap from the moving vehicle, but I was afraid of the scarring the inevitable road rash would cause.

She climbed forward, bracing herself against the sides of the van with her palms, and then plopped herself into the passenger seat to look at Isadore. He glanced over for a moment, but then set his eyes back on the road. In no great hurry, she leaned back against the window, watching him intently. She was waiting for him to talk. When he didn't, she folded her arms across her chest in a show of defiance and patience, occasionally glancing out at the road. It was ridiculously noisy in that van. If Isadore had wanted to say anything, he would have had to yell at the top of his lungs to be heard. Finally, he spoke.

"Shit," he said. "Shit. Shit. Shit!"

A car was coming towards us on the highway. At the moment it was just a gleam in the sunlight, barely distinguishable from the wet road, but as it got closer, Isadore grew more and more agitated. He looked back in the rearview mirror, picturing himself doing a quick U-turn, knowing that at the van's present speed we would most likely careen off the road, over the cement rail and into the briny sea.

As we got closer, it became clear to us that the approaching vehicle was in fact another Volkswagen van. They were not uncommon in quiet seaside towns. What you may not know, and I certainly did not until I became whatever it is I am now, is that there is an odd custom between drivers of Volkswagen vans.

They always wave at each other. Always. To not do so is a social faux pas on the scale of farting in a tent. Westfalia drivers sometimes try to work their way into the tight-knit circle, but they are repeatedly shunned and viewed as try-hards when they wave. I have never seen any other specific mode of transportation ritual like this anywhere else across the Omniverse.

The reason for the wave is simple. It is because there are a variety of quandaries unique to the ownership and maintenance of a Volkswagen van. The first reason I already mentioned: Volkswagens tend to be so loud that you have to bellow each syllable to maintain a conversation. The next is the constant reeking and belching of exhaust, which has even killed a few unlucky owners by asphyxiation. Finally, they are constantly breaking down, with hard-to-reach engines tucked way up in the back. When it comes time to make the necessary roadside repairs, you'll often see young and old people hunched next to their vans, looking haggard and exasperated. So the wave is one of camaraderie, a recognition of a similar burden. They understand, man.

Thus, when the older couple approaching us in the other van got close enough, they waved. Everyone waved back, including me. Isadore instinctively waved with the hand holding the gun; he waved a big shiny gun at them. We could not see their reaction as we were speeding as fast as the shaky van could carry us down the highway. Realizing what he'd done, Isadore dropped the gun into his lap. He looked very embarrassed, and shot us a sheepish sideways glance. She sat leaning against the opposite window and laughed a little. I was just confused. I had no idea why everyone was waving, or why she was laughing. Finally, she said to Isadore, "My name is Jahanara."

I sat dumbfounded, Isadore too. We both just stared at her, though he was watching the road out of the corner of his eye.

Jahanara.

Jahanara.

JahanaraJahanaraJahanara.

Her father was a short, stern man, and devout Muslim. In that culture, her name means Queen of the Universe. Let me tell you, she just might be queen of more than one of them.

In the United States of America, there was an annual event called the Miss Universe pageant. It was a sham. Never were the Sadeekaninians consulted or propositioned with applications. The Sadeekaninians look like giant shimmering manta rays, and glide through the pink fog of their planet with an unparalleled grace. The males of the species are quite hideous, which is why they sing a song each evening that causes a visual hallucination in anyone who hears it, so that they see the most desirable, sexually attractive thing they could ever possibly see. Thus these majestic creatures willingly blind themselves, knowing full well that when the song ends and the ugly lights come back on, the illusion will be over. Now you tell me who would win the talent competition.

And just why was this twenty-six-year-old gas station attendant more radiant and beautiful than those magical creatures four solar systems over? Because I say so.

"But everyone calls me Nara," the Queen of the Universe said.

Isadore looked at her and said, "Isadore."

"So, Eeeesadooor, where are you taking us? Cuz I got things to do, okay?"

"Somewhere good," Isadore replied, picturing his ceremonious arrival back at the Children of the Second Sun compound and the accolades that would follow. He sounded giddy, the little bastard. He was excited that she had told him her name, and again had visions of the two of them, but not at that far distant beach or movie theatre. No, he was picturing an impromptu encounter some time much sooner, where they would be rolling around in the back of his coffin-like crusty van, on top of a big sheet of bubble wrap.

A note about my life up until this point; I had always thought of myself as being an almost entirely sexless creature. The sight, and even the thought, of my own naked body had never prompted me with the urge to rub it against anyone else. The few times that I had engaged in any sort of sexual experience, excluding the time an orderly named Gerald had gotten way too intimate with me at the mental hospital one evening because he thought I was catatonic, had all left me exhausted. I had tired myself trying to navigate the human psyche enough to get the sex, then exhausted myself in the act itself. It all amounted to work the more I thought about it. And I never had a job I cared about.

As a result of this, I have never been a jealous person. I have watched happy couples and handsome men with rampant revulsion and foreboding, but more as someone watching wild dogs tear apart a gazelle on the plains of Africa, never as an equal. Certainly not as someone who stood a chance or gave a damn. Well, now I cared. I could feel my jealousy towards Isadore in my throat and chest. It choked me, bile was rising. How dare he get to talk to her? Just because he had a gun. I oozed my way to the front of the van, crinkling and squashing refuse in my path.

"My name's Hank," my bag of skin blubbered. She turned and looked at me in a way that said, "I know. I've always known."

"I know," she said. I stared back at her, my jaw dropping visibly. I let whatever light was in me come flooding out of my face like a blazing headlight. "You're wearing a name tag."

I looked down, and there it was. My big, paranoiac letters, upside-down, but still very legible. I looked back up at her and she smiled.

"Did you just come from a wedding or something?"

"No."

"Then what's with the nametag?"

Decisions.

Is it best to mention you are petrified the car will explode, that one of the wheels will fall off, that a whale will accidentally fling itself into the road, that the roof has leaks in it and acid rain is seeping onto the seats—that you spent the day experiencing waking nightmares involving serpent shit-demons, deadly umbrellas, that you cut peoples noses out of magazines?

Do you mention that you are nuttier than squirrel poop and you just came from a tiny, smelly room where you sat around with a bunch of other people that are nuttier than squirrel poop and blathered incessantly until spittle formed on your lips about this doom-filled planet, its rapid-fire karate chop of horrors—which you know could be nothing less than a science experiment gone wrong with the technicians asleep at the wheel?

Most would say . . . no.

Having no idea how to hide such an omnipresent thing, despite my years of bold attempts, my vessel gurgled, "I came from group."

Nara paused. "Group? Group . . . therapy?"

"Yup."

There was another pause, Isadore looked back at me, seemingly taking me in for the first time. Now I was the wild card. What would I do? Something wild? Something crazy? The short answer is, nope. I would sit there like a kid on field trip, not sure where I was being taken and not doing anything particular about it.

She adjusted her position in her seat and looked at me. I felt uncomfortable under her gaze, but it was not the excruciating rectal scrape feeling I got when others stared at me, I felt like I was being bathed in a warm glow, a glow that I did not deserve to bathe in. What Jahanara was thinking then was, *So that's why he pissed his pants.*

"What have they got *you* in for?"

The way she said it was nice, emphasizing the "you" only slightly, like we were fellow inmates at the funny farm. I opened my mouth to speak, but she interrupted me.

"Forget it. Words. Just tell me this. . ." She threw a mischievous glance towards Isadore, then leaned forward and whispered loud enough for him to hear, ". . .are you . . . violent?"

In those long years before I jumped off the bridge and died, I had been involved in at least twenty acts of violence. But most of these involved pushing children and old ladies down in my rush to escape some peril just behind me, and most of these occurred in the supermarket. I found supermarkets horrifying due to their garish colored mazes, fluorescence, meat products, and Muzak chock full of subliminal messages.

Being more susceptible than most, I heard each one of those stupid messages. And they were stupid. "Buy more cat food," and the like. I didn't even own a cat. Cats scared me. Elurophobia.

Of course, I would say this to the cartons of tinfoil in my shopping cart, I'd mutter, "I don't even own a cat."

And the Muzak, knowing that I might say this would follow with, "Buy a cat," at which point I would get so scared and angry that I'd run screaming past the meat section of the store, ignoring my usual ritual of poking all the packages, and straight for those huge sliding doors, knocking down old ladies and children in my raving mad dash.

The process of subliminal messages was first thought to be used by Tony Vicar in the 1950s in his movie theatre. He spliced snippets that said, "Hungry? Eat popcorn," and, "Drink Coca-Cola," into his movies. Let it be known now that I have witnessed the Greeks using their version subliminal messages in their theatre, long before then. The Greek method involved a man with a long horn standing next to the audience and whispering things into the audience's ear. These things were, "Plato is a hack," and other such slanderous musings, most often not pertaining to the play at all.

I was saved from having to tell Nara about the supermarkets—and the old ladies I have pushed—by Isadore's erratic driving as he swerved the van over to the side of the road suddenly. I thought that maybe he was going to shoot me. He didn't say anything. He just left the van running and hopped out of the car, ran over to the ditch, and unzipped his pants.

We waited. Our eyes locked. Was this it? Our moment alone to establish our profound connection and pledge allegiance only to each other? It was not. Nara looked over her shoulder and saw Isadore's back as he held his inherited-from-Ezzz-jizz penis in preparation for urination. Then she looked back into the van, not at me, but at the empty driver's seat. I followed her gaze. A look of understanding must have slowly leaked across my face, because she smirked at me and started to move towards the driver's seat.

A loud tapping stopped her. Isadore was pointing the gun at her through the window with one hand down his pants.

Outside the van, Isadore struggled with his belt and business while focusing the gun on the window. He opens the door to get better control of the situation while shifting his weight from foot to foot.

Nara moved her butt back to the passenger seat and watched the sad display of his flailing with his fly. She rolled down the window slowly, never breaking eye contact.

Isadore still had a measure of modesty and so turned away as much as he could while keeping the gun trained on the vehicle. We waited. He was having a hard time making the pee come out. It had been so long that his bladder and lower abdomen ached, yet he could not go. Turning his head to one side he said, "Make some noise or something, I can't go with you watching me." He looked back at the ground he intended to urinate on, and that was when the Queen of the Universe uncoiled and struck.

Nara grabbed his extended wrist, yanked it up, and with the other hand ripped the gun from his sweaty distracted grip. Isadore spun around with his bursting bladder and exposed weenie for us to see.

"Shit!" Isadore said. He raised his hands like he was in a western. Nara lowered the gun so that it was pointed at him.

"My turn to be the asshole with a gun, okay?" she said. "Hmm . . . three things. . ." She shifted in her seat so that she was facing him squarely through the door. "One: Put your bits away please . . . Hank and I don't need to see that. And before I turn you over to the cops, what the hell did you plan to do with us? And last," she moved her head back and wrinkled her eyebrows slightly, "what the fuck is with that head in your van?"

I was so proud. Isadore started to lower his hands. "Uh-uh . . . keep em up cowboy . . . and start talking." Jahanara had also seen a lot of movies. She pulled a strand of hair from her face and leaned forward with her other arm on the window.

"Can I piss first?"

She considered this. Then she turned and looked at me, her gun arm still poised. Not waiting for my answer, she turned back to him. "No. No you can't. I think soggy pants are in your future, shitface." Isadore groaned. He tucked his gear back into his jeans.

Just then, winding through the heavy salt-laden ocean air, we heard the eerie wail of distant police sirens. Isadore peed in his jeans. It formed a starkly visible kidney-bean-shaped dark patch near his groin.

CHAPTER ELEVEN

The Night of the Geckos, Dear God! the Geckos!
and
the Creature that Eats Worlds

Cops and robbers.
Cops and robbers is a game I played as a child. Yes, I was a child once too, but I try to avoid having too much of my ethereal consciousness dwell there. It was a lot of black socks against skinny white legs under the aching sun; a lot of harnessing the power of that sun to burn hapless insects with a magnifying glass; a whole lot of horrible things I did and said; and the catholic school system. Cops and robbers being the slightly modernized and moderately-less-racist version of cowboys and Indians. When it came time to play that game, I always had to be the Indian, or the robber. I didn't mind so much, I was just happy to be included.

When Jahanara used to play that outdated game, she always had to be the Indian. She had darker skin than most of the kids in her predominantly Caucasian seaside town, so it was far easier to suspend disbelief. But when it was cops and robbers, she always chose the cop. Things change, people change. A teenage existence spent skirting the edges of the criminal element made her more empathetic to the lawbreakers. If she chose to play it now, she would most definitely pick the robber.

As an adult, she had never met a police officer that she liked. And she had met many during her adventurous youth, including Officer Brent Cohen, whom she found repugnant. She called him a pig in her head every time he came into the gas station for jerky and chocolate milk.

Isadore turned and looked at Nara as the sounds of the approaching cops grew louder and louder. Nara was not used to holding an actual gun and she kept marveling at the weight of it, shifting it around in her hand.

"Please. You have to help me. I don't want to go to jail! I'm sorry!" he pleaded.

Nara really did feel sorry for him. I mean, he had just peed in his underwear, so it was a serious effort to not pity the guy, even if he did kidnap her at gunpoint.

"I'll tell you everything, I swear!" he said, his hands still in the air and his eyes going back and forth from the approaching cavalcade of cops and his captor. Nara took no immediate action. She was hungry, and Isadore had ruined her solo dinner plans. The cops at least would give her a doughnut or coffee or something, perhaps a blanket to drape over her shoulders.

"You shot that guy."

"That was an accident! Please! I was never going to do anything to you! I would never!"

"You're an idiot. A dangerous idiot. Say, 'I'm a dangerous idiot.'"

"I'm a dangerous idiot! This is a mistake! I never meant to. . ."

The sirens grew louder but my gaze was locked on the drama unfolding in front of me. Did it occur to me to hop out of the car and run towards the cops and safety? Not even for a second.

"Please," Isadore pleaded, "haven't you ever made a mistake before? I can't go to jail!"

"You should have thought of that before you started pointing guns at people!"

And then we saw them, the blue and red symphony of light. It was seconds later that the noise became the shrill *Weeeeooo! Weeeooooooo! Weeooooo!* that would end Isadore's wild ride.

Nara had made a mistake once, a big one. And even if her conscious mind wasn't keenly aware why the sweaty wild-eyed dweeb in front of her made her brain's memory banks dredge up that mistake, the noise of it grew louder than the police sirens.

The Ancient Greek view of time was much different than the one I was raised with. In my head I was always staring wide-eyed and full of horror into the future, as if strapped to the front of a careening and thundering locomotive bound for the what lay ahead, whereas the Greeks saw us as staring fully at the past and stumbling backwards into the future. The past and its memories can sometimes seem so loud, and the forthcoming a low-level easily ignored hum.

"Alright. Get in. But I drive." She hopped over the driver's seat, barely waiting for Isadore to get seated.

Within seconds we were off, the van whining like a wounded animal, and the cops hot at our heels! Isadore sat sweaty and soggy, poised on the edge of the passenger seat and facing backwards, his eyes fixed straight past me at the approaching lights. Nara was clearly enjoying herself. She had never had a chance to be in a high-speed chase with the cops before, and now she was completely innocent; if they got caught, she was the brave hostage. She looked in the rearview mirror and smiled, the lights were gaining. Of course they were gaining, it was a Volkswagen van.

"We gotta get off this highway," she said, her eyes narrowing. "There!" she exclaimed. Casting one look in the rearview mirror at me, she cried, "Hold on!" as the van whirled around a corner. I fell hard and smacked my skull against the bust of Totten's head as I went down and it made a loud popping noise like gunfire as the tiny bubbles on the surface burst upon impact. Isadore spun around and gave me a sneer as I pulled myself off the floor and braced my bulk against the safe.

Then we were bouncing and heaving down a very uneven, very narrow road. It was paved, but with large potholes spread across it like a paranoiac minefield. Nara gripped the wheel tight and never took her foot off the gas pedal. The trash on the floor was thrown around in a sea of noise and motion and I fell onto all fours, bombarded from every direction by pop bottles and crinkling cellophane wrappers.

Looking at it now, it reminds me of the universe right next to ours. The chip packages would hover and spin in the air in a manner most similar to the misshapen planets of that universe. There isn't a single spherical structure there, just cragged, twisted rock and matter, all chaotic and spinning wildly. The pop bottles flying through the air and smacking against the shiny bags are similar to the meteors that whizz and punch holes through the planets. Beautiful and alarming in its chaos.

Behind us we could hear the squadron of police cars whizz along the highway. They were not following us down the minefield road.

"Do you think they saw us?" Isadore asked, one palm against the roof to keep himself from cracking his head against it.

"Naw. . ." *bump, bump.* "That highway is too. . ." *bump,* "curvy."

We carried on in this way for a while, the road on either side thick with trees and broken-down wooden fences. Nara made two more erratic sudden turns, almost launching the van onto its side both times. We were now racing down a dirt road, turned to mud by this afternoon's sudden downpour. The trees on either side whipped past us in a frenetic green blur.

Finally, we came to a paved street surrounded by farmland. Nara cranked the van onto this and kept pace. She was an excellent driver, minus the occasional grinding of gears.

It's been a while since I drove stick, she said to herself. The sun was on its way down and we were still chugging noisily along when the van suddenly started to sputter and choke, and then, within moments, die. Nara guided it over to the ditch, letting it coast, and lifted her hands off the wheel to demonstrate that she was not at the cause of its death. And indeed, she wasn't.

Isadore had forgotten to fill the tank with gas while at the gas station. He had been so preoccupied with the robbery, shooting Murray, the safe, the escape, the police, and planning to have sex with Nara, that gasoline had never seemed a priority.

"We're out of gas?" Nara said, looking at the meter. She laughed her sudden raucous infectious laugh of one syllable. Isadore looked down, and to no one in particular quietly said, "I'm a dangerous idiot."

That body o' mine pulled open the sliding door and wriggled its way out, eager to escape the tomb of the van with its bubble-wrapped head, spilling pop cans in its haste. The other two followed, and we all stood looking at the beginnings of a glorious pink and orange sunset with a variety of clouds—Cumulonimbus even. The light cast on the field of long grass next to us was a deep orange as the air around us started to cool.

"What now, Fugitive?" Nara said to Isadore, who looked panicked. This had been his resting face almost entirely, except for rare moments of almost sociopathic bravado with the gun in his hand. Unfortunately, things were about to get a whole lot worse for this pee-soaked gas station robber, because it was just then that we heard a strange cacophony of sound coming towards us through the grass.

It sounded like hundreds of people beating wood together.

"It's the cops!" Isadore cried. We turned and looked in the direction of the noise, which Nara and I knew was definitely not the cops. And then we saw it: an undulating horde of tiny blue tokay geckos hopping, barking and clicking their way noisily across the field towards us.

"No, it's. . ." Nara started, and then stopped, squinting in the direction of the mass. We all stood dumbfounded. Isadore had never seen a lizard before, except behind glass, Nara had only ever seen geckos as a child during her family's vacations to Mexico, and the only lizards I had seen before then had been newts and salamanders. They were a clamorous and active bunch, with Zulaikha barking her orders and sending out her sister lizards to keep the horde together, but with little success.

It's safe to say that we all reacted with a strong fight, or in this case, flight reaction to the site of that many strange, blue and red yipping lizards in the middle of a farm field in rural North America. Herpetophobia is a very common fear, so I was not alone in my wish to escape the reptiles. Nara was the first, hopping into the passenger side of the van and slamming the door shut. I followed after one more long, awe-stricken stare, with Isadore close behind, using both hands to seal the door. When it wouldn't close all the way, he pushed and hauled on it. It was closed, mostly.

Once we were all stowed inside, he climbed up into the driver's seat, turned to us, and said, "What the shit?"

Nara just gawked out the window, her earlier naked fear of the unknown dissolving into a look of wonder, the orange light of the sunset on their blue and red scaled skin was quite striking.

"Ohhhh . . . Look at them all! They're all around the van! They're so cute . . . look! There's a bay—yahhh!" Her sentiment was disrupted when a bright blue lizard with red spots, approximately one foot long, yellow eyes blazing, leapt onto the window and clung there, barking. It crawled its way up the window and was working its way into the van, when instinctively, Nara put up her hands to block it. It wriggled its way through her fingers and landed on her lap, looking up at her.

"Tok! Tok!" the gecko said, turning its head this way and that.

Zulaikha was not happy with the losses sustained at the hands of a certain dog in the field by the trees. The number of geckos now hovered at thirty, and she longed for the safety of the water-logged crate on the sea. The Volkswagen van now seemed like a glorious haven and she urged her followers towards its solace.

The Queen of the Universe almost lost her cool. Most humans and cats she could handle with expertise, but this was different. She picked up the lizard by its end to fling it out the window, but she soon found herself holding a wriggling, detached tail, with the gecko still in her lap. She screamed a loud burst of alarm and threw the tail away from her, which happened to be at Isadore, who yelled and brushed it off onto the dashboard, where it continued to thrash and twist. The gecko scurried off her lap and onto the floor. My pouch of carbon and electrons scrambled for higher ground, I was most definitely terrified of barking tailless lizards.

"Where is it?" Nara said, jumping up onto the seat.

"I don't know!" Isadore replied, sweeping his foot through the sea of trash at his feet.

"Behind you!" I yelled, pointing wildly at Isadore's open window, where two more bright blue lizards were scurrying in. He spun around and grabbed one by the middle. The gecko responded by latching onto his index finger with his tiny gecko mouth and biting down. Isadore let loose a loud yowl, trying to shake the thing off his finger. But once a Tokay gecko grabs you, it is hard to convince them to let go. Nara and I watched with horror as Isadore flailed frantically.

In a truly gruesome moment, he started bashing the gecko on his finger against the steering wheel. While he was busy doing this, I saw another gecko scamper in through a crack in the door, and I pulled my legs up to my chest. Nara put one hand up to her mouth in horror as Isadore beat that little lizard savagely. Finally, after an uncomfortably long time, the gecko decided that being thrashed was not worth revenge and released its grip, falling down by the gas pedal. Isadore looked over at Nara, his eyes wild, his hair flurried. He was panting heavily.

At my feet the garbage was rustling. I swore I could see a patch of blue skin under a pop can near the safe. There were at least four lizards in the van now. I put my hands and shins against either side of the van in an attempt to lift myself off the floor. Then came the "Tok! Tok! Check-to! To-ka!" sound of the barking lizards reverberating in the tin can of the Volkswagen. I squealed and reached for the sliding door handle and freedom.

"Hank!" Nara said, one hand shooting towards my chest to stop me. "DO NOT!" She slowly moved her other arm around the passenger seat to intercept the door handle. I leaned forward, to heave the door, and she leaned forward to stop me, so I backed up. She seemed to relax. I tried to relax. But I was in a strange van with a strange man, and a gun, and bubble-wrapped heads, and didn't that empty potato chip package just make a noise? Fear had me by the short and curlies, and this time in a way that was justified. I leapt at the door like a wild animal, peeling it back with all my might. It crashed open, bouncing along its hinges with a scraping noise, to reveal a landscape of yellow eyes, blue bodies and rapid-fire barking.

"*Maldita sea*," Nara swore in the language of her mother.

We saw geckos climbing over geckos. Geckos poking their heads around the roof and looking at me with their slitted yellow eyes. One gecko screamed at another, and a gecko scream can make every hair on your mammalian body stand on end. Zulaikha was large and proud amongst them, swiping her tail at one of her sisters to initiate a charge for the suddenly available van. And all of them bright blue and gleaming under the thick orange sunset.

I had a vision then, of the geckos running for me and up my pant legs, working their way around to my butt. Then I had the sickening thought of ten or twenty snapping, angry geckos, working their way into my anus. I realize I don't have to share every single thought that went through my head on this day, but this one was particularly . . . vivid. I put one hand over the crack of my butt and backed away from the open door, pressing against the wall of the van and trying to slide the safe between me and the approaching lounge of lizards. The bust of Totten's head jabbed me in the back. I had nowhere to run to. Absolute horror ripped through me and I felt my vision going dark—which was a rare mercy my body had created for a level of fear it could not handle—when, for no apparent reason, all the geckos froze. They stopped barking, stopped scuttling, and all lifted their heads in the direction of the sky.

We stared at the geckos for a while, and then couldn't help but follow their tiny gaze skyward, feeling very much like god was about to descend upon us and punish Isadore for bashing that lizard.

And all around the planet at that moment, lizards were stopping what they were doing and turning their heads towards the sky. And I look now too, even though I am the sky. Because there was a reason, a reason not apparent to a human, but apparent to a lizard.

Three galaxies away, which is not that far, and very, very far depending on how you look at it, something wondrous and terrifying was happening. A creature whom we will call "Hord" had just enveloped an entire solar system with his solid black mass and crushed it, almost instantaneously. This sent ripples throughout our universe, through all matter, as it created a vacuum a solar system wide. The cosmic web shuddered and moved slightly closer together. On that ice-planet this causes the tiny ice-bugs to gag on their Slurpees, on Mercury it causes small plumes of fire, on New Elvis's new home planet it causes him to forget the words to "Love Me Tender."

The sudden death of this system effects Earth in a variety of ways: Fish suddenly change direction, trees creak even though there is no wind, humans get a sudden ringing in their ears, and all the lizards of the planet will look in the direction of the faraway demise. It is a form of silent tribute that they themselves barely understand.

How do the lizards sense this? It's their third eye. Scientists have long been trying to explain why certain lizards like the turantura, and the tokay gecko have faint remnants of a third eye between their two usual ones, sometimes fully developed and functioning. Until now, the function has been only guessed at. What the third eye sees is matter and space—ether. It sees the fabric of the universe. So naturally, it sees when this fabric is altered significantly. Which doesn't happen very often, but is rather noticeable when Hord eats a solar system.

I feel the loss of that solar system with its four suns and happy creatures like I had the wind knocked out of me, back when I had lungs. Those creatures lived in near constant sunshine. How could they not be some of the happiest beings in existence? Their joy was pandemic. There are some nasty things out there, but you can't blame Hord really, he was hungry, and he happens to eat solar systems.

We moved slowly from the van looking sometimes at the frozen-in-place lizards and sometimes up at the now ominous orange-with-tinges-of-purple-at-the-edges sky. Nothing was descending from the heavens. We were standing among the critters when Nara leaned down to closely examine one by her feet, marveling at his tiny lizard breaths as his light-colored neck craned upwards.

Zulaikha raised herself up and shook her body. She was the first to snap out of the third-eye spell. She barked and clicked, and pretty soon the rest of the geckos were barking and moving again. Nara took this as a signal to wordlessly run, and Isadore and I soon followed. We ran down the road, looking back to see the throng of blue tokays swarm over and into the green van.

When we had been running for a while, the two of them up front keeping pace and me lagging behind. Nara shuffled to a stop and I barreled into Isadore full tilt, almost knocking him to the pavement.

"Watch it you . . . weirdo!" Isadore said, recoiling slightly from me.

"I'm sorry, what?" said Nara, catching her breath with both hands on her knees. She stood up and pulled a sweaty lock of hair from off her face. "Did you just call Hank a weirdo?" Isadore looked at me—I was puffy, disheveled. Gray wolf sweatshirt and sweatpants, I definitely had an air of weirdo about me.

There are moments I want to hold onto on this day, to grab it with my ghostly matter-gripping fingernails and pull it desperately towards me. This is one.

The pink twilight on the right side of Nara's sweaty face; the slightly running mascara from her left eye, now luminous and gray; the sweat stains barely showing through her red polyester gas station shirt; her hair voluminous and wild in the fading light. She looked at me as my mouth gaped open like a deep-sea bass, and her countenance took a look of deep sadness. She bit her top lip from the inside slightly.

I want to take you inside her head again, to ride that lightning, but there is no need. I know what she was staring at, ancient Greek-like, in her past. It plays across her eyes as they shimmer in the fading daylight—that potent mix of regret, empathy and shame.

"Everyone's weird," she said flatly, and then turned and started walking again. "Let's get the hell out of here, okay?"

CHAPTER TWELVE

How it All Began,
and
Gladys Wants a Stink Bomb

I had nothing to say about our encounter with the geckos. It seemed to me at the time like just another unspeakable horror on the whirlwind carousel chock full of calamities we call daily life. What I was concerned with now was the fact that it was getting dark, the geckos and wild dogs could easily sneak up and maul us. And while this was a concern, it was not the one of paramount importance.

We had abandoned running for a brisk power-walk with no purpose or destination other than away from the van. I ran up to Nara, who was clearly the leader in the situation.

"We should get inside somewhere."

"Breathe that night air, Hank. It's invigorating."

"What if there are more . . . lizards? Or dogs?"

"Or spaceships. UFOs. I mean what the hell were those lizards even looking at? There was nothing there. That was so . . . eerie."

"Spuh . . . spaceships?"

Nara kept walking; movement was important. She glanced over at me and my wild sweaty terror. Then she took in Isadore, clutching his lizard-bitten finger and scanning the ditches by the side of the rural road for more hordes.

"Yeah, somewhere safe sounds good."

A word about alien spaceships. With a few exceptions (the one that came and cloned Elvis and the one that brought the hairy Ezzzz all those years ago), aliens have no interest in coming to Earth. The only ones with the cooperative skills necessary to build telescopes powerful enough, and spaceships fast enough, have better things to do than confer with a bunch of locust-minded mammals. That is why we haven't been openly contacted—it's not because our militaries are covering it up, it's because of our militaries. They have watched the descendants of Ablaya Mookdi for a long time, and they are, quite frankly, a little put-off. We are not very popular with the creatures we share this planet with, let alone the neighboring galaxies.

The whales, specifically the humpbacks, have been talking to the same aliens that made New Elvis for years. They do this by simultaneously singing all over the globe in a unified chorus. It's a song that bears a resemblance to a nuanced version of "Wooly Bully," and when all the humpbacks sing together the vibration echoes into the atmosphere so that the alien mothership hiding off-world can hear it. Being fans of music, it was the humpbacks that first heard the songs of Elvis from a radio on a freighter and pointed the aliens in his direction.

That night, Nara had flooded my head with visions of anal probes and eyelid removal. I ran up to her and walked close, Isadore striding up to her other side.

"We should get off the road, the cops will find us," he said.

"Nope. After those Lizards, I'll be staying on the yellow brick road thank you very much."

Isadore started patting himself down frenetically. "Shit!" he said.

"What now?"

"I left the gun in the van!"

"You left the safe in the van too. After Hank and I busted our asses carrying it. And your creepy head thing."

"We have to go back!"

"Fuck no. You wanna go back. . ." she glanced in his direction, ". . .go."

And that was that, women are born leaders. Isadore's whining about the cops, and my whining about the wild dogs in spaceships had convinced Nara that we had to find shelter somewhere soon.

So we never found out what was really in that safe. It wasn't money at all. Oh how Isadore, Totten and the Children of the Second Sun would have been disappointed! Oh how Jahanara would have laughed her sudden raucous laugh. Oh how I would have stared.

It was porn. The thing was full to the top with Nara's employer's collection of pornographic magazines. There were magazines about women with big breasts, women with extra-long fingernails and big bottoms, men with extra-huge hairless snakes, old women, young women, old women with young women, young women with old men, nothing too adventurous, but a real cornucopia. Totten most likely would have found some use for all that porn, some new clever torture, but alas.

"So, what's your name again?"

"Isadore."

"Right. What's with the head and shrine in your van?"

"It's uhm. . ." Part of Isadore's duties in the cult were to entice people into joining, but he was no Ryan Totten. What followed was a shotgun approach to discourse peppered with turns of phrase that he had been programmed to recite. The only time his language seemed at all genuine was when it came to describing Totten himself.

"So, you're in love with this guy?" Nara asked.

"No! Of—of course not," he replied unconvincingly.

I found his talk about Ryan Totten and his Children of the Second Sun very illuminating; many of the religion's theories corresponded with my own, but not enough of them for me to even remotely consider enrollment. I was terrified of flying, let alone in a spaceship. The whole concept of being strapped inside a metal tube hurtling through the air sounded to me like lunacy. Also, stewardesses.

One of the reasons I wouldn't fly was because I knew there was a slim chance the airplane could fly too high, break free of earth's gravity, and get pulled into space with no chance of coming back. I pictured my face pressed against the small oval window of an airplane as it slowly rotated through deep space, a stewardess standing over my shoulder smiling her empty smile, my silent scream lost in the vacuum until the spinning plane is no more than a speck against a sea of blackness.

Nara waited patiently until Isadore had explained the last part, about the bubble-wrap and the anal-oral sex. She looked over at him for a moment, then stopped walking, hunched over, and started to laugh. She grabbed her sides and shook silently. It was a release of tension, and a direct reaction to the recent absurdity she had faced. Tears were welling up in her eyes. Isadore looked at her in dismay.

"It's better when His Highnessedness tells it," he said.

"Who?" Nara gasped, looking up at him.

"Our leader."

She stood, suddenly composed. "I went to school with Mormons, people believe some crazy shit. I'd almost like to meet this leader of yours one day. Almost. But right now, I'm freakin' starving." She left her hands on her stomach and massaged it. "And cold," she said, moving her hands up around her bare arms. Isadore gallantly took off his jean jacket and offered it to her.

She grabbed it quickly. "Now you'll be cold."

"No I won't," he replied, hunching his shoulders together.

It was definitely starting to get cold. It's always cold in seaside towns at night, even in the summer. We walked in silence for a while, not seeing any houses, just the now ruddy reddish-brown color of the sky and the dark shapes of fields and trees.

"A cheeseburger. With gravy fries," Nara said, staring wistfully ahead. She was a vegetarian. "What about you Hank? What's your favorite food?"

Timidly, I replied, "Tapioca."

"Pudding?"

"Yup."

Tapioca was served in most mental hospitals in that area, usually on Tuesday afternoons. Having spent most of my life in mental institutions, my repertoire of food items was limited to cafeteria-style cuisine.

"Mine is Spaghetti!" Isadore piped in. Nara looked briefly at him, then turned back to me. She was not normally one for small talk, but the hunger was distracting and she was afraid to crack open another hornet's nest regarding religious beliefs.

"So what do you do Hank?"

I looked back at her, silently taking stock of my activities of the day. I had woken up, numbered my cereals, arranged all the cushions on my couch, watched TV, washed my hands a couple times, put another layer of tape around all the edges of my windows, coated my apartment with odor-eater, re-arranged the cushions on my couch, cut out people's noses from People magazine, eaten a giant tub of blue Jell-O with pretzels in it, and washed my hands a couple more times. Then I had gone through the lengthy preparations necessary to leave my tiny apartment, including restacking all the cushions from the couch into a cozy pyramid.

From there, I'd walked the long way to my therapy session (avoiding any potential squirrel-housing trees), sat in my group therapy session where Carl and I had engaged in a bitter psychic war over who got to sit next to the window (he had won). After that, I had a near-death experience at a stoplight just outside, and had celebrated my survival with an ice cream cone, got kidnapped, been attacked by blue lizards, and was now walking with a beautiful young woman and my twenty-year-old kidnapper in the darkening night air, down some mysterious road going god-knows-where, and ready to encounter god-knows-what.

"Do?" I said.

"Yah, yer job."

My mouth opened. Then closed again. No words came out. When enough time had passed for it to be awkward, Nara moved on to the next question.

"Okay, your hobbies then."

"I don't have any." Which was true. All those things I just mentioned were most definitely not hobbies. I *had* to do those things. The consequences would be dire and lasting. I would fixate on something, one thing, that I'd failed to do, and I would have to go back, usually at four in the morning, to set things right as best I could. If I couldn't, it would continue to haunt me.

"Well," she continued, already bored of her attempt at small talk, "some people, they have a . . . a *thing*. Something that they have to *do*, some sort of . . . purpose. My aunt used to say she heard a voice, it told her that she had to buy ceramic dogs. Do you ever get that?"

She knew. She knew too much, too fast, and I should run away now. I desperately needed to run away. And look, there I go!

"Wait!" Nara called into the damp night air.

I see my body bouncing, shimmying to and fro. For a large guy, I can really haul. I am around a bend in the road in mere moments. A line of ants narrowly avoids demise beneath my flat slappy feet. I can see exceptionally well at night, now that I *am* the night. I see one of my white sneakers with the missing aglets snag on a root and my body tumble sideways into a thorn bush.

"Hank!"

"Let him go. . ." Isadore says. Even then I could hear him. I had not made it very far.

"Hank, I'm sorry! No more questions, okay?" she says. She has one hand up to the side of her mouth in an effort to make her voice sound louder. I shift and a thorn stabs me in the thigh, causing me to let out a short, fast yelp, and ruining my clever plan to remain quiet until they pass.

"Oh. There you are," she says, walking up to me and crouching down.

While Nara is pulling thorns out of my extremities, I will tell you about the voices. This one's a doozy.

Some of the voices in people's heads are very real, and there is a very scientific explanation for them, though perhaps not the one that you are thinking of. They are what happens when there is a misfire in the circuitry of the brain's radio. When it starts picking up static from the Omniverse.

We think of the brain as a computer, a central processing unit, but the more scientists investigate, the more it seems like an FM receiver. Brain circuits can tune into the frequency of other brain parts deemed relevant at the time, and initial evidence is found that the brain has a tuning knob that is actually influencing our myriads of messed up and practical behaviors.

At least that's what the voice told me. Her name is Gladys. I'd introduce you to her, but I just don't want to. For the longest time I thought she was just the nagging voice of my mother, my internal conscience or something. Alas, my mother is alive, well, and possesses limited psychic powers near as I can tell.

No, Gladys lives in a universe that is attached to ours. I am hesitant to call it a parallel universe, as it's not all that parallel at all, it's definitely more of a diagonal. First off, there is no sense of smell in Gladys's universe. When she does manage to get through to my brainwaves through the static, she loves nagging me about the smells here. How did Gladys get through to me way over here on this lil dirtball we call home? She wasn't trying to, her brain radio misfired at the same time as mine, and a connection was made. She is largely incomprehensible and easy to ignore as her world is so different to ours, but *phewf*! That woman can talk! I'd say I'm glad to be rid of her now that I am dead, but that would be asinine, as I now have her and an infinite number of others located where my brain radio would be if I still had a head.

Question: Parallel Universes and places where smell doesn't exist?

Answer: Yes.

Question: Did you really think we were going to just let that slide with no further mention?

Answer: I suppose not.

 To explain this, we will have to start at the beginning, how things really began. I know that you've been told over and over about the Big Bang. *Bing badda BOOM!* Then there was light, that sort of thing. Truth be told, explosions are great, but they aren't everything. Our universe, and many of the others, *grew*. Like plants. Like a Chia Pet.
 Where the little universe seeds and the little chia seeds differ is in their respective growth rates. Chia grows fast, while universes grow ridiculously slow. It takes eons for a universe seed to sprout, and many more for those roots to form other universes. Inside the universe there are some periodic fast growths and deaths, but that's all extremely relative. If you were to view the novel Chia Pet explosion in 1977 in geologic time, it would look exactly like an eruption as the decorative terra cotta critters and their sprout coats appeared in many homes across the US. These little spurts and wiltings could be called explosions, which could resemble a big bang.
 In fact, I am watching now as Nara yanks the thorns out by their roots in order to release me, and I see all the spindly tendrils,

and YES! It looks like roots. If Nara were to have an infinite number of those, intertwined and in every direction possible, then you would have a good model of the Omniverse.

So Gladys and her universe are similar to ours because they are touching, they are cousins. It's a good thing I don't have to spend eternity with just her, as we had long ago exhausted all of our conversation topics. What Gladys really wanted was for me to find the worse smell in the world and make it into a ten-ton stink bomb. She's a bitter old broad and she wanted me to punish my planet for flaunting its smells in her non-existent, vicarious nose. She wanted me to take my stink-bomb act on the road too, to transport it to as many planets in the solar system as I could. I had no interest whatsoever in the project, but she was very persistent.

Alas, the worst smell on Earth was constantly evading me. Every day I would smell a new combination that would make me want to retch. But retch *enough*? I had a few close encounters during my experiments with decaying fish and chicken feces though, and that bathroom in the gas station. The big problem with my and Gladys's plan was the bomb part. Both of us were entirely clueless on how to build a bomb.

Having never had an interest in science except for how to avoid diseases, I had limited knowledge of chemistry, biology or even geology. This was largely due to an acute case of Hellenologophobia, which is a fear of Greek words. Much to my dismay, Greek and Latin words are commonly used in science to describe things like fears and phobias.

My avoidance of Greek culture was partly due to a film entitled *Zorba the Greek*, which my mother forced me to watch at a tender age. The particularly scarring scene involved one of the main characters being stoned to death by the villagers. I was too young to remember why they did that to this poor woman, but just old enough to remember the music and the clothes and the stones—which explains both my fear of Greek culture, and my fear of geology.

Gladys was a crusty, old, noseless spinster in her alternate version of something that resembled Nebraska. All she knew about was making flavorless biscuits and needlepoint, so stink bomb-building was not in our collective futures.

The worst smell in the animal kingdom is created by the zorille of Africa. It is a black and white weasel-like thing, that when threatened releases hormones from a set of glands near its anus. It then proceeds to swing its bottom back and forth in front of its attacker. If only I'd lived in Africa!

The worst smell ever, in the entire Omniverse, is on a planet many universes away from ours. There is a tiny creature there, about the size of a pea, with underarms that could peel the sclera off your eyeballs.

As Nara was hunched over, picking thorns out of my leg and attempting to untangle me, I sniffed her hair. It smelled sublime.

"Ah!" I cried, as a new pain in my right leg pulled me from my reverie.

"Why did you run?"

"I . . . get scared." Concise. That's good, past me, real good. I approve.

"Scared of *me*?"

"No!" I blurted, because I actually wasn't. "Scared of bugs. Of clowns." I usually started with those two relatable phobias. But before she could assuage and relate, I kept the list going, "And umbrellas, acid rain, and eyeballs, of sewer snakes coming up the toilet, and jigsaw puzzles, and definitely lizards."

"Yeah, that was intense." She pulled another thorn out and I winced.

"Yeah. So many lizards!" I said, like a man-child.

"So many." We shared a smile, both of us looking down.

"I'm starting to think that's enough excitement for one day." She grabbed another thorn branch from my calf and I reached down to assist, accidentally moving the branch so that it stabbed her. "Dah! I got this, hold still, okay?"

She was right. That was certainly enough adventure for one day. And if only it had stopped there in that quiet moment under the crepuscular sky, huddled in a thorn bush.

I wish we could all just stay here, by the side of the road, but we know how this day ends, shuffling toward the void, some of us faster than others.

CHAPTER THIRTEEN

The Fear
and the
Blue Light Way Down Low.

Once Nara had pulled all the thorns out of my corpus, she helped me to my feet.

"Look," Isadore said, pointing at a faint light off in the distance. "What do you think it is?" he said warily. I opened my mouth to gesticulate my theory about the military base and the possibility of a giant glowing shit snake ready to be unleashed in the sewers, but Nara interrupted me.

"Hank, I can guarantee you, it isn't whatever you're thinking."

Looking closer, we saw that the light came from a tiny wooden shack, a dull blue glow pouring out of one crooked window. Nara suggested we go over there and say hello, to which I replied that I would most assuredly rather not. Well, what I actually said was simply, "No!" in a sudden startled burst as if someone had caught me squatting over the toilet bowl. They were both slightly taken aback and looked at me in surprise.

"You can stay out here. I'm going to check it out."

I looked around to see that fog was starting to creep its milky way across the dark grass, and I am most definitely homichlophobic. I had seen that movie once, *The Fog*, and that was all it took. The mental hospitals I had lived in were even more careless with their television monitoring than my mother was. I had been one of the many patients up all night after a showing of *Herbie the Love Bug*. As far as I know, the doctors have not yet made up a word for a fear of living cars, though it won't be long. It wasn't hard to trace my fear of cars back to this seemingly innocuous Disney movie.

My nyctohylophobia, or fear of dark wooded areas, was a low-level hum on my strained psyche, moving me towards the other humans with a largely uncharacteristic urgency. I walked extremely close to Isadore, at one point stepping on his heels as we headed down the winding driveway.

"I wish I had the gun," Isadore said.

Nara let out a noise of derision and frustration. A twig snapped under my foot and I jumped, bashing into her shoulder. She didn't push me away, but put her hand on my arm to brace me. "Lizards and tigers and bears, oh my," she said. I had seen Wizard of Oz, so I attempted a smile back at her—my first.

Once we were at the top of the driveway we found a dilapidated blue house with a large rotten porch and two empty white wooden chairs gleaming like the bones of a fresh kill. The light we had seen from the road was coming out of a tiny shack adjacent to the house, partially hidden by a proliferation of blackberry brambles. There were plants coiling and streaming off of every part of the structure, giving the house, and particularly the windows, an overwhelming sense of sentience. Surrounding the foreboding abode was thick, tall grass, up against the sides which had not been mowed for years. Upon seeing the house, we all stopped.

Was this house alive? In essence, yes. The many human and non-human residents inside of it had spent so much time with their complicated electromagnetic fields and positive and negative ions that a fair amount of residual psychic muck still clung to its walls. This mishmash of influences is very similar to a genetic code, as if the house had many parents, each person that walked through its walls leaving a small energy imprint. In a manner of speaking, it could feel, and it could think. And there is of course the many things inside the house which had a life force before mobile creatures even entered the picture. The wood, for example. Right now the house is afraid of us. It's been a long time since it had visitors, and is feeling slightly embarrassed about its worn condition. I can relate to this house and its difficulty communicating. What the house does is send off a subliminal "go away" message loud and clear. I never seemed to need this ability, as people generally steered clear when they saw me coming.

"The crickets are loud tonight," Nara said steadily, a noble attempt to draw our attention away from the ominous looking building. She cocked her head slightly to one side, "I mean, *real* loud. It sounds like hundreds. . ."

"Maybe we should try somewhere else," Isadore said. Her clever ploy hadn't worked on him, his eyes, wide and white in the darkness, were fixed on the hanging porch door.

"Where else?" she said, starting to walk towards the house. Is she brave, or stupid? Watching from my bucket seat in every atom, I know that Nara was also put off by the house, but she was hungry too. It was seventy-thirty hunger-to-bravery.

Nara sidesteps her way up to the porch, pulls aside the squeaky screen door, and knocks, thrice. *BOOM, BOOM, BOOM*, goes her fist on the door, loud and hollow through every corner. The sounds seems to go on for far too long, most definitely spooking the bejeezus out of all of us. Isadore and I are still standing where she left us in the yard. She motions with her hand for us to follow, and we shuffle our way forwards, moving slowly, but in small fast steps. We stop when we get to the edge of the porch just as Nara knocks again.

Then, we hear it—a sound like a tiny circus very far away. Slowly, it grows louder, filling the heavy air with a manic swooping music.

"Over here," Nara says, stepping off the porch and into the long grass. The music is coming from the shack, where it has reached a frenzied crescendo, cutting through the buzzing of the crickets. She works her way up to a slanted window and is soon bathed in the blue light spilling out. We follow, fumbling our way through the cool, long grass. Isadore keeps almost touching me, partly from his clumsiness and partly from my jerking, hesitant steps. I am afraid of long grass, there is no telling what could be hiding in there. Nara stretches up to peer in the window, her eyes widening at what she sees.

"Oh . . . my . . . god. . ." she breathes.

"What?" Isadore asks, his voice a hoarse whisper. All of a sudden, the swooping bombastic music stops cold, and a voice calls out.

"Who's out there?"

"Fuck. Run!" Nara says, turning to face us.

I am always ready to run. I spring into action like a mighty gazelle on the plains of Africa, like a hlethlan on Rilfex's moons, plowing right into Isadore and knocking him flat as I bound away. Nara is attempting to leap her way through the grass too, but it's slowing her down so it looks like she's moving underwater. I take one fitful glance behind me. There's nothing I can do for her now, for either of them. She would want me to escape, to live my life in memory of her.

"Hey! Wait!" the voice from the shack calls out, but I have no intention of stopping and waiting. I notice the others are now far behind. I take one last look over my shoulder, and not paying attention to where I'm going, trip on an abandoned tire and stumble headfirst into the grass. After a moment of quiet contemplation in the dirt, I roll over.

The stars are out now. I feel it start to creep from my toes all the way to my chest: The Fear. Not just any old fear. *The* Fear.

I would shut my eyes, but it's too late. The cycle has started, the gaping maw is yawning wide, and before me I can see the novas, quasars, pulsars—so many stars.

During the day I was often looking down to avoid what I came to call Big Sky Syndrome—the feeling that the sky is impossibly huge and you are impossibly small and alone. But Big Sky Syndrome is amplified tenfold when you are faced with the night sky and its many stars.

I know now that the number of stars you can see from Earth with your naked eyeballs is three thousand six hundred and twenty-three. The most you can see with a telescope is only nine thousand one hundred forty-three. Which is not that many really.

But sprawled in the grass it was like I had come face to face with the infinite. And it was this notion that horrified me. My little brain could not handle the thought of being that little. A completely crippling fear of the infinite is called apeirophobia, and is the grandaddy of fears largely because it is so very much beyond our control. A clown you can avoid; no circuses, no clown porn. The infinite is a concept that humans have devised countless ways to avoid pondering, using the clever constructs of lights, television, and complicated romantic relationships. The night sky has a way or ripping all of these constructs aside and forcing you to stare into its jeweled abyss.

Many humans share this phobia, but not all of them are induced to vomit when confronted with it. When faced with the immeasurable, my first reaction was to reach for the Gravol—an anti-nausea pill—as I was also emetophobic (or afraid to vomit). I normally kept my Gravol, my towelettes, my nose plugs (for when I felt like defying Gladys), and my assortment of anti-psychotic medication, in a fanny pack around my waist.

A fanny pack is a small satchel worn around the mid-section. It was especially popular in the 1980s, and came in a variety of colors, usually fluorescent. Mine was absent that day, in my rush to arrange all the cushions on my couch I had neglected to arm myself with it.

My second tactic, which does little to disparage the vestige of mental illness, is to repeat a mantra I cultivated after years of terror. There's no one around to hear it now, so I burble it out into the cold night air.

"Infinity schminity," I say.

"Infinityschminityinfinityschminity…"

The words rise in urgency and tone, like consecutive key changes in a 70s ballad until I am close to screaming out loud. I am sweating hot bullets in the cool night air, and very soon I'm going to vomit all over myself. I see the sky beneath me, like the earth has turned upside-down and I am hanging over the stars. I can feel myself start to fall and keep falling forever. When I close my eyes, there is no escape, just more infinite darkness, stretching and yawning. Oh, the stars.

A word now, as I writhe in terror in the long grass, about all those people who decide their actions by the whims, fancies, and paths of the stars: Astrology. All I really have to tell you is that astrology, star signs, horoscopes and all that are a *system*. And, like all systems, were created by people who are searching for order, structure, and predictability in an effort to make some sense of their surroundings.

Do the stars millions of lights years away affect our day-to-day life? Of course they do. However, the advice they give is not as practical and full of common sense as the weekly paper or updates would have you believe. It is just as chaotic and nonsensical as everything else in the Omniverse. While a typical horoscope, for example, might tell you to be understanding with your co-workers next Wednesday, to be gregarious and social on the 22nd, and that you should enjoy quiet time with a loved one on the 27th, an *actual* horoscope would read decidedly different. It might tell you to go ahead and wear that bunny suit all day on Thursday, make sure to poison your neighbor's dog on the 26th, and engage in every opportunity you can for an orgy before Friday. If everyone followed what the stars were really saying, the world would be a different place indeed.

And, as I open my eyes to find an anchor or any kind of foundation, I see it, just to my left. It is a spaceship, with a green landing light, blinking its eerie way across the spacious speckled sky.

It's not a spaceship. It is a man-made weather satellite. It is one of two thousand six hundred and fifty-three that were in the sky that night. One of the eight thousand one hundred and ninety-four pieces of man-made wreckage whirling around in our atmosphere. Yes, there is litter in space, a whole lot of it. I told you humans were filthy. There are even a couple of dead bodies floating up there, but we'll save that story for another day. For now, it is enough to know that it distracted me from the fathomless chasm of the infinite and drew my attention to a fear far easier to digest and far easier to explain.

Had I known it was a satellite and not an alien spaceship, I still would have been terrified, but most likely not to the extent where I got up and started running and screaming like a four-year-old girl. Maybe not Nara, as she was never much of a screamer, but some other four-year-old girl.

Satellites: That was part of why I coated my apartment in layer upon layer of tinfoil, in an effort to shield myself from the x-ray, cathode ray, heat sensor, and laser beams that were flooding down from above, watching me from all directions at all hours of the day. See, I was afraid that *They*—the same ones who decided when the walk signal should end and the big scary orange hand should appear—had somehow discovered my and Gladys's plan, and were using satellites to watch me, to watch us, in preparation for our eventual capture and subsequent torturing.

"Naraaaah!" I bawled, hysterically running in the direction I had just come from. Bounding and leaping, arms flapping wildly at my sides, I see Isadore and Nara standing by the shack bathed in dim blue light. Just beyond them I see another figure. No, two. One really small. "They're coming!" I holler. "They're—" and then I trip again over something big, black, and hard.

It is another discarded rusty tire. Underneath it lives a delightful colony of small black ants that were resting comfortably until I came along.

Moments later I land on something small, gray and hard. There is a sickening smack sound.

A rock. Under it lives another colony of ants, but these are the big, red kind. They are at that moment making plans to take over those tire ants once and for all.

It hurts in big white splotches of pain. I moan and clutch my head. There is blood, hot and wet blood, my own blood. My seal has been punctured, I am dying. I hear Nara's sweet, slightly husky voice, angelic and soothing. She is lifting me up off the ground. Her smell. I will not open my eyes. I will let her take me to the afterlife, to somewhere else, buoyed up by her careful embrace. It's not a bad way to go. Better than a slap in the face with a freezing cold wall of water that kills you instantly.

CHAPTER FOURTEEN

Ventriloquism for Dummies, the Silver Teapot
and
Invisible String Theory

Instead of falling off the Earth and into the infinite stars, I find myself being led blindly into a place which reeks of animal musk and booze. I sniff deeply, taking note of the combination of aromas. There are two voices besides Nara. No, three. I am being lowered into a soft smooth chair. The blood is running down my forehead and over my eyes, making it difficult to open them. Nara starts to wipe it off slowly, pushing my hands away when I move them towards the searing pain on my head. All the while she makes little shushing noises, and thanks someone when they give her a cloth. The cloth is cool and wet on my face. Wincing and squinting, I open my eyes a crack.

We are all inside the blue-lit wooden shack, a TV is silently flickering in the corner, and there is a man seated on a crate in front of me. He is a large man with large black-rimmed glasses and gray hair that curls and twists straight up. He is wearing a red plaid shirt with the sleeves cut off. In one hand he holds a pewter mug, while seated on his lap—and presumably, his other hand—is a small ventriloquist dummy made to be an exact replica of the man himself, only smaller, complete with the hair, the glasses, and the exact same torn plaid shirt. It is holding a small red accordion.

I leap up from the chair and back away from the man, knocking over a rake and pressing myself against the far wall of the shack. It's hot in that room, extremely hot; I feel it rising all around me.

"Hank," Nara says. She is seated to my left, extending a comforting hand to me, but I cannot look at her. The dummy is fixed on me, boring into me with its plastic eyeballs. I cannot speak, I stammer continually but form no intelligible words. It is a symptom of my automatonophobia, or unbridled fear of ventriloquist's dummies.

Isadore is also staring at the dummy and the man. He is standing next to the door, one hand still clutching the doorknob. The dummy is unblinking. Out of all of us, it is only the man with the glasses and Nara that appear somewhat relaxed. Nara has taken off Isadore's jacket and draped it over her lap.

"I'm Lloyd. Lloyd Bilk," says the man, giving a nod with his head in my direction and Nara's. "And this," he says looking down at the dummy who looks up at him, while I cringe and cower closer to the rake as it turns its head, "is Lil Lloyd."

"I can introduce myself, old man," the dummy says. It extends its hand to Nara.

"Heh. Cool," she says, attempting to appear like this is a fun and ribald turn of events. She reluctantly takes the odd little wooden hand in hers.

I whimper slightly. Plans are forming in my head, and some of them involve violence. I want to grab the rake off the ground and thrash the little abomination within an inch of its deranged little life. The dummy can read my thoughts. It cocks its tiny head up towards me and says, "Easy there, little man."

Nara laughs warily, not the boisterous sudden laugh of earlier, more of a titter. She turns to me and puts out her hand again. Slowly, I take it.

"Sit down Hank, let's look at that gash on your head." And ever so cautiously, I move forward with my eyes never leaving the dummy. I ease myself down onto a plush blue rocking chair. As I am doing this Nara decides it would be a good time to make pleasant small talk, to try and establish some normalcy for her sake and ours.

"So, what's with Lil Lloyd?" she says, careful to keep her eyes away from mine and the puppet's, lest my fear rub off on her. The man chortles quickly and loudly, like he's never been asked such a ridiculous question, then stops suddenly.

"I'm a puppeteer actually. Lil Lloyd and I are part of a show tonight at the fair down the road."

"Ohthankgod," Nara breathes out quickly.

"What?"

"Nothing. I've just had a long day. I didn't know if I could handle another nutjob at this point." Isadore and I chuckle nervously in agreement, then realize she's talking about us and fall silent. Lloyd takes a sweeping glance at us, then locks onto Isadore, who looks away timidly.

About random events: tokay lizards, car accidents, bizarre men with puppets, that sort of thing. From where I sit, nothing seems random anymore. It all feels like there are invisible strings attaching things together in a complex web that looks like a funnel spider's. You tug one invisible string, and the rest bend and flex. You can predict a whole lot if you pay close enough attention. Often you can tell what people are going to say if you watch them intently enough, you can become a student of body language. Nara was a big fan of doing this when she sat in bars alone.

It is the same with the Omniverse. Knowing it like I do, I can often predict what is going to happen to any one person or thing. Those lizards had been encountering food shortages steadily over the past thirty years, it was only a question of time before they left for greener pastures. And Hord hadn't eaten a solar system in two thousand years, it had been slowly encasing the one that it did eat for just over a thousand years. So both of those events were not spontaneous, erratic occurrences. They were a lonnnnnng time coming.

There are an infinite number of so-called "random" things happening right now, all weaving that glorious fabric we call fate, but for the sake of brevity, we'll focus mainly on the ones that my jumble of meat stumbles into on this one late summer evening.

For Nara, today had started off like any other in her seemingly dreary doldrum but not altogether unpleasant existence. She had awoken to the early afternoon sunlight bearing down on her, making her large white bedroom unbearably hot. She had gone into the kitchen in search of liquid, but found mostly empty beer cans as she had attempted to get drunk last night but lost the enthusiasm for the project multiple times. She was still hungover despite this failed attempt, and poured herself a glass of lukewarm tap water, being too impatient for the water to run cold. Then she sauntered over to her large window, heaved it open, and leaned against the sill, watching the people pass below her. The day had started calmly but took on an inkling of the unusual when she left for work to discover that someone had stolen her bike, and then left it two blocks down the road.

How's this for random intertwined invisible strings: It was my therapy session nemesis, Carl, that had stolen that bike. He had stolen it, then realized that it was girl's bike and left it. Carl had gender issues.

Then she'd gone to work to find the Slurpee machine spitting out brown sludge into a massive pool the shape of Texas. After she had cleaned it up quietly and diligently to the sounds of Top 40 alternative radio, a young Filipino man with a gun robbed her and took her hostage. Then lizards. Now this.

"Oh? What was so odd about today? Would you care to . . . talk about it?" Lloyd asked. "Lil Lloyd and I are great listeners." Both of their heads clocked slightly to the left simultaneously.

"Not really, no," Nara says, glancing once at Isadore then moving the cloth up to my forehead.

"Are you sure? I mean, I don't normally pry into people's secrets, but your friend there looks like he's seen a ghost." With that both Lloyds looked at me again.

Ghost. I had the sudden thought then that this Lloyd Bilk had to be a ghost. Why else was he sitting with a wooden copy of himself in this tiny wooden shack in the middle of nowhere if not to lure people in and . . .

My fear of the undead, or phantasmophobia, had always been pretty vague and listless. Most often just the thought of seeing them would be enough to spike some adrenaline. Occasionally I could picture them attempting to gnaw on me with their ghostly intangible lips, but it was more of an established visual fear.

Usually, if I had any suspicion that someone might be a ghost, I would quickly excuse myself while they were in mid-sentence and run away as fast as I could without turning back. A ghost with a ventriloquist dummy was a horrific new twist on a twisted being. I had to escape. Set fire to the place. Quote the Bible. But Nara's firm pressure on my aching head kept me still.

Also, the stars: Best not to think about the stars. Best not to think about the aliens. Best not to think about ghosts, and pick a spot on the wall and stare. So I did that, just behind the man at an old poster on the wall. It was wrinkled almost beyond recognition but Lloyd looked exactly the same, same gray hair and glasses. It read, "The Breathtaking Bilk Brothers! Tonight at Circus Gotti!" in meticulously ornate swirling letters, giving it a definite old-fashioned look that was complimented by the wrinkled yellowed edges. How old? Twenty? Thirty? Fifty years? He looked the same. Had to be a ghost. I turned abruptly to Nara and leaned in to whisper this ghost-theory to her, but Lil Lloyd swiveled his head at that moment, staring straight at me so that I squealed and pulled back.

"What?" Nara says.

I couldn't respond. She turns to look in the direction of my horrified stare, but the dummy has already turned away and appears to be excitedly whispering something in Lloyd's ear. They are chattin' a while, which is especially strange when you realize it's actually just a monologue. After a moment, they both look up at us.

"Can I offer you guys some tea? Lloyd Bilk asks. I don't have to be at the carnival for another hour." He is already taking an ornate silver teapot off a crate next to him and placing it next to an arrangement of pewter mugs, all with one hand; the other is stuffed up the ass of the miniature version of himself. The dummy's head and gaze are fixed on Isadore, who is frozen, much like a deer caught in the headlights of a ventriloquist-dummy-shaped truck. Nara is the only one capable of any response, so she responds to fill the silence.

"Suuuure," she says.

Soon we are all seated, except for Isadore, who remains hovering by the door like a hummingbird by a feeder. We are sipping a pungent yet not altogether unpleasant tea, and listening to the voices of the Lloyds sing country hits of the 1940s with accordion accompaniment. Lil Lloyd's accordion only has two notes, an in-note and an out-note, so it is more of comic relief to the plaintive songs the bigger one sings. They break into a song by Hank Williams Sr., which reminds me of my father, kind of.

I don't remember my father. He gave me my name, lingered for a couple years, and then he hit the open road for greener, more childless pastures. Mom said that he was crazier than a junebug and had thrashed Big Bird within an inch of his life in the middle of a busy mall when I was two years old.

Big Bird was a man inside a giant costume of a big yellow bird from a TV show called *Sesame Street*.

Mom said that Father had an untreatable condition called xanthophobia, which as a child I took to mean a fear of giant birds. A very understandable fear, you have to admit. It wasn't until recently that I had learned that xanthophobia meant a fear of yellow. The color yellow, the word yellow, all things yellow. Years after thrashing Big Bird, he got arrested after setting fire to a Subway restaurant and was somewhere locked up, though Mom never bothered to find out where.

I did bother to find out once I was dead, because it was bothering me. He was in a tiny room in a halfway house, chainsmoking as if his life depended on it. He used to be very handsome, that I can tell. Like an aged moviestar. I parked my ghostly butt across from him for a while as he stared into space, and tried really hard to think of something to ask him. Seeing as I now know everything about his short, problematic life, there wasn't much for us to discuss. I just stared into his frightened, busy eyes as he stared through me and felt a sadness like I had been hollowed out.

Whatever closure I had been looking for was not happening. Closure is a fallacy. Life gets messy and then messier, and then you sweep it under the rug for a few years until you trip over it.

Was I just a hapless victim of nature? Or was I nurtured into being afraid of almost everything around me?

Question: Do our genetics decide our actions?

Answer: Our genes give us a basis, yes, but it may surprise you that our actions can actually modify the way these genes are expressed. If we think of our cells as actors, and DNA as a script the actors are supposed to follow, it still needs a director. Someone to call the shots and change things on the fly. If you give the same script to Steven Spielberg that you give to weirdo auteur John Waters, you are going to get a very different movie.

So we have some control over what we are handed by our ancestors. Unfortunately, some of what our ancestors hand over to us are ingrained fears and inherited traumas and reactions. Why are babies afraid of snakes? Even pictures of snakes. What did a snake ever do to that baby?

I was not afraid of yellow. Lay it on me. Purple, however, purple was a different matter entirely. Porphyrophobia. Whenever I wanted to feel close to Dad in a socially acceptable manner, one that didn't involve doing things I knew made me appear crazier than a junebug, I would listen to country music. Which means I know the song that Lloyd is singing now. It's one of my favorites, "Hey Good Lookin'" by Hank Williams Sr. He has a powerful yodel, and for a brief period of time, I forget to be afraid of the dummy and the strange shack with its rusted hooks and phantom posters, of the bizarre man in front of me, tokay geckos, Isadore's eyes, of almost everything. Music is a powerful force in the universe.

From the look of hazy rapture on Nara's face, she is not afraid either. She looks over at me, and I can only smile. She smiles back, then reaches over to place her hand on my arm, but misses and her arm falls in between our two chairs, and she giggles. That was weird, I thought at the time.

Isadore suddenly keels over. His pewter mug falls to the ground, and he is lying in a heap by the door. That was also weird, I thought.

"Isadore-ore-ore-ore. . ." Nara says. Her voice is sluggish and huskier than normal. The Bilks have stopped playing. "I feel so . . ." Nara says, she looks at him, then down at the cup, and suddenly her eyes widen; she is awake again, wide-eyed like the dummy, ". . .fucked up! What did you do asshole?" she shouts, standing shakily.

"Nara-ah-ah-ah?" I say.

"He drugged us-sus-sus!" The Lloyds watch motionless, still holding their accordions. "Come on, we gotta. . ." She hauls up on my sleeve, but it slips out of her grasp. Then she spins towards the door, hunching over Isadore. "Get the fuck up-up-pup, okay?" She grabs the back of his shirt and lifts him a half-inch, then drops him heavily onto the hay-strewn floor.

I feel so sleepy. It's been a big day, I can rest now if I want to. There is definitely something in the tea.

The something is a highly potent combination of Yohimbe from South Africa; Lactuca Virosa from Zambia; kava kava from the South Pacific; huge amounts of valerian root from Northern Asia; a powerful cough medicine; marijuana from Vancouver Island, British Columbia; sleeping pills, and chamomile. Lloyd likes it strong, but this batch was made special.

The dummy starts to titter and chuckle with increasing frequency until his flapping mouth starts to cackle, a shrill maniacal laugh that penetrates my skull, the top part of his little head thrown back and shaking.

"Now, Lil Lloyd, you stop that," the big one says, looking concerned.

This is more than I can take. I leap up from my chair poised to strike. Having spent many years doused on a herculean myriad mountain of prescription drugs, whatever was in that tea will not stop me now. I grab a rusted pitchfork from where it leans against the wall to my left, and point it at Lloyd and the dummy, who stops cackling.

"Whoops," it says in its tiny voice. I am ready. Frozen, but ready.

"Here!" Nara calls from the doorway. Her voice sounds loud and booming like she is at the far end of a cave. I heave the pitchfork at her and she catches it, in the next motion she charges forward, ramming it through Lil Lloyd, so he is pinned up against the wall of the shed. She drops the pitchfork and staggers back. We make a great team. Big Lloyd has narrowly escaped the same demise, but is clearly in shock, staring at the still form of the punctured puppet.

"Run-un-un . . . move! Okay-ay-ay-ay?" Nara says. She grabs one of Isadore's arms and starts to haul him out the doorway. I stumble, knocking over the teapot and chair, and grab his other arm. Together we start to lug him through the long grass and into the night. But he is so extremely heavy.

I am not frightened at this point of the Lloyds chasing us, I am just trying not look like a wimp in front of Nara. It's okay though, because near as my fogged brain can tell, no one is chasing us. We are sinking into the grass like it is a delicious ocean of cool, refreshing blades. And beneath that, the damp inviting soil, calling me into it. It was so hot in that room. There are magnets in the ground. I don't even have time to consider my barophobia, or fear of gravity, because we are going downnnn. Naptime is imminent.

I always wondered what I look like when I'm asleep, and it is rather unfortunate. There is drool streaming out of my mouth, and my nose is making this whistling noise with each breath. Nara, of course, looks beautiful. Her hair is strewn across her forehead, her full, sensuous lips are parted slightly. Isadore is face down next to a pile of deer doo doo.

CHAPTER FIFTEEN

The Big Beautiful World of Lloyd Bilk.

Lloyd walked up and stood over our still forms as they lay sprawled in the grass like abandoned marionettes with severed strings. He took a deep breath and slowly raised up the puppet on his arm so that it too could survey the scene.

"I wish you hadn't started that laughing, I feel bad enough," he said to Lil Lloyd.

"The fucking bitch just impaled me with a pitchfork! How about a little sympathy *my* way?" Lil Lloyd leaned over Nara and made a hacking and then a spitting sound, but of course, no spit came out as he was just a dummy.

"I hope we're doing the right thing," Big Lloyd said.

"How can you even say that? The little cunt was obviously in on it from the start."

"Don't call her that!"

"Aw shit. Here we go again."

"What do you mean by that?"

"You know damn well what I mean."

"No . . . I don't, or I wouldn't have said it."

"For chrissakes. She's not *her*, Lloyd."

"What are you even on about?"

"And here you come running to her defense, even though cunt-face here is obviously an accomplice to armed robbery!"

"I said don't call her that! Besides, we never even got to hear their side of the story. Maybe her boss was a real asshole. Maybe that place deserved to be robbed. We could have just asked them."

"Rrriiiiight, and live off Mr. Noodles for the next two years, but have the remembrance of that one sparkling conversation. Pull your head out of your ass, Lloyd."

"How do we even know if there's a reward?" Lloyd asked.

"Hellohhh . . . he shot a guy! There's gotta be *some* kind of reward! You need to listen to me Lloyd. This is just like that night at the circus. . ."

Lloyd took another big breath. "Do you really think she was in on the robbery?"

"Naw . . . hostages always wander around with their kidnappers in the dead of night. *Of course* she was!"

"And the fat, squirrely guy?"

"He must be the brains behind the whole thing."

"He doesn't look that smart to me."

"Look who's talkin'!"

"Good one."

"Enough hemming and hawing, standing here like two dummies flapping our tongues in the breeze."

"Shouldn't we take them to the police now? That tea wasn't that strong."

"You're for*getting* Lloyd. . ."

"What?"

"The *showww* tonight?"

"Crap! What time is it?"

Lloyd set Lil Lloyd on a stump in the grass where, though no longer capable of moving his mouth, he micro-managed instructions on how to load our incapacitated bodies into the back of the Puppetmobile—a converted ice cream truck. Lil Lloyd also let loose a litany of expletives in Nara's direction over his puncture wounds.

The Lloyds, like so many residents of that small seaside town, (when not out water-skiing, having barbecues and eating salads with marshmallows in it), watched a lot of television. About one hour before our arrival, the evening news had shown a tape from the security camera of the gas station, complete with the scene of Isadore shooting Murray in the arm. They had notified everyone to be on the lookout for a green Volkswagen van, as they had not found it yet.

They also had a picture of Nara taken from the staff room, which they flashed across the screen every few seconds. She looked extremely bored in the picture and yet somehow still vivacious and radiant. The TV station was also enamored with her image and kept a picture of her in a little window through every following broadcast.

It was this picture that had revealed our identities to Lloyd. He had been about to ask us about the whole thing when Lil Lloyd had whispered his plan to drug us and deliver us to the police in the hopes of getting a reward.

After much dragging and grunting, Lloyd managed to haul us all into a heap on the grass near the back of the converted ice cream truck. As he was in a rush to get to the carnival and set up for the show that evening, we were piled unceremoniously atop one another.

Lloyd pushed up the sliding door to reveal a mass of red curtains and various puppet limbs. Hanging puppets of different sizes and personalities dangled their heavy feet in the air while a mess of wires interlaced across the ceiling. There was also a series of gears on the floor, as the side of the van opened and lowered to form a small stage complete with a hardwood floor and curtains that rose and fell.

A painting of the Bilk brothers during their time with Circus Gotti was emblazoned on the side, their two faces aglow with spontaneous joy and excitement. The truck had been Lloyd's home for many years and had seen countless strange towns across the continent, but money had been tight lately for the brothers, as they had been without work for some time. Lloyd had taken to painting houses to fill in the gaps between circus tours, but the money was never more than the price of a few week's supply of Mr. Noodles. Circus Gotti had fallen on bad times after an unfortunate mishap during one of its performances.

I will attempt to take us there while Lloyd attempts to drag my bloodied bulk up into his truck. It is with a similar, lurching and clumsy motion that I can travel to two different places in space and time with any accuracy.

And here we are, strapped inside this tiny airplane named Electra, next to a beautiful young woman as she goes hurtling towards the ocean. She is expertly pulling back on the controls, while bracing herself for the inevitable impact. The man next to her, Fred Noonan, is shitting bricks, hollering over and over,

"Oh my god Amelia, this is it!" He looks at her frantically, his fist-sized heart thumping spastically in his chest, but she is busying herself with trying to save their lives. "Amelia! If we live through this, promise me we'll live alone together on some tropical island for the rest of our lives! No one else, just us together forever!"

She reaches over and flicks a couple switches angrily. There is no noticeable effect.

"Promise me!" Fred says, grabbing onto her arm.

"I promise," she replies, not looking at him. His nattering in her ear is distracting and she would say anything, even this, to shut him up.

"Do you mean it?" Fred cries.

"Yes!" Amelia replies in a frustrated exasperated tone. And then the plane hits, and all is spray and chaos. But don't worry, she's alright. There is a fish near the surface when the plane hits, the fish is far from alright. It's fish paste.

Darn. That wasn't the Circus Gotti at all. I told you my control over time and space was shoddy. Hold on, I'll try and steer us towards that night at the circus, because it will help to explain a lot of things better than I ever could. It just takes some focus, and I won't be able to hold it for long as I don't want to lose my grasp on that moment by the Puppetmobile.

Ah. Here we are, the Big Ring during the final days of the shoddy Circus Gotti. We are watching a greasy, mustached man by the name of Vincenzo Gotti, whip a large tiger named Devaki, in an effort to get her to jump through a hoop. The tent is dark and orange with a few gaping holes letting in the slowly shrouding purple light of an August evening in Portland, Oregon. It is opening night, so there is a healthy crowd including some local reporters! Lloyd is celebrating a great set earlier that evening by eating beans backstage, just to our left, next to the wire fence of the tiger cage. Mmm, beans.

Vincenzo is really hitting that tiger, which greatly angers Lloyd, whose face does not move much, but twitches with every lash of the whip. He sets down his beans, having lost his appetite. Lil Lloyd the demonic puppet is there too, looking sparkly and new and not all that malevolent.

Devaki the tiger is unresponsive to the whipping, even when the hoop in front of her gets set alight with a *shwoof* noise.

"This is bad," Lloyd mutters to himself.

"You ain't whistlin' Dixie," replies Lil Lloyd, "Say something. Do something, Lloyd." Lloyd puts the tiny puppet aside on a bench nervously and looks around. There are no other humans around to see him talking to his puppet like a real human.

Suddenly a *HRUMPF!* comes from behind Lloyd and a grizzly bear wearing a tiny fez pushed over to one side of its head comes staggering over. Lloyd steps out of the way as the hulking mass of brown fur rears up on its two hind legs, towering over Lloyd and leaning against the chain fence of the tiger enclosure from backstage. While Devaki the Tiger and Bubba French the Dancing Bear have never really got along, Bubba is upset by the intense beating Vincenzo is unleashing. As much as the bear mistrusts the tiger, he would actively snarl at the weasel nephew that was running the Circus Gotti into the ground.

Owch. And under the stars many years later Lloyd misjudges the distance between the ground and the truck and smashes Isadore's head into the side. It makes a loud noise that rings through the chirping night air. Isadore remains asleep and drugged, but despite himself, and despite his knowledge of Isadore's violent crime, Lloyd feels guilty. He has always been a man of solid moral fiber, if not always a man of action. Which we are about to witness.

"Alright you stupid beast. . ." Vincenzo grumbles, "leap!" Devaki does not move, but instead snaps irritably once in his direction. In response he cracks the whip hard across her back and she lets loose a yowl, making a clumsy leap away from him, stumbling slightly. A low growl comes out of her that not many have heard before. Vincenzo hits her again. She stops growling. Lloyd sets down his beans and moves toward the cage. The crowd is growing quiet with only a scattering of murmurs reverberating around the tent.

"Lloyd," a tiny voice in Lloyd's head says, "do something. Yell, scream, get help."

"I'll lose my job," he says to himself, looking over at the puppet on the bench.

Vincenzo hauls back on the whip, bringing it far back to his left, then he cracks her again as hard and fast as he can, so that she starts to gallop forward weakly, tripping over her own feet.

When she leaps, she does not make it, falling heavily onto the ring, and the fire spreads quickly over her body. The assembled crowd lets loose a sickening gasp that turns into screams. Vincenzo recoils in horror, dropping the whip to his side and grabbing onto the locked door of the cage to start fumbling with the door.

"Lloyd! Listen to me! Do something!" the little voice says.

"Yes," he replies, and grabs a large mat from the floor, then kicks open the door, which knocks Vincenzo aside. He rushes forward and tries to dampen the flames, but it is already far too late. He waited too long.

Vincenzo jumps up to his feet and runs out of the cage, where Bubba the Bear is waiting for him with a snarl and hefty lunge. When Vincenzo falls, Bubba grabs him by the leg and hurls him like a rag doll towards the center of the ring. The crowd begins to panic and rise, flooding towards the exits as if they themselves were ablaze.

The papers write about this and it becomes a national story with the catchy title, "Tragedy Under the Big Top." This phrase is like a virus and soon thirty-six different late-night news reporters on thirty-six different stations are heard saying, "Tragedy under the big top tonight in Oregon," in a theatrically somber, yet whimsical tone.

I saw this broadcast, because I watched a lot of TV during my stays in different outreach centers. I don't recall this story, but I'm usually pumped up with enough drugs to waylay a pachyderm.

So Lloyd and Lil Lloyd leave the Circus Gotti not long after, and take Bubba the Dancing Bear with them. For a while they travel together in the south of the United States and Central America, but they have a falling out in Baton Rouge, and head their separate ways.

Before Nara, Isadore and I stumbled in, Lloyd spent a lot of time alone in his shack. The performance at the carnival tonight will be his first in years so he is understandably nervous, even if it is unwarranted—he is a top-notch ventriloquist and a very accomplished singer. This quiet seaside town also doesn't have the most discerning taste when it comes to live performance. As a result of his nerves, he would rather forget about kidnapping us altogether, but Lil Lloyd can be very persuasive.

Once we are all finally loaded into the back, he scoops up Lil Lloyd from the stump and puts him in the passenger seat of the truck. He checks to see if the keys are still in the ignition, where he always leaves them, and is surprised to find them missing.

"Do you have the keys?" Lil Lloyd pipes.

"I always leave them in the truck," Lloyd replies, his face full of panic.

"Just jokin'. I gottem right here."

Lloyd sighs and turns the dummy over, reaching into the cavity up his backside and pulling out a small ring with two keys on it.

Are we going to address the pachyderm in the room? The question that I am sure has flickered across your mind at least once? No, Lil Lloyd the ventriloquist dummy did not put the car keys in his backside; Big Lloyd the human being did that. Does Lloyd have multiple personality disorder or is he just incredibly method in his approach to performance? Unfortunately, it's a combination of both options that leans heavily toward the first one. Some truly upsetting childhood trauma and that horrific night in the circus had given Lil Lloyd more and more control in the past few years, without the socially acceptable outlet of comedy and gargling whilst singing country songs to off-gas this neurosis. Which is truly unfortunate, because Lil Lloyd is a bitter, angry, jaded entity out to hurt the world in all the ways he feels hurt himself, and he is quite literally holding the keys.

Soon the truck is roaring out of the pothole-puckered driveway, puppets swaying wildly to and fro over our unconscious bodies as Lloyd cranks it onto the winding road in the direction of the carnival lights, their orange and yellow glow cascading up against the tall trees on the horizon.

CHAPTER SIXTEEN

The Puppetmobile
and
the Funless Couple.

A particularly large wooden octopus puppet falls off its hook and lands on my stomach. My adorably chubby-wubby container of flesh jerks awake, but is almost immediately rendered catatonic at the sight of so many puppets hanging eerily above me. That fragile mind of mine cannot even piece together my location, being constantly assaulted by all those smiling, sad, or angry puppet faces. I pull my legs up to my chest, plug my nose, and start to slowly rock back and forth. This is what I do when things are too much and vomiting is not an option. It doesn't help necessarily, but habit has rendered it similar to a biologic reaction, like a sneeze when one encounters dust. There are many things we think of as biological reactions that aren't, and vice versa.

For instance, there is a biological reaction in the mind which dissuades the brain from thinking too hard about itself. Try this: Picture your big juicy brain sitting in your head. Now imagine your brain thinking about itself. This is different than a standard passing thought about the nature of existence, but a concentrated and prolonged effort to unify the idea of blood and tissue with self-awareness and a higher consciousness. Most often this exercise will cause a slight ache to form near the top of the head. Why?

Because, dear friend, the brain is like a muscle in many ways, and certain parts require continued use before they can be used without discomfort. In most humans, this part of the brain goes unused, as even slight pain tends to divert action. What happens to those who use this "brain-awareness muscle" all the time? Well first off, they are poor conversationalists. Secondly, they start to see the world slightly different than most. Once the pain subsides there is a feeling similar to a gentle pulse. This is a shortcut method to the long dormant mammalian version of the third eye. Alas, I say they see the world only *slightly* differently because the connections to this third eye appendage were long ago severed evolutionarily, and the eye itself is missing. So, we don't get to watch Hord eat galaxies or watch atoms spin before our eyes, which is probably not such a bad thing, as it could be distracting, if say, a saber-toothed tiger or shit demon was coming for us.

I slowly move my hand up to the bleeding wound on my head, which hurts the outside of my skull, not the inside, as the pain was caused by a rock with red ants under it, and not by my lazy brain. It all comes back to me then, through a haze of cough-syrup-spiked tea; Lloyd, the lizards, the impaling of the dummy. At least now I know why I have "Hey, Good-Lookin" playing over and over in my head.

"Nara. . ." I whisper. She looks so peaceful, so resplendent that I almost don't want to bother her. Her lips parted, one arm is over her head, chest rising and falling with a gentle rhythm like the lapping of waves on the shore . . . but she is the only one who can help me escape the puppets. "NARA!" I holler.

I am all of a sudden terrified that Lloyd might hear me. That the door would open and that creepy little dummy will have me executed in a most horrible way. They will strip me naked, laugh at my genitals, splay me in acid rain with a purple umbrella on my head and feed my incoherent mess headfirst to the toilet snake before finally digging up my corpse to have me join their unholy legion of ventriloquist undead.

I lean over Nara and shake her, but she won't budge. She lets loose a little moan and then rolls over onto her side. The truck veers around a corner and I grab onto something to steady myself. It feels odd. I slowly look to see what I am holding to discover the nose of a puppet with bulging eyes and straggly purple hair, a large toothy grin forever plastered on its face. I yank my hand away with a small yelp and stare up in horror at the swaying bodies and little people all around me.

The carnival is a sea of lights and noise in the middle of a bumpy field. It is so bright you can't see the stars above, thank god. Families and lovers abound, wandering aimlessly or rushing towards the many stands and rides. For a small oceanside town, it is impressive in its scope, including a large performance tent and a Ferris wheel! Officer Brent Cohen rips off a swab of hot-pink cotton candy and shoves it into his mouth so that his lips smack around like a mustached cow.

The cops had found the Volkswagen van and were staking out the nearest gathering, which happened to be the travelling carnival down the road. There was even a lady cop and a man cop dressed up like your average strait-laced, stiff-backed, funless couple at a carnival. She is in a peach-colored sweater and blue jeans, he is wearing a yellow short-sleeved golf shirt and blue jeans, with a baby blue sweater tied jauntily over his shoulders. He has sunglasses resting on the brim of his baseball cap, even though the sun went down hours ago. People didn't do that thing with the sunglasses and the hat in this quiet seaside town—the occasional tourist from California yes, but never the locals.

They paced around with the lady cop holding a large pink pig made in China, which the male cop had won after spending thirty-five dollars at the ring toss booth. She had gone behind the lines of porta-potties, ripped a hole in the pig's bottom, emptied the mixture of sawdust and plastic stuffing from inside onto the smelly grass, and stuffed her gun up inside it. Now they were standing next to the stage where Lloyd was due to appear at any moment, like two eager lovers of ventriloquism acts, with no display of said eagerness on their funless faces. The male cop was pretending not to look at the lady cop in her tight sweater. She was not looking at him; it was just business.

The other cops were wandering in actual uniforms, holding pictures of Isadore and Nara, but for some reason no pictures of me.

I can postulate on the reason now of course; I was Caucasian and almost quintessentially nondescript. Picking me out of a police line-up would have been next to impossible in this town with its high ratio of bland-looking Caucasians. I had spent so long trying to make myself invisible to my fellow humans that I had almost verily succeeded.

Lloyd pulled up to the gate in his Puppetmobile and explained who he was, as if an explanation was necessary considering the giant mural on the side of the truck which stated in large luminous letters, "Lloyd Bilk! The Vanguard of Ventriloquism!" The guard at the gate was a local kid named Jackson that had never been put in a position of authority before, so he was doing all he could to make everyone else feel small and worthless. It was as if he had been given machine-gun hands for one brief day.

Also, Officer Brent Cohen had just been telling Jackson all about the robbery, and how he was to check every vehicle for anyone who looked like Isadore or Nara.

"Could you step out of the vehicle Mr. Bilk?" Jackson said in his mightiest teenage voice.

"I'd love to son, but I'm running late. I have a show to play in fifteen minutes. Lil Lloyd and I need that time to get ready!" Lloyd was damp in the armpits with sweat trickling down the small of his pasty back in fine rivulets over the fact that he had three drugged people (one bleeding from a wound on the head) locked in the back of his truck, but he tried not to let it show. He was a performer; he could be very intimidating when he needed to be. Jackson stood confused. This man was disobeying him. As much as he wanted to seem powerful and in control, he also knew that it was his first day on the job so he should avoid any trouble. Lloyd's bizarre countenance had trouble written all over it. He stared at Lloyd for a long time trying to decide what to do.

Lloyd, for his part, did nothing, he let it appear like Jackson had the upper hand. Finally, almost ten seconds had gone by and Lil Lloyd was starting to belittle the boy in his tiny voice from over Lloyd's shoulder,

"Oh come *on*, you little weasel."

Lloyd put his hand up to his mouth and coughed loudly in an effort to mask Lil Lloyd's comment, also hoping to snap the boy awake.

"Alright, well, move along then," Jackson finally said.

"Thank you," Lloyd said, gunning the truck past the gate and to the right, veering along the dark backbone of the carnival.

The stage was next to the pony rides, and a distinct potpourri of animal feces and hay brought Lloyd screeching back to that horrid night at the circus, but he blocked it from his mind by busily searching for his equipment. He grabbed a suitcase from the front, tucked Lil Lloyd under his arm, and rushed for the stage, taking one last fitful glance at the back of his truck.

When the truck stopped, Nara began to stir. The constant motion had kept her lulled, but now she was coming around. That, and the fact that I was shaking her continually.

"Papa Smurf, no, stop. . ." Nara groaned sleepily.

She opened her eyes with a start, those big luminous steely eyes, and then squeezed them together again. I waited five seconds before I started babbling hysterically at her, gripping her arm tightly.

"Stop it," she said, her eyes still half-closed. She opened them again and looked at me.

"Andthenanoctopusfellonme andallaroundmethe eyes. The eyes, I just know that he'saghostNara. Theybotharefeedme to somekindof ghost snake!"

"Hank. Stop. You're hurting me."

I was not aware that I was squeezing her. I looked down, pulled my hands off and continued ranting. "Anthelittleone, he knows! HeknowsIknow. They're goingto kill us! Wegotta. . ."

She stared at me for a moment and then slapped her hand square on my mouth.

"Where the fuck are we Hank?" she said, looking around. She tentatively removed her hand,

"I—I . . . I think we're dead. I think we're in Hell."

"Trust me, we're not dead. Not yet."

"Buh. . ."

"Where's Isadore? Oh wait, there he is," She looked down to see that she was sitting on his leg.

"Hell," I muttered.

"Phew! You guys really reek like piss, you know that? Mannn. . ."

"N' the glassy orb eyes. . ."

"Fuck. Look at all this. Must be the creep's storeroom." She stood up and looked around. Then she started lifting things, kicking the octopus puppet out of her way. Its wooden tentacles landed in a heap next to me so that I scurried backwards, slamming against the door of the truck which made a loud clanging noise.

"We're in the bastard's truck!" Isadore groaned and started to shift in his sleep.

"Hey! Get up!" she yelled. He did not.

"Deh—demon," I said, looking down at the octopus.

Nara stepped over to where I was babbling, and squatted, noticing a crack of light coming from under the door.

"Hank, wake up that little shit . . . I'm going to try and get us the fuck out of here."

Lloyd was busy hooking up his accordion onstage, but soon found that he had left all of his cables in a bag in the back of the truck.

"Durnit," he swore.

"What?" Lil Lloyd asked.

"I left the patch cords in the back of the truck!"

"Well, borrow some."

"From who? The guy who makes balloon animals?"

"Do not go back to that truck Lloyd."

"They're probably still asleep anyway."

"Well, I'm going with you."

The two cops in disguise witnessed this heated exchange each with one raised eyebrow. Unlike myself, Lloyd was socially permitted to be crazy, as he was a ventriloquist, so they admired his commitment to the craft of ventriloquism as he ran off the stage like a man possessed.

"Crap!" Nara was trying to pry open the door with a puppet limb when it snapped in half and caught her on the hand.

"He won't wake up," I said while hunched beside Isadore. Though still in a state of high agitation, now that I had a mission to accomplish, I could tear my eyes away from the puppets. Nara cradled her hand and turned to face the two of us.

"Stand back," she said, her hair falling in thick reddish strands over her face. She pulled her foot back and let loose a savage kick into his side. Isadore was awake now.

"Ow! What the fuck?!"

"I'll tell you what the fuck you little shit! First you fucking kidnapped me, and now the fucking puppet man drugged us and locked us in the back of his fucking truck!"

Isadore rubbed his side and started to process this information. Just then we heard two voices outside the truck, one really low and baritone, and one high and sneering. "Shit! Hank, lie down," Nara whispered.

There was the sound of Lloyd fidgeting with the padlock, and then the sound of him turning the handle on the door. Finally, the back door slid up with a clattering noise. The smell of pony poop was immediate and nasty. I saw Nara's nose wrinkle slightly next to me.

"Shut up Gladys," I whispered.
"Did you hear that?" Lil Lloyd squawked.
"What?"
"One of them spoke!"

Nara took this as our signal. She pushed with her hands, slid herself forward while raising her knee, and then slammed her booted foot as hard as she could into Lloyd's jaw. There was a lot of frustration, anger and righteousness in that boot. I clambered up to a standing position, anxious to escape the unholy parade of puppets surrounding me. Isadore pulled himself up and staggered forward, falling heavily out the back of the truck and onto the ground below. Lloyd staggered back, clutching his jaw in shock, Lil Lloyd limp at his side.

I moved forward to the edge of the truck with my hands poised in front of me like an animal ready to strike. I was suddenly halted as Lil Lloyd was being raised up to eye-level, bearing down on me with his wide glassy eyes of inherent evil. I was stuck like a fly in sap, paralyzed with my mouth gaping open.

"That's right fatty," Lil Lloyd jeered, "stay right where you are."

"I-I didn't want to do this," Lloyd said, looking down at his arm. "And if you'll just get back in the truck there won't be any trouble. I'm really sorry." I saw those ghostly glass eyes, I felt them, despite their obvious glassiness, and was terrified of their wrath. Nara looked sideways at me, then back at the Lloyds.

"Oh for fuck's sake," she said, and leapt off the truck, bending her knees to cushion the fall. She strode over to Lloyd, who recoiled as she drew near, and wrenched Lil Lloyd from his stunned grip, then heaved the dummy over a fence where it landed face first in a massive pile of pony shit.

"Let's go," she said to me, yanking Isadore up by the elbow. I crawled down and ran past Lloyd, who was staring forward with his mouth open in silent protest.

Soon the three of us were running behind the games booths, bobbing and weaving like we were drunk. The effects of the silver teapot were still palpable. My eyes were wide with wonder at all the noise and lights pouring through the spaces between the stands. Then I thought I saw a glimmer of a clown so I decided to focus on keeping up with Nara and Isadore. Finally, Isadore called "Stop!" and we all stopped. He was hunched over and swaying. "What the shit, man?" he gasped.

"Don't you know any other words?" Nara snapped.

"Where are we?"

Nara looked around, she put her hands on her hips in the way that her stern father used to do. "Some kind of state-fair thing. Fuck those hotdogs smell good."

"I have to get back to the compound. I have to tell His Highnessedness what happened!" Isadore said, straightening himself. Nara looked at him for a moment.

"Well, go then. I won't stop you. Me, I need a hotdog." She held out one hand, palm up. "You. . ." she demanded.

"Isadore."

"Isadore. Give me some money." He pulled a wad of bills from the cash register out of his jeans and handed it to her. "Hank, you want a hotdog?"

"I don't eat hotdogs," I said. I was afraid of lips and assholes, particularly those of the naked mole rat, which is neither naked, a mole, nor a rat. I had heard from a homeless man once that most hotdogs were made of naked mole rats. My doctor dubbed this one zemmi-carnophobia. Although I couldn't help but poke the variety of meats in the supermarket, I would be damned if I was going to eat any of them. It was more of a horrid curiosity that made me do that.

"Suitcherself," she said to me, and started to walk away.

"Wait!" Isadore called.

"What?!" she said, turning. Isadore just stared at her, looking desperate. It was a common look on him, a common look on both of us. She breathed a derisive sigh and started walking again in the direction of the nearest food truck. We followed, like her little urine-steeped ducklings.

CHAPTER SEVENTEEN

The Carnival
and
the Locust Seed.

Nara ordered her hotdog from the concession stand while Isadore and I huddled beside the dunk tank. There was no dunkee present.

The dunk tank is a game people play where someone sits on a seat over a tank full of cold water. Then other people throw baseballs at a target which, if hit, triggers a switch dropping the unfortunate person into the water. It is only really fun if someone hated is sitting in the dunkee seat. Once, at an elementary school fundraiser, the principal of my school sat in the seat and charged all the students five dollars for a chance to dunk him. He was unpopular and raised a lot of money for a school that loathed him that day.

At that moment I had briefly entertained the idea of strapping Isadore to the vacant seat. That was the only thing I could think of when someone angered me—submerging them in water. I had spent all morning imagining Carl's weasel head completely submerged in toilet water as he sat there gloating in his chair by the window. Once Nara had her hotdog, she walked over to us. I tried not to watch her eat but was captivated by her carnal hunger. I was normally revolted by anyone eating anything, ever, and I was curious of how I would respond to her eating ratdog in front of me.

I know now what hotdogs are actually made of and it is not the naked mole rat. It is not by accident that you won't find the phrase "floor scrapings" in the ingredients on most hot dog packages. I've said too much already. You think you want to know, but you don't. You can always follow Nara's example: Take a hearty bite and remain blissfully ignorant.

I was distracted from watching Nara by Isadore, who kept jabbering about the Leader and his mission and such—how he needed to get back in time for "the ritual cleansing." He was trying to work the Lloyds into some kind of conspiracy to silence the Children of the Second Sun, that Lloyd was hidden agent of the president of something, but his heart was not fully in it, I could tell.

Totten had told everyone that the President of Nicaragua didn't want anyone leaving the planet and ripping a hole in the space-time continuum. The President was so determined to quash their efforts that he had placed agents around the world of every race, creed, and occupation. Totten knew it was necessary for his people to have an enemy. He was waiting to unleash the news that the President of Nicaragua was actually a human-sized reptile in disguise, and that the reptiles were indeed in a power struggle to thwart the Children of the Second Sun.

I have some bad news. Totten was on to something there in his drug-fueled ramblings, though he was wrong about the President and the reptile fiends. It's actually a whole lot more complex than that. The Ezzzz folk—the same interstellar beings that brought us the penis—left a legacy of another sort behind, buried deep in our cells. In our genes. More specifically, in a little gene which I have come to call the "locust seed," and which has been called by others the "selfish gene." This gene's whole function is self-preservation. The space-reptile part of our make-up wants us to fuck and fuck, and breed, and kill and eat, to such a point that we destroy everything good about this planet. We are our own worst enemy.

But here's the kicker: The locust seed gene's mechanisms are so powerful to such a point that we are deceiving even this basic greedy part of us; all of this pollution, spraying of hairspray, driving of cars, rampant destruction of all things chlorophyll-giving, farting of methane, exhalation of carbon monoxide... all these things are the work of our selfish gene working to save our hapless lives. They are all self-preservation. Self-preservation is the only goal of the selfish gene, and just as locking your car door is preservation against the lazy criminals, we are saving ourselves from an eventual lazy death that was surely coming.

This lazy death I refer to is the Ice Age that *was* very much on its way. See, our bodies either could feel this change in the air, and our inevitable icy demise. That was up until our collective subconscious, our selfish gene, kicked in and said, "Pollute! Pollute! Drive that jet-ski! Log that forest!" and we were spared a sudden change in the atmosphere. The air on Planet Earth started to heat up, the ice started to melt, the planet started to balance itself by using us. We circumspectly called this "the greenhouse effect," which is a nice image—a delightful little glass building in a country courtyard.

Did the locust seed go too far and lay waste to the very thing it was supposed to be protecting?

Are greenhouse gases going to actually bring on yet another Ice Age, but from a different cause?

Yes. In closing, we're smarter than we look, but no less evil; It's nice to not be a human anymore.

Speaking of humans, Nara is growing steadily irritated with Isadore's frantic, continuous prattle about lizard men and rocket ships, and rightfully so. She diplomatically sends Isadore to go get soft drinks. Then she turns to me.

"Well, I feel much better. We should probably phone the police and turn that puppet weirdo over to the cops . . . fuck I hate cops. Also, they would probably throw numbnuts Isadore into jail, but that was fucked. He can't just go around drugging people."

I nodded.

"Screw it. We're here, we might as well have some fun. Whattaya say Hank? Feel like . . . cuttin loose?" She reaches forward and mimes tickling my sides.

"Uh, maybe?" my unticklish self responded.

"Just this once, I'm going to take 'maybe' to mean yes." She looks around at the dizzying array of spinning machines around us.

"What'll it be? The Zipper?" I follow her eyes to a vertical ride with tiny spinning cages on it. The people inside are screaming in absolute horror as the devil machine whips them into human-shaped butter. I shudder involuntarily.

"I can't. I have eithrophobia."

"What's that?"

"Fear of enclosed spaces."

"Right. But you're not afraid that one of those things is going to rip off and hurl up into the air . . . Okay, how about the Fun House?"

Directly behind us is a mural featuring the leering figures of ghosts and witches, and below that, people lined up to climb into tiny two-seated carts. I didn't need to make that mistake twice.

"Eisoptrophobia."

"Come again?"

"Fear of mirrors."

"You don't say," she replied, eyeing my stained tracksuit. "Okay . . . the Gravitron." She pointed to a saucer-like thing that whirled around and around, rising slightly off the ground. I clutched my stomach.

"Illygnophobic," I said.

"I see. . ."

"Fear of vomitting."

"Well fuck! That rules out almost every ride here. The merry-go-round? It's slow..."

I followed her eyes over to where a group of squealing children were clambering onto the tiny painted horses.

"Pedophobia."

"Fear of pedophiles? Jesus."

"No, fear of children. M—mostly when they sing."

"Children..." she seemed to consider this. "You know, now that you mention it, you don't seem like the dad type. Okay, okay, that bouncy thing over there, you *can't* hate bouncing."

Just over the heads and stands undulated the face of a giant inflatable clown, bobbing and rising as the people inside bounded off of its billowing innards. I quickly shut my eyes and looked away.

"Coulrophobia," I said, hurriedly.

"And that is?"

"Fear of clowns."

"You too huh? Well, can't blame you there." She put her hands on her hips and looked around. "It is just an *inflatable* clown mind you. Fine, let's see, I'm running out of options here." She looked over my shoulder. "Ferris wheel?" I turned and looked at the Ferris wheel.

"Sure," I said.

"What? You're not afraid of heights?"

"No."

"Good." She grabbed me by the hand and started to haul me over in the direction of the massive spinning wheel and its many light bulbs.

Lloyd was attempting to push Mr. Giggles the pony away from the giant pile of poop, but the pony was intent on sniffing the strange object there, and stubborn as a pony could be. Finally, Lloyd used all his weight and Mr. Giggles let out a snort and trundled off. He slowly bent over and fished Lil Lloyd out of the mass of steaming crap. Hesitantly, he used the edge of his shirt to wipe clean the eyes and small thick-rimmed glasses. Even Lloyd leapt back in surprise at the fury contained in those glassy blue orbs. One word erupted like a buzzsaw ambulance siren: "Rrrreveeeenge!" Lil Lloyd screeched.

CHAPTER EIGHTEEN

Something Good Has Got to Happen to You. A Little About Nara, and the Drunken Wildlife.

Isadore was holding two plastic cups with white-and-red-striped straws, happily pretending that he and Nara were on an impromptu date to the carnival, which was only interrupted when he saw two uniformed police officers questioning a clown directly in front of him. His hamster-sized heart cramped up briefly in its wheel, then started pumping blood to his extremities as fast as it possibly could. His body knew something was up, and that now was the time to act, but instead Isadore stood immobile and stared. The clown looked at the picture and shook his head. One of the officers looked up and over her shoulder.

After a quick turn in the other direction, Isadore attempted to sink his infamous head down into the folds of his t-shirt. He started to speed-walk away as fast as his stiff legs could carry him, being careful not spill any of the soda from the cups. He had been raised to be frugal and didn't want to waste any, even though the pockets of his frayed jacket were lined with at least two hundred dollars in stolen cash. When he saw another cop standing next to the bumper cars, he dropped the cups and broke into a run.

Nara and I stood in a long winding line of people all facing in the same direction underneath the giant wheel with its twinkling lights. The other couples were cozying up to each other in the night air, encircling their arms tenderly around one another. My awkward mess of bones and meat thought briefly about entwining its limbs with Nara's, but was abruptly reminded of the wooden octopus from the Puppetmobile, and so declined.

"Isn't this romantic Hank?" Nara said, resting her head upon my shoulder for comedic effect.

"Guh?" I blurted.

She laughed. "Oh, the things you say, you're such a Casanova!" She slapped me on the shoulder, then leaned in close and smiled to herself.

Giacomo Casanova was born in Venice, Italy, on April 2, 1725. He was a sickly boy from actor parents, and went on to have sex with a great many people, including a mother and her daughter, a woman pretending to be a man, some priests, and a nun. He traveled a whole lot considering there were no airplanes. However, cities were closer together then. He died poor and alone, despite his many lovers and admirers.

What is love?

It's complicated.

For example, pheromones and their role in genetic selection: They did an experiment once where they lined up smelly men's armpits with blindfolded women and had them sniff heartily, to see which potential mate they would choose. Almost without fail the women would select the men whose immune response genes were different than their own, thus creating stronger, healthier potential offspring. Is this all there is to love? Of course not—it also helps if they don't lose their cool during a road trip when you get lost late at night in the wilds of Northern California searching for a motel that is open. Can you fall in love with someone that smells repugnant to you? Not likely. Friends, but not lovers.

I had never been called a Casanova before, not even as a joke, but the truth was I smelled impossibly good to Nara because of our opposite immune response genes. She didn't even mind that it was a complicated potpourri involving piss, disinfectant, and whatever the chemical cocktail in my bloodstream was making me secrete. Her first whiff of my essence had been way back in that gas station. Was this why she put up with so much of my nonsense? It certainly wasn't my wit and charm.

In response to her proximity I started to shake, my whole body convulsing in uncontrollable waves of spasms almost to the point of seizure. This was my rare response to the possibility of sexual congress.

"Are you cold?" Nara asked, leaning away to look at me.

"No," I replied.

We are inching our way through the line, the lovers unloading, and new lovers taking their vacant seats.

"Crap!" Nara says.

"What?" I ask in a panic, looking behind and above me, chipmunk-style.

"I forgot to get tickets." She puts one hand on my elbow to steady me. "I'm going to go get them." Then she turns to walk away.

"Wait!" I say.

She looks back at me, waiting.

"I'll come with you!" My hands are in the air in front of me, fingers out stretched, ready to grab something. I look like a crazy person and the other people in line start to notice this. Nara doesn't seem to care that I look crazy.

"No, you save our spot in line. I'll be right over there." She points at the ticket booth which stands thirty feet away. Seeing the utter terror on my face she adds, "Nothing is going to happen to you in the next two minutes, I *promise* you. I'll be right back." And then she is gone.

Isadore runs past the stage and in front of the gathered crowd, doing a piss-poor job of keeping a low profile. He is looking over his shoulder, not in the direction he is moving, so he bumps headlong into the funless couple with the pink pig. He apologizes. The lady cop is about to snap something curt and abrasive at him when recognition floods over her face. She fumbles with the pig. The male cop turns and starts groping around for his gun behind his back, cleverly hidden by his jaunty blue jumper. He hollers that favorite of all law enforcement phrases,

"Freeeeeze!"

The lady cop holds a big pink pig up to Isadore's face, its googly eyes wobble menacingly before him as she tries to wrestle the handgun from its fluffy innards with little result.

Lloyd and a filthy, shit-caked Lil Lloyd explode from behind the stage at that same moment. Lloyd is staggering and weaving like he is drunk. He is not, he is just extremely disarrayed. Someone in charge of something appears in front of him and tells him how glad they are that he could be there, that they remember seeing him in the circus all those years ago and wasn't sure if he was still alive, but he's glad he is and is it okay if they skip soundcheck, because they're on a schedule and the kids from the hospital have to be in bed by ten o'clock at the latest. Lloyd shoves him aside, and Lil Lloyd squeals

"You!" with such vehemence and conviction that both the cops and Isadore turn and gape in awe.

Isadore wastes no time, he pushes the (stuffed) pig out of his way, knocking it from the lady cop's grip. The male cop is still distracted by the muck-coated dummy with its razor voice and crystal blue eyes, so he misses his chance to grab Isadore and haul him in. By the time he can holler "Don't move!" Isadore is red hot and running, pushing children from the hospital out of his way. Past the crowd around the stage, past the Tilt a Whirl, past the big inflatable clown room, over popcorn and pop cans, through families and couples, under and over tent wires he leaps, bounds, and scrambles along. Run! Isadore! Run! Because he knows he's probably going down anyway, Isadore pushes a clown holding a bunch of balloons that he could have side-stepped with more effort. The balloons scatter into the air in a colorful explosion of rubber and helium gas. Isadore doesn't like clowns either. Poor clowns. They just want to entertain you.

Officer Brent Cohen with his magnificent moustache does in fact like clowns. His Aunt Trudy is a clown in Nebraska. He sees Isadore send that poor clown sprawling and he says "Heyyyy!" in a hurt but angry tone of voice. Then he sees Isadore run around behind the line of the Salt and Pepper Shaker—a giant two-armed whirling machine with green cages on either end. He steps forward to go after him and is almost knocked aside by the two plain-clothed officers in hot pursuit, one wrestling with a giant stuffed pig. Close behind them, and running with a steady, long stride, follows a stern bespectacled man holding a stinking, cackling ventriloquist's dummy.

Isadore is smarter than he looks in his frayed jean jacket and rocker t-shirt. He rounds the corner of the Salt and Pepper Shaker and heads for the line up to the concession stand. Once there, he takes a fistful of bills from his pocket and hurls them into the air.

The selfish gene of the people gathered there makes them swarm on the cash instinctively. Within moments it is a scene from a classic painting of writhing bodies, but with decidedly more white trash fashion. Mothers push down sons, boyfriends push aside girlfriends, children slip their deft child-size fingers in between their grandparents fumbling digits, all in a sudden mass of money-grabbing. Some toes get pinched and some hands get stepped on, as Isadore uses the chaos he has caused to melt into the crowd and shimmy under a nearby tent flap.

When he looks up, he finds himself in a small room face to face with a hulking grizzly bear in a tiny hat. The bear moves forward and sniffs at Isadore as he presses his body back up against the side of the tent. The bear's breath reeks of gin so strongly that it makes his eyes burn and start to water.

Officer Cohen stands firm, feet spread, and scours the mass of greedy people for any sign of Isadore. The nervous rookie cop beside him, a young black man named Neil Torren, breathes out an emphatic "Damn!" and kicks some dirt. They have lost their prey momentarily.

The lady cop and her date cop with the sweater tied around his neck run up to them, only slightly winded. She finally wrestles her gun free of the stuffed animal and tosses the pig onto the ground, then turns to Officer Cohen. "Where the hell'd he go?" she says, checking her handgun for any residual fluff.

"I don't know," Cohen says.

She turns to her partner in the polo shirt and sweater, but his eyes are locked on the discarded pig lying in the dust. "Simmons, call for back up."

He mumbles an incoherent response, looking away.

She gives him a puzzled look and accepts Cohen's offered radio. "Calling all units," she says, her voice ringing with authority, "suspect has been sighted, I repeat, suspect has been sighted at the fairgrounds."

"You go that way, I'll go this way," Cohen says to the cop with the sweater around his neck.

"Fine," the cop says sulkily and storms away.

The pig lies gutted and forgotten, and is soon trampled by the money-grubbing mob.

A word about toys. Toys are a little bit alive too, much in the way houses are. But you don't have to watch what you say in front of them, they won't tell anyone.

That poor, discarded pig would go on to a life of happiness with a young girl named Tuula, who would rescue it from the feet of the mob and give her a good home for the next twelve years. So let it be said that there are two happy endings in this tale.

And on the other side of that tent, panting and out of breath, Lloyd and Lil Lloyd are engaged in yet another one of their theological debates.

"I think this has gone far enough," Lloyd says.

"I can't believe you lost him!" Lil Lloyd sneers, or rather, would have, if he had lips.

"The cops have him now, let's forget about it. There's no more reward money."

"Forget about it?! After they impaled me and shoved my face in *shit* Lloyd!" His little wooden hand raises and shakes. Lloyd recoils slightly from his own arm. Suddenly the squeaky voice takes on a gentler tone, "Come on Lloyd . . . after all we've been through," he pleads, "don't you give a damn about me at all?" More textbook narcissist manipulative behavior from Lil Lloyd. Break the cycle Lloyd! Run free! Love yourself, you spineless waste of space!

"Of course I do," Lloyd says as he looks away, hoping desperately to avoid conflict.

"Then come on! We're not stopping until those bastards pay!" The gentle voice is wiped away as all that wrath comes bubbling and gurgling upwards, threatening to choke the words from Lil Lloyd's imaginary throat.

A brief word about Lil Lloyd's malevolent streak, which would actually be a word about Lloyd's lack thereof. The word is this: balance.

Despite appearances to the contrary, the Omniverse knows how to achieve balance. This is much easier to notice when viewed on the grand scale, taking a broad general view of the situation. With the exception of Lloyd-like situations, most often it is hard to see any balance whatsoever, as certain people, planets, and solar systems really do seem to get all the luck. Earth is more than a little off-balance, and I'm not talking about the axis. Right before I died, there were definitely more have-nots than haves living and dying there. But rest assured, however crappy someone is doing, or however much ill-will they spread around, you should know that they have a counterpart life-form out there somewhere, who is doing the exact opposite.

Once again, I don't expect this knowledge to make you feel any better about anything, particularly if you're doing crappily.

Murray Macdonald is doing pretty crappy at this moment. Since he got shot in the arm he has learned that the repairs to his body require intensive surgery he cannot afford, he has just been questioned for the past five hours by a team of burly belligerent policemen asking repetitive questions, and his bratty son is whining next to his hospital bed because they're going to miss the carnival. His gum-chewer of a wife is cunningly pretending to ignore the child's nasal whining by flipping idly through a home-decorating magazine while making large swooping motions with her lower jaw like a cow in cud-heaven. Murray is in a great deal of pain from his arm, so he is pushing the little button to trigger the nurse to bring more drugs, but no nurse is coming. He is growing steadily more and more irritated and wants nothing more than to smack his child so that he will shut the hell up, but his smacking arm is immobilized and throbbing. The hospital bed has a steel bar going down the middle, so no matter where he positions himself, it is uncomfortable. The TV is showing a baseball game, and Murray's team just lost. He's extremely hungry, but the food is new levels of lousy.

"Irene!" he says.

"Mm?" she replies, not looking up. *Flip, flip*, go the magazine pages.

"Irene!" he yells.

She looks up from the magazine.

"Get him out of here, will you? I mean, fer chrissakes! I've just been shot! I don't need to hear his bitching about some freaking carnival! And where is that gahdamned nurse?" He leans forward, "Nuuuurse!" he bellows.

"I'll find her dear," Irene says with a sigh, setting down her magazine and grabbing their son by the arm.

"Julian!" Murray hollers once they get near the door. The boy spins around. "You put that back this instant!"

The boy lowers his head and takes a stethoscope out of his pocket, placing it on the nearby counter.

"All of it!" Murray warns.

The boy empties out two rolls of gauze, a thermometer, three pairs of latex gloves, and a container of petroleum jelly from his pockets. The small counter is soon crowded. Murray sighs and leans back, cradling his arm and looking upwards at the stained ceiling. He is thinking, *Why me oh god?*

The answer we could give him is something about balance. How somewhere out there, someone or something is having a real swell time, so it only follows that he should suffer, and suffer with no seeming end in sight; that he should spend long, shadow-drenched nights asking himself *Why god?* until he succumbs to the only escape, and a meager one at that: fitful, sweaty sleep. Why it's balance, Murray! But that's not much of an answer is it? Answers are supposed to *take away* the question. They rarely do, as you may have noticed, most often they spiral into even larger questions.

Ryan Totten, for instance, was at that moment experiencing his third orgasm of the night with two young female followers; one, a stunning Asian woman named Kiko, and the other, a sultry Swahili woman named Kalifa. He is craning his neck back and hollering "Oh god, oh god!"

Totten's metaphysical balancing point is not Murray though, it's actually a breadbox-sized snail creature with a honed sense of smell, many light years away. It has accidentally fallen into a den of those pea-sized things with the staggeringly smelly armpits.

Murray's counterpoint in the Omniverse is actually the King of the Thludnesensenites—a race of warm-blooded aquatic creatures on a water planet of perpetual twilight. At the same moment that Murray is shifting around in his uncomfortable hospital bed, the

King is cascading over the massive waves towards his kingdom to find his long-dead family restored by the miracles of modern science. They are all gathered and waiting there with his long-dead wife—also recently revitalized and seated in a majestic silver throne turned purple by the twilight. At her feet are the singing, dancing people of the kingdom, their large, manta-ray-like necks stretched tight in an exultant harmonious ode to new hope, prosperity and homecoming. The King's cat-sized heart feels like it will burst from joy. He too cranes his massive, slippery and muscular neck skywards, letting loose a triumphant trumpeting noise that echoes across the giant purple sea.

Gladys, the woman that lives in my head, has a balancing point of a flea on a dog in India, on the planet Earth. If I knew that while I was alive, I would have found that flea and tortured it in a variety of excruciating, flea-sized ways, until Gladys was so happy that she forgot all about me, and stink bombs, and everything except being irresistibly happy.

Nara's is a thin, fingerless creature on a city-world ten solar systems over, waiting in line at the World Bank for an immeasurable length of time.

Isadore's is a giant desert worm, sunning itself idly in exactly the same spot it has for twelve years.

Mine was a teenager on Gladys' planet. One of the cool kids. And while that kid is cruising the hallway with his acne-free, noseless face up in the air, I am neurotically scanning the throngs of people for anyone wearing a tight red gas station uniform.

There is no sight of Nara anywhere. She has been gone too long. The ticket booth is not that far away. The dread rises up from my stomach, in a nasty churning knot. Now that I can see into my stomach, I realize that feeling of dread comes from a slew of digestive enzymes priming my body for action. It is amazing how much body mass I have considering how many times a day this chemical reaction occurs. At the moment of all this stomach action, my mind is replaying that horrible afternoon when my mom lost me at the mall, so I don't notice the Lloyds appear from behind a robust and slow-moving family of five.

Lil Lloyd has spotted me and is weaseling his way into the line-up with Lloyd in tow. Most people when they see his penetrating glass eyes and shit-stained miniature eyeglasses recoil slightly, which makes his weaseling even easier. Within moments he is almost behind me, the eyes and glistening poop on his wooden face sparkling under the lights of the Ferris wheel.

My internal spotlight goes haywire, zipping and flashing across gray face after gray dismal face, none of them young brown and beautiful. Each one greets my desperation with an impassive mask, and I like to think that had I been a child, the situation would have been different. Someone would have seen my obvious distress and taken me by the hand saying, "Are you lost little feller?" or, "Can I help you?" As a grown man I know that the most I can expect is a hurried look away.

Sucks to be old.

Meanwhile, not far away, Bubba French the Dancing Bear has a few more gray hairs on him, and a few less in the bald patch near his rear end, but in general he is the same surly, cantankerous lout that he was all those nights ago at the circus when we last saw him. He leans forward and sniffs Isadore, but recoils in disgust and backs away. Isadore smells very much like stale piss. The grizzly cannot resist the opportunity to scare the bejeezus out of him though; he leans forward again, putting his massive head right in front of Isadore's gleaming face and wild, white eyes.

"Boo!" Bubba says, in his snorting bear language.

The expression, "BOO!" common across the world as a method for one person to frighten another, comes from the name of the Norse god, Boh, son of Odin, whose appearance was so frightening that to even say his name was to cause panic in whoever heard it.

It prompts a similar reaction in Isadore now, he yelps and leaps for the tent flap, yanking it aside so that it slaps loudly.

Outside the tent, the cops are gathering together near a hot dog stand and speaking their cop-talk about sealing perimeters and combing crowds. Bubba sniffs deeply and smells something quite different to stale piss. He smells hot dogs! While normally a finicky eater, Bubba is just drunk enough to eat floor-scrapings and he lumbers past Isadore, who does nothing to stop him.

Why wasn't this giant animal chained up? Bubba had of late been so despondent and immobile that any bonds were unnecessary. There was a cage in the tent, but the door was largely left open and unlocked. He still had a collar around his neck, to demonstrate the yoke of his oppressor, but it was largely for show. Even still, the short answer to why he wasn't chained up was negligence. While it was terribly exciting to have a dancing bear as part of your travelling roadshow, PETA and a variety of other organizations had seen to it that the public generally looked upon Bubba not as a source of wonder and delight, but as an uncomfortable harkening of a bygone and more slave-friendly era.

The cops look at the grizzly bear with its tiny hat and demonstrative collar plodding towards them out of the small amber-colored tent, and one of them draws his gun. Bubba does not take well to guns, having been shot with a tranquilizer dart more than once in his wilder, younger years. He raises himself up on his two legs and snorts. The other police pull their pistols amidst a cacophony of human shouts and screams. The mob of money-grabbers spread like so much oil up against bear-shaped vinegar without an emulsifying agent like friendship and understanding. The money has mostly been grabbed anyway, so the selfish gene kicks it up a notch, propelling them away from the sight of more immediate danger.

Isadore uses this chance to slip out along the side of the tent behind the massive bear. He rushes down a makeshift alleyway and upon emerging knocks over a small child standing there eating a big blue swab of cotton candy. Does Isadore stop to help up the child? Nope. But he looks back for a second, considers it, and then hurries off as the kid starts to bawl, their eyes on the cotton candy lying on the dirty, dirty ground.

Back at the foot of the Ferris wheel, Nara comes weaving through the crowd towards me, clutching two tickets triumphantly in front of her. I see her refreshingly radiant face and once again start to wish that the world was in slow motion.

What the hell . . . I'm going to slow things down so that we can watch her ease past these people and come towards us. All I have to do is reach out my nonexistent arms and fingers and squeeeeze them together on this moment.

Hnnnnnngh!

Her shirt seems instantly more red, and the color-streaked locks of hair coil and sway by her shoulders like she is underwater. She twists her hips as she passes a man wearing a baseball cap, narrowly avoiding him as he steps backward. The man is methodically and slowly scratching the inside of his ass, and her subtle twist now seems to be a simple ballet of sanguine grace. Her eyes are on ours, and she is smiling a warm, playful smile.

And in slow motion I see Lil Lloyd pull a small glittering knife from behind his accordion. He hides it from Lloyd's eyes by sliding his little hand down to his side. His wooden mouth parts slowly, slightly damp pony shit still hanging off of where his lips should be; a small fleck of it falls almost tragically to the ground.

Bubba French roars in slow motion, the spit hanging off of his maw and swaying languidly back and forth. The cops gradually stumble backwards, collapsing over each other, with their mouths gaping in half-formed words. Bubba slowly seals his massive jaws of death, licks his lips, and gradually cranes his mammoth head towards the hot dog vendor. The light captures his matted filthy fur like a tinseled tree on Christmas morning.

And here comes Isadore. He's actually running as fast as he possibly could, so he looks pretty ridiculous. His eyes are wide and his lips are pursed together and jutting out. He is rolling and tumbling tediously forward, his feet rising up next to his buttocks.

Alright, Nara is now by my side and we are celebrating our reunion by exchanging a compassionate look into each other. She holds up the tickets between us and we slowly turn to face the stairs in front of us, her arm sliding in next to mine as we climb them, step, by step, by step.

Isadore runs up to us and goes, "Foooshhhuhhh deeerrrrr muhhhhh wuhhhhheeeeee. . ."

Hold on, I'll speed this up again.

What he said, only slightly more coherently, is that the cops are here, and they're right behind him. And indeed they were.

CHAPTER NINETEEN

The Ferris Wheel

With nowhere else to go, a very desperate and irrational Isadore rushes up the stairs, pushes past me, grabs Nara, and slams the two of them down into the little cart of the Ferris wheel, lowering the metal bar.

"Let's go!" he yells at the man standing next to the controls.

The man running the Ferris wheel is a short surly guy in grease-stained clothes, named Tylissus. Most of the other carnies called him Tyler, which is slightly more efficient for fast-talkin' carnies to say. Tylissus is responsible for only three aspects of operation on the Ferris wheel: taking tickets, pushing buttons, and loading and unloading the lovers and children. He is not aware of the shoddy job that his fellow Ferris wheel people have done in their assemblage earlier that week. While he knows that a couple of the carts are squeaking, he does not know this is because two of them are dangerously loose. He usually does Tilt-A-Whirl.

He successfully loads Nara and Isadore into the cart, giving Nara a twice-over with his eyes, as he imagines his greasy hands upon her tender young body.

The Ferris wheel was invented by George W. Ferris and first demonstrated at the Chicago World Fair of 1893. The original was a mammoth thing, with carts that held up to forty people. This particular version is much scaled-down, with carts that hold two, it is made of hastily constructed pieces of metal. They just don't build 'em like they used to.

Nara looks at me standing there with my mouth open, and then turns angrily to Isadore. "What are you doing?" she says, lifting the bar. Tylissus pushes it back down.

"Please keep the bar down sweets," he drawls. He hits a button and the car starts to squeak away with them inside. I am left standing there in my resting state of confusion and bewilderment.

I have no time to form a plan of action to counter this hijacking of my magical moment in the sky, as I am suddenly and forcefully pushed aside and start to fall backwards down the stairs by an unseen assailant.

I see who it is now. It's Lloyd's right arm. It's that freaking puppet. The stairs are metal and grated, and the people standing on them do everything in their power to part like the Dead Sea before Moses when they see me hurtling down at them.

Moses was a prophet of the Lord. The Lord returned the favor by helping him escape from the Egyptians. God supposedly parted the water of that sea, enabling Moses and crew to walk across the ocean floor.

The people on the stairs are escaping from being crushed by my tumbling sweatpanted self, enabling me to smack my body on almost every metal step on the way down. After much flailing and bursts of sudden pain, I land with a thud on the sodden, muddy grass, amidst a chorus of "oohs" and intakings of breath.

Tylissus goes through the pageantry of expressing concern, calling down to the bottom of the stairs, "You alright bud?" before turning back to face the interloper. And while Tylissus saw Lloyd push me, he doesn't want to fuck with the mentally ill; this was a common sentiment of people of the time. To him, a man holding a stinking puppet and riding a Ferris wheel by himself couldn't be anything but mentally ill. In truth, Lloyd is probably the most level-headed out of all of us. His arm though, that's another story. He lets Lloyd budge into line and sit down in the cart, even though he doesn't have a ticket. Lloyd pulls down the bar and gives Tylissus a plaintive, trapped look. Tylissus looks away quickly, busying himself with the elderly couple that are next to board.

"So this is your escape plan? Because it's truly terrible," Nara says to Isadore. They are busy arguing with each other, so they don't notice the Lloyds climb into the cart in front of them as the Ferris wheel slowly ratchets skyward.

"At least up here I can see where the cops are. . ." he says scanning downwards.

"Yeah, and they can see you!" her scratchy voice rails.

"No they can't."

"Well, they will."

"Man, I wish I had the gun."

"Why? So you could shoot yourself in the foot? Or maybe shoot me?"

"Maybe," Isadore says irritably.

"You know . . . Isadore," her voice dropped down an octave to its more husky, dulcet tone. She looked across the fairground with its twinkling lights and slowly diminishing cacophony of noise. "At first, I was pissed off, then I felt bad for you, but you really are a menace. You probably should be locked up somewhere."

Isadore is silent. He is having a flash of introspection amidst his dread and adrenaline.

"And you just left Hank down there," she says.

"Hank! What's the deal? Why are you so nice to that fat psycho? You don't even know him."

"Ha! *Him!* You're the gun-toting cult kid! I mean, do you have any idea how fucked up today has been? And it's all because of *you!*"

Of course, Nara is wrong, it's not Isadore's fault. He was just one sloppy organic compound in a seemingly random chain of events, which is almost sadly predictable. Even if Isadore wanted to stop it now, he couldn't. Which brings us back to that notion of free will. Do any of the creatures in the Omniverse have it? The simple truth is: Yes.

The un-simple truth is that it is rarely ever exercised. Most creatures have a genetic niche they are born into, or in the case of those things without genes, they have a rut that they know all too well. But the great thing about all this matter and space around you? Genes aren't everything—even selfish or immune response ones.

While you and I didn't choose our parents, or our country, or our social-economic background, or even our planet, we often don't get to choose what we eat, or if we get to eat at all, or the fact that we have to defecate after eating . . . but there is hope! Somewhere above and below all that, there is a part that can change, can run wild and unfettered. What you try to do with the genetic and cultural niche you've been given, whether you live by it until the day you die, or whether you reject it and go against the seemingly unstoppable flow of biology is a decision that resides somewhere above and beyond the mass of goop stored in your head.

It is tempting to jump back into the analogy of the brain as a computer, it has programming and patterns, but as stated earlier, the brain is a lot more like a radio than a hard drive for data. Imagine it like you're building a transistor radio at home from a kit. If you follow the instructions exactly, you will get a transistor radio and it will work, but which frequency you tune it into is up to you.

It takes a brave soul to grab that knob and crank it into the noisy static; to use all your resources to rebel against the very thing that you are and always have been can seem tricky when there are countless forces working against you. True free will takes a great deal of mistrust and skepticism towards your given lot in life.

What terrified Nara so long ago on that swingset was her first step towards free will. She just knew that something was wrong, but not what.

What was wrong was this (and a common occurrence in our chaotic SNAFU universe): She was an accident. Another cosmic "Situation Normal All Fucked Up." Nara was supposed to have her matter and energy formed into a jellyfish here on Earth, but at the moment just before her conception, Hord let loose one unbelievable explosion of cosmic matter that he had stored for eons—in short: a cosmic fart. So things got blown completely out of whack and she ended up a little confused and misplaced, but not altogether bad. Had she sat on that swingset longer and fully leaned into her detached and dissociative state, she might have come to learn how to reject her niche in a healthy and constructive manner. What she was left with was a disinterested psyche and bored demeanor resulting from a feeling of residual cosmic displacement.

Isadore has never rejected his lot, being obviously more of the follower type. He will tonight though, and he won't even realize it. This happens to people more often than you'd think. It is usually accompanied by some sort of mental collapse, which is then treated with drugs.

So despite the fact that none of this is Isadore's fault, that he is merely going through the motions of a complex system he will never understand, he apologizes to Nara on the Ferris wheel.

"I'm sorry," he says, looking down. But just then the cart slid backwards again, and the squeaking drowned him out.

"What was that?"

"I said, I'm sorry."

"Should be." Nara was not satisfied with this apology, but could also tell this was the best that Isadore could do, and so she let it slide. She looked down at a family of carnival-goers peacefully ambling to her right. The daughter of the family ran ahead to a booth, while the son stayed glued to the mother's arm.

"I'm nice to Hank because he reminds me of someone," she said.

"Who?"

Nara had a younger brother once. His name was Sabahat and he died of spinal meningitis when he was only six. He was a sickly, timid child, surprisingly clever and yet still afraid of his own shadow. Nara was his only friend on the planet, and she took this job very seriously. However, twelve years old can be a harrowing time to be a female in North America, there are a lot of bizarre obstacles to navigate, including high school, mean girls, boys, puberty, and disillusionment with one's parents. She pulled away from the grim reality of her brother's situation in the last year of his life almost to the point of cruelty. Her last memory of her brother before he was terminally hospitalized was him whining for her to turn his night light on through a crack in the door, and her chiding him for being a baby.

"My brother," Nara said heavily, cocking her head to look at Isadore. "You kind of look like him." Her countenance shifted, "But you don't act like him. He was six years old and still had more common sense than you do."

Isadore was silent a moment, his black hair blowing just above his eyes, "Hank reminds *me* of a big smelly hamster. Enough about that guy! Can we please figure out what the shit I'm supposed to do? Those cops are going to shoot me!"

"Well, what did you expect? I mean, maybe you should have thought of that before you put a gun to my head, robbed a gas station, and then shot some stupid tourist!"

"This wasn't how it was supposed to happen!"

"Right. You were supposed to escape in your creepy van, go back to whatever mad-scientist lab thing your leader has, and hop into a rocket headed for the sun! Have you ever thought that through?" She raised her hands off the bar of the cart, "I am all for appreciating people's beliefs or whatever, but it's just so. . ." she looked at him, "dumb."

At this, Isadore is silent again. His whole reality is increasingly unreal with each movement upward of the cart on the Ferris wheel. He is well on his way to his moment of free will. They are almost at the top now, the carts are almost full.

While below, my bruised and battered head is ordering my recently pummeled body to lift it. I stand up and wobble back and forth like I am drunk. I don't drink, as it doesn't mix well with my meds. I did once and it took me long time to figure out what city I was in and how I got there, making me one of the only people in the town where I lived—and damn near the entire planet—who said "never again" and actually meant it. Of course, I died tonight. If I had lived, I most definitely would have needed a drink after all this.

Squinting up at the wheel which is not yet in full circulation, I see Nara and Isadore waving their arms at each other. And then, in the cart just behind them I see the Lloyds, and watch powerlessly as Lil Lloyd raise something small and glinting in the light of the wheels. Even then I knew it was most likely a knife not meant for spreading butter.

"Naraahhhh!" I shout. She can't hear me from way down there.

Regardless, she does hear the little dummy cackling, and she cranes around in the cart to look backward and find the ventriloquist dummy with his tiny shiny knife. Isadore yelps like a poodle that's had its tail stepped on.

"Oh *come on*," Nara says. Moments later the Ferris wheel starts turning.

The cops are gathered around staring at Bubba French as he sits there munching happily on a hotdog. Every time one of them makes a move towards him, he grumbles menacingly, so they adjust their hats and belts and talk about whether or not the bear is in their jurisdiction seeing as how he's an out-of-town animal.

"You're not supposed to disturb them when they're eating," Torren, the rookie cop says.

I push my way through the lineup, ignoring my deep-seeded phobia of bodily contact, and force my way up the stairs. Isadore and Nara are wheeling down towards me as I approach the top. Isadore looks scared.

"Hank! Get us off this thing!" Nara calls, looking at me and then up at the cart above her where Lil Lloyd's piercing eyes and gleaming knife are hanging over the edge.

And then they are gone, whirling away in their squeaky cart. From above I hear the high-pitched cackling getting louder as the Lloyds come coasting down with Lil Lloyd waving his knife in the air at Tylissus and me. Big Lloyd is just sitting there, his head slumped forward, so there is no question who is in control. And then they are gone too, receding away from us. I turn to Tylissus and manage to stammer out, "S—stop the ride!" We're both a bit shaken by the cackling dummy. Tylissus is slow to respond. He puts his hand over the brake button, but hesitates.

In a rare act of, well, action, I reach over and hit the button under his hand. There is a shrill screeching and grinding noise as the Ferris wheel starts to slow in its rotation, unleashing a flurry of sparks all the while. It wasn't moving all that fast, but it had a lot of force behind it—centrifugal force.

And due to its shoddy reconstruction, the brakes are less than efficient, so it continues to lurch forward in a series of spurts, all the while making a horrific noise like an elephant in heat. The lovers in their respective carts cling to each other even tighter.

Two carts down from Nara and Isadore are Charles Kissinger the Third and his girlfriend Tamsyn Lee Dennis. Both are seventeen years old.

"I love you Tammy," Charles says, "If we died right now, I'd be the happiest I've ever been."

Tammy is looking down at her feet, where one of the straps on her sandals has come undone. She purses her hot pink lips together in frustration. "Oh Chuck, that's sweet," she replies absently, reaching forward in an attempt to fix her sandal which is just out of reach due to the bar holding her in place. Just then the cart lurches forward and she screams, clutching at Charles' arm. "Chuck. . ." she coos, burying her face in his sweater vest.

Nara and Isadore's cart has some screws loose and one side of it shakes and shimmies its way right out of its moorings, bending ever so slightly downward with each lurch of the wheel. Nara's hand tightens onto the bar in front of her, but this does little to reassure her, knowing she'll have a tight grip on the cart when it falls. Behind them Lil Lloyd crows, "I have you now bitches!"

Nara spins around and snaps back, "Bring it on you little turd!"

The cops come crawling out of everywhere when they hear the elephant-in-heat noises. They are all gathered below the Ferris wheel, looking up at its crooked dangling cart and panicked people.

There is an old couple, Agnes and Wilbur Sosnowski, seated in the cart just below Lloyd's. They were obviously unnerved by the lurching of the wheel and have pretty much stopped talking. They had been discussing how much they have seen in their lives, and how much everything has changed. When they were children, people didn't walk on the moon, or seriously consider building rocket ships. People read more books, watched less TV, and felt entitled to hate whomever they chose for no other reason than the pallor of their epidermis.

From my perspective of seeing the earth as a cute lil baby planet stumbling through its first steps, not a lot has changed.

But to them, it seems like a whole new world compared to when they were youngsters like Tammy and Chuck. Agnes looks down at the cops, "Oh Wilbur!" she exclaims, her delicate hands grabbing his arm.

"Now stay calm Agnes, I'm sure they're looking for someone else."

Agnes and Wilbur run a large marijuana growing operation from their small house less than a mile from the site of the carnival, and are known all around the quiet seaside town as having the best product and prices in the area. Wilbur's pension was not quite enough to keep them from starving to death, and Agnes has always been a real whiz with the plants, so it wasn't long before they started growing. And after that, it wasn't long before they started going to Florida twice a year instead of once every three years. As a result of their primary income source, Agnes is constantly on the lookout for law enforcement, whom she calls "the fuzz." Growing marijuana was illegal at this point in time and subject to all kinds of draconian punishments. I know, it's just a plant; I don't make the rules.

"Then what are the fuzz doing here Wilbur? Just what the Sam Hell are they doing here?"

"Oh shit oh shit oh shit," Isadore says, looking at all the blue uniforms milling below. He hunches down into the cart, pulling up the collar of his jean jacket as the cart sways from the residual kinetic motion.

"Oh you're fucked now boy-o!" Lil Lloyd cackles. He is waving the knife back and forth, as Lloyd stands up in the cart. "Hey coppers!" he yells, "We gotcher guy right here!"

Officer Cohen looks up. Squinting, he sees a figure hunched over in a cart at the very top of the Ferris wheel seated next to the beautiful Jahanara, who has her arms folded across her chest. Then he turns and yanks a megaphone from a younger officer who was clutching it tightly to his chest. Cohen's voice comes out loud and cop-like:

"Isadore Abella, stay where you are."

Nara laughs. "No Isadore, run. Run far away. Stupid pig."

Isadore stands up. "Don't come any closer, I've got a gun!" he shouts.

Nara hits him hard. "Are you fucking crazy?!" Nara says, "You want them to shoot you in the head?" She leans over the side of the cart, "No he doesn't!" she shouts.

"Yes I do!" Isadore says, grabbing Nara and jabbing his index finger into her side, with a superfluous thumb up so that his exposed hand resembles a pistol.

"No!" She yells down, then turns to face him, "...he doesn't," she warns through gritted teeth.

"Yes I do!" Isadore covers Nara's mouth with his hand. She bites him. He shouts. They are doing a good job of appearing to be kidnapper and hostage. In their struggling, the cart gives a squeak and shifts sharply to the left. They both immediately stop moving and look at each other, eyes widened.

From my spot at the bottom I can see Lloyd climbing out of his cart and for a second I wonder what he's doing, but then I see him grab onto the huge metal spoke of the wheel, pulling himself towards Nara and Isadore. Lil Lloyd inches forward along the top as Lloyd huffs and puffs below the metal beam.

"Nara!" I yell, and before I can think of anything else I am scaling the small fence next to Tylissus, then shimmying up the cold metal infrastructure on the other side, scrambling upwards. I set my big, sneakered foot on the nearest beam and inch my way along, reaching up with my hands to grab onto the one above me. There are large greasy patches in front of me, which I do my best to avoid. Soon I am at the hub of the wheel, craning my neck to see what's going on above.

What's going on is this: Lloyd is wrapped around a metal girder, crawling his way along and all the while Lil Lloyd is sliding forward and unleashing a harangue of death threats at Nara and Isadore, who are scouring the cart for something to throw at him in an effort to slow him down. Isadore interrupts his search occasionally to look down at the fuzz, who have grown in number and are now surrounding the base of the wheel in an effort to move the gathered crowd out of the way.

I start to inch my way diagonally up towards the outside of the wheel again, but much higher. I brace one foot on the side of teen lovers Tammy and Chuck's cart in an effort to thrust my bulk upwards.

Chuck spins around. "Hey! What the hell are you doing?" he asks, pulling Tammy to his side.

I look down at him and swallow hard, "I. . ."

For a moment I start to wonder myself. Then I hear a gun go off, ringing through the night over the noisy sounds of the carnival. There is an instantaneous *ding!* and a vibration I can feel in my hands as the bullet ricochets off a metal rung. Nara screams, a short loud exclamation of surprise. One of the cops has fired a warning shot at Isadore.

"Nara. . ." I say to Tammy and Chuck, and push off their cart and onto the beam above their heads, hugging it with my arms while kicking and scrambling with my legs.

"What the hell are you doing?" Nara yells down to the cops.

"Isn't it obvious? They're trying to kill us!" Isadore yips hysterically.

"Kill *you* maybe. I'm the fucking hostage!" She looks back down at the cops, then huddles closer to Isadore, away from the edge. "Why did you tell them you had a gun? Idiot!"

"What the hell are you doing?" Officer Brent Cohen hollers at the lady cop in the pink sweater, who is standing with her feet spread, both hands aiming a large rifle upwards. She lowers the rifle to her side, stands up straight, and turns to him.

"I was aiming for his arm."

"Well you missed! Are you *trying* to kill the hostage?" He turns away and runs up to where Tylissus is standing.

"We have to get those people down."

"Can't," he responds.

"Why?"

Tylissus nods his head towards the wheel. "There's some looney tune crawling around up there with a puppet."

"A puppet?"

Tylissus shudders instinctively, recovers, and then says, "A puppet."

Cohen shakes his head and tries to look up through the spokes of the thing and catch a glimpse of me. He sees my gray-sweatpanted self inching along a strut towards the center of the wheel. I'm very high up now, if I slipped, I would most certainly die. But don't worry, I'm not going to.

"Hey! You! Get down from there!" Cohen calls into his megaphone.

I look down to see who is yelling at me and slip on big patch of grease that I failed to notice. My feet come out from under, and I fall hard onto the bar before I tumble off the side. On the way over, I manage to wrap one arm around it. I find myself dangling from one arm, nurturing my brand-new fear of heights. The people in the carts all scream and murmur.

"Hank!" I hear Nara call, but I can't see her, I am busy holding on with everything I got. I try to swing my leg up onto the beam as I feel myself growing hysterical and frantic, I can't seem to get the momentum and strength needed to lift my leg that high. I am panting and wheezing, and if I didn't know better, I'd say I was going to fall to my death.

"Do something Chuck!" Tammy cries from below.

Chuck decides that the best course of action would be some practical advice. "Don't let go!" he says. He then moves on to motivational speaking. "You can do it!" he declares.

I grab onto the arm that is around the beam with my free hand. The weight of my own body is almost unbearable, all that pudding has come back to haunt me. Using my new handhold I finally manage to swing my body enough to get one foot on the strut above me, and then inch my sneaker onto it, searching for traction, but the surface is still just as greasy as when I slipped off of it.

I manage to work my foot onto the other side and gracelessly clamber my way up so that I am straddling the beam and panting heavily. I look up and see Nara's face looking down at me, her long, red-streaked hair is falling around like a waterfall. She looks worried and gorgeous.

"Are you alright?" she calls.

I raise one hand and give her a weak thumbs-up sign, but feel myself slipping again and quickly hug the beam tight.

"Stay there, I'm coming down to get you," she shouts.

"What?" says Isadore, "What? No you aren't! You're staying here! They'll shoot me for sure if you *leave*." He grabs onto her arm; she yanks it free.

"Do you have any idea how sick I am of being your hostage?" They glare at each other, while behind them Lloyd crawls along.

"Please?" Isadore says.

Nara breaths out quickly in disgust. "And how sick I am of listening to you whine." She leans over and looks down at me, trying to decide what to do.

Lloyd is almost at them.

"Behind you!" I shout.

They spin around as Lloyd grabs onto their cart with his free arm. His head is still down, he's not all there. Lil Lloyd swoops in with the knife and Isadore jumps back just in time to avoid being slashed by the tiny wooden hand. Nara kicks Lloyd's hand off the edge, and Lil Lloyd lets loose an ear-splitting howl.

I stand and start to climb again with newfound puissance, biting my bottom lip in determination.

"So you're back for more are you?" Nara calls to the puppet, reaching forward to grab him and hurl him once again, but the noxious smell of pony shit slows her down slightly.

"Hey listen man, we don't really have time for this right now," Isadore says, looking past the puppet in an attempt to reason with Lloyd. But Lloyd is not listening, he is looking down, his face a dark mass of curves and shadows.

"Hey! You! Leave them alone!" Agnes the weed dealer calls to Lil Lloyd.

"Stay out of this old bag!" Lil Lloyd flaps. Lloyd sticks his arm up into the air over his head as he slowly stands on the girder, towering over them. The puppet looks down, its glassy eyes swelling with malice and depravity lit from below by the lights of the Ferris wheel.

I arrive just in time for the Lloyds to leap off the girder and into the cart, sending the whole thing listing down on one side. Seconds later Nara grabs Lloyd's arm at the elbow and grits her teeth in anger and defiance as she falls towards him. Isadore starts to tumble backwards out of the cart, his arms flailing out in front of him, catching nothing but the summer air.

CHAPTER TWENTY

Showdown atop the Wheel
and
Isadore's Act of Free Will

Philip Coover the septic tank guy is drunk and running out of money. No one wants to have sex with him, in part because he dresses like a Sunday school teacher, and possibly because he cleans up shit for a living. Well, at least he used to. Ever since his accident with the hose two days ago, he has been unable to work. His confidence dissipated the moment the shit erupted, and in this line of work, confidence is everything.

He stumbles out of the back door of the noisy bar, after deciding that he can't bear to go into the bathroom because the familiar smell would be too much for his newly deflated ego. Once he is out in the cool night air of the nearby parking lot, he sways and pisses, spraying a convoluted zig-zag pattern at his feet in the gravel.

And above him, amongst the stars and near the edge of our milky way galaxy, the moon of Gunro got hit by a meteor half its size, knocking it out of orbit. Before long, the inhabitants of that moon, the criminals and degenerate exiles of the planet Gunro, would be forced to fend for themselves, forming their own government and social customs very different from those of their mother planet. One of the new rules was the immediate execution of anyone found drunk. The reason being that their very small community needed everyone in good working order.

Unfortunately, this law completely backfired, and the small moon's population was pretty much decimated within a year. But all this happened many light years ago. I only mention it because at that moment, if mankind had a telescope powerful enough, you would see quite the spectacle—you'd see a meteor smacking into a moon and knocking it out of orbit.

It takes a long, long time for light to travel towards us. This much we were right about. Alas, seeing things by light is a very mammalian method, and not the most efficient. As I mentioned before, lizards had their third eye to help them see the universe more accurately. According to our rules of light and human logic, the universe could have ended already and we wouldn't even know it yet, because it would take so long for the news to hit us. As if that makes sense.

I just want to calm your fears: It hasn't ended yet, and I don't foresee it dying off anytime soon. If anything, it's growing at a rate you can't imagine.

And below Philip, whose life will end all too soon, far, far below him and his pool of whiskey-piss, is a stream of molten rock racing along to where it will erupt from a small fissure just beside Philip's trailer. This fissure and the sulphuric gas it releases will form a new hot spring from the little creek it hits, which will suddenly make Philip's property worth millions in tourist revenue dollars. This will allow Philip to leave the septic-tank-emptying business once and for all. However, he will long be plagued by a fear of defecation.

The paranoid beaver living in this creek at the time will be S.O.L., or shit-outta-luck.

Philip Coover finishes pissing and mutters to himself as he weaves away from his zig-zag pattern of pee. He says,

"Wendushmalyfshtart?" And then he belches a small hiccup-like "urp!" sound. All of which, when translated, means "'When is my life going to start?"

The depressant effects of alcohol tend to make every small setback a desolate windfall of misery and hopelessness. It also makes you dizzy.

Spinning in a circle makes you dizzy. And it's FREE!

The rides at the carnival are all built in an attempt to make the humans dizzy, too. Humans dedicate a whole lot of time into constructing devices that make them nauseous. The aliens hiding behind the moon that came for Elvis and spend a great deal of time monitoring human activity do not understand this at all, as they have no inner ear, and are thus incapable of feeling dizzy.

Philip is so dizzy that he barely makes it back to his truck, which he plans to drive home. He is wrestling with the foolishness of this action, but then cleverly rationalizes that his trailer is straight down the highway with only two turns, one of them his driveway—a simple task easily performed even by a circus monkey.

"I shnofrigginmonkey," Philip proclaims to the night air.

The septic tank truck, still full of poop and chemicals from two days ago, rumbles and chugs to life. After a few moments of fumbling, the big, bug-coated headlights flick on, and the truck pops and grinds its way over the gravel towards the exit of the parking lot and onto Interstate 12-A.

Just as that truck lurches onto the highway, Isadore's foot catches on the bar of the Ferris wheel cart, saving him from splitting his skull like a ripened cantaloupe on all that cold metal and space beneath him. The cart is groaning and squeaking under the weight of the three—four if you are counting puppets—people now moving around inside it.

I am inching my way along the very top of the Ferris wheel, trying to get to where Nara and Lil Lloyd are engaged in their deadly struggle. Nara is clutching Lil Lloyd's throat with one hand

and batting at Big Lloyd's face with the other, occasionally landing some solid blows, but even this is having no effect as he is a very large man, currently deep in a hypnotic zombie-state.

I am crawling as quickly as I can, but after recently acquiring my consummate fear of heights, I am not moving especially fast. "Hey!" I yell, trying to draw the bloodthirsty puppet's attention. It works. Lil Lloyd's piercing eyes and dirty wooden head swivel to face me.

"Stay where you are fatty!" the puppet calls, and in one motion Lloyd's big wide arm pulls Nara in close up to the puppets tiny knife. "Or the girl gets it!"

All those movies I have seen come flooding through my brain—all the times I have heard the nefarious misogynistic villain howl of "or the girl gets it." I try to recall just what the hero did in these cases, but all I remember is the look of grim determination on Clint Eastwood's face and not his corresponding actions. So I stop moving and draw forth my best imitation of a look of grim determination, which, as I can see now, looks like I suddenly have to go to the bathroom.

For her part, Nara does not have the countenance of a Hollywood damsel in distress. She looks irritated as she tries to sever Lloyd's headlock.

Meanwhile Isadore is hollering and yelping as he dangles, drawing an even bigger crowd around the base of the ride. "Somebody!" he calls, "Help ME!"

"Say," ponders Agnes to Wilbur, "isn't that the robber off TV?"

"Of course it isn't," Wilbur says, looking up at Isadore's upside-down face as it hangs a few feet above them.

"Nooo. . ." she says, dragging out the word thoughtfully, ". . .now I saw it just as we were leaving, I checked on the plants, and the TV was on . . . and there was a picture of this young East-Indian boy. . ."

"It ain't him Agnes." Wilbur sighs, he is now looking down at the police as they seem to multiply exponentially.

Isadore is not East Indian, he is more Filipino than anything else, but Agnes has poor vision, and is ignorant, so we'll just let that slide for now.

I am really high up. It's scary. This is something familiar, the well-worn channels and grooves of fear in my brain run deep and fast. Unfortunately, rather than coming up with an ingenious plan to save all of our lives, ole Fear-Brain starts thinking about how I forgot to check the bathroom door in my apartment and make sure it was locked. I always locked it in case of shit demons. No one wants shit demons trampling all over their bedspreads.

"Hank!" Nara says. I look up at her, snapping awake. "Just grab the little fuck and toss it!"

I crouch down on the beam and waddle towards them, hunched over like a frog. Or a fierce jungle cat, ready to pounce. I am so close.

Lil Lloyd presses the knife into her neck. "Uh uh uh!" he warns.

"It's just a fucking puppet Hank, do it!"

Lil Lloyd screeches something, a caterwauling shriek I couldn't really understand the first time, and that I still can't discern, despite my omniscience. The only reason I have any idea is because I know Lloyd's subconscious thoughts. Like most expressions of the subconscious, what he says makes little sense when said out loud, but I might as well try and translate it for you. What he meant to say was, "All my life people have been telling me what to do! Why did you let that tiger die? I am tired of being a puppet." After that, he lets loose a long howl and lifts the knife high to stab Nara in the chest.

His incoherent shriek is startling when you are trying to focus on crawling across the top of a Ferris wheel, so I slip a bit, stumble back, and then over-compensating for the backwards motion, I tumble forward landing face-first into the tiny cart definitely not meant for four large people, particularly one of my stature. The whole thing groans and comes unhinged on one side with a snapping sound.

This time, we all scream: Agnes and Wilbur, Tammy and Chuck, the mob gathered below. Isadore yelps, Lil Lloyd yowls, I wail. Even Nara explodes with a short, piercing gasp of terror.

My face gets mashed into the seat and then I tumble out, catching onto the bar with one hand, which saves me from somersaulting to my death. The weight of me holding onto the bar squeezes onto Isadore's foot, leaving him swinging painfully upside-down, but saving him from dropping to his death.

Nara deftly grabbed onto the side of the cart, which was now the top, as it went down, which meant she's safe for the moment, hugging the plastic with all her might. Lloyd fell forward and shoved his arm between the seat and the back of the cart wedging it in—the left arm I mean, as Lil Lloyd was shrieking hysterically on his right.

Down below, Officer Cohen was barking things into a megaphone—there was suddenly a whole lot to do. He had to phone the fire department, get some people up to rescue us, keep the crowd back, and stop the trigger-happy undercover lady cop from killing Isadore, and more.

"I want some people up there now!" he yelled, but none were forthcoming. It turned out that a number of the cops were afraid of heights. Most of them were standing with their heads tilted upwards, holding their hats onto their heads with one hand.

Hanging by one sweaty hand on the metal bar, I was now experiencing the full extent of my fear of heights. Isadore kept clawing at my flailing legs in an effort to pull himself up, which wasn't helping.

"Hold on!" Chuck hollered helpfully from below.

Nara looked down and noticed Lloyd's arm sliding out; he didn't have a very good handhold. If he fell, he would most likely knock me and Isadore off as well. The puppet was hanging down just near my hands.

Lil Lloyd had recovered from the fall and was now barely missing my sweaty fingers with erratic slashing movements of the knife as Lloyd's puppet-bearing limb swung listlessly left and right like a tire swing. I brought my other sweaty hand up and proceeded to do a little polka with my fingers as they squeak around the plastic of the cart, avoiding the knife while still clinging for life.

"Ahhhh!" I said.

"Lloyd!" Nara said loud and clear, trying to penetrate the passive face just below her knee. "You *have* to *ditch* the *puppet* or we are all going to *die*!"

I have very few good ideas in my adrenaline-addled brain on this day, but this is one. I grab the bar with my other sweaty hand. "Sing the song!"

This confuses Nara. "What?"

"Heyyyy. . ." My voice cracks. I am a terrible singer. "Heyyy gooood loookin. . ."

Lloyd blinks behind his large black glasses. He acts as if he has just woken from an afternoon nap to find himself hanging from the seat of a Ferris wheel by his fingertips.

Thanks, Dad. Thank you for waking me up those misty mornings with your own off-key version of that Hank Williams song. How could either of us have known that one day it would save lives?

Lloyd looks at Nara as if for the first time. Then he looks down at his dangling feet, and beyond that my sweaty red face and Isadore's twisting frantic body. Finally his eyes fall on the puppet. He raises the filthy, small version of himself up to his eye level.

"What are you doing?" Lil Lloyd howls, "I had them!"

Then Lloyd grunted and you could see he was straining to hold himself up. He grimaced as his grip started to give way.

"Now!" Nara yelled.

"Don't listen to her!" Lil Lloyd shrieked in his ear. Well, would have, had he possessed a voice of his own.

"I'm sorry. . ." he whispered, and swung his hand violently down. But Lil Lloyd was stuck on there pretty good, so Lloyd had to thrash him around, smacking him against his leg in an effort to get him off. All the while the demonic thing was howling and screeching. Finally it fell off, and landed with a clanging noise on the bar right by my hands.

"Ah!" I said.

"I'll get you for this!" it shrieked, it's eyes parallel with my own. Then the cart swung suddenly as Lloyd grabbed onto the seat with both hands. With this movement Lil Loyd tumbled over the bar and fell shrieking downwards into the metal and blackness below, his little voice getting quieter and quieter, until suddenly, his limp little body ricocheted of a beam with a *dung!* and bounced to the right, sailing right over Tammy and Chuck who clung to each other in fear. He came cascading down, and hit a metal fence like a trampoline, rebounding and gaining momentum, and all the while shrieking and yelling in anguish. After catapulting off the fence he clanged once more off a metal girder before sailing between Officer Cohen and Tylissus, landing heavily on the control panel of the Ferris wheel. They stepped forward slowly to examine the strange object.

We all followed his beleaguered descent, and after a moment, breathed a small sigh of relief.

"Hey," said Nara to Lloyd dryly, "I saw your lips move."

Just then Lil Lloyd's small wooden hand, the one holding the knife, slipped off his tiny chest and fell to his side, smacking onto the brake release button. The wheel instantly creaked into life, rolling forward with us hanging between the spokes. Again we screamed.

Isadore screamed loudest, as his head was dangling down and rapidly approaching a large metal beam which would no doubt decapitate him. I was kicking with my legs, and managed to bear-hug the side of the cart with my left leg hanging dangerously, the crack of my ass showing clearly from my sweatpants. My tender arms were burning with exhaustion and felt damn near ready to let go and follow that dummy down into hell.

Lloyd is very helpful now that the psychotic puppet is off his hand. He reaches down with one of his long arms and grabs Isadore by the belt, hauling his scrawny butt up and into the sideways cart. The metal beam grazes the hairs on the back of Isadore's head, which is still attached to his body.

Tylissus swipes the knife away and smacks the button again, but the brakes do not engage. Instead there is a loud groaning noise that rips through the wheel as the whole things starts to shudder.

"We have to jump!" yells Nara, and she's right. If we don't, we will get squeezed into jelly between the metal grate and the damaged cart with the force of the wheel as it comes down, and then get ground up and smooshed into human paste as the wheel drags us under and around.

"I can't!" says Isadore, as he and Lloyd try desperately to wrench his leg free of the bar.

"I can't!" I yell, my eyes wide with horror as the grate comes rushing to meet me. I am at the bottom now, so I will be the first to get turned into pâté.

And here is where Isadore's moment comes. His shining second of freedom of choice—that free will I mentioned earlier:

All his life Isadore had been taught to be selfish, and not just by his genes, but by every creature he interacted with. When he joined the cult—by all intents and purposes a collective with aspirations beyond himself—it was only in the hopes of some really great payoff in the end. His every action, like those of many biped menace humans, was an effort to save his own skin.

What happened here happened so fast, Isadore himself didn't realize it. He wasn't trying to impress Nara, as he had been since the moment he met her. He was responding to Lloyd saving his life mere moments before. The gratitude was so deep and immediate that he didn't have time to reflect on it or even know it was there.

At that instant, with death so near to him, Isadore decided to sacrifice himself for someone else. He took a deep breath and closed his eyes before pushing Lloyd, real hard. He didn't have to do that. It was a small action, but it sent Lloyd flying off and away from the cart towards safety. Lloyd hit the metal grating with the grace of someone who is suddenly pushed without warning; like a giant sack of potatoes, knocking Tylissus to the ground and collapsing beside him, cracking his skull against the side of the control panel as he went down.

A lot of people banged their heads today. I clocked Nara in the gas station with the big metal disc; I hit my head twice: once in the van and then once on the rock outside Lloyd's house; Lloyd smacked Isadore's skull against the bumper of the Puppetmobile; and now this nasty head-walloping. It explains a lot actually, our actions etc.—we all had mild concussions.

Nara was looking down at me with pooling lucid eyes, and I up at her, separated by the sideways two-seated cart of a Ferris wheel. There were no words, no time for words, just her with one arm out-stretched as far as she could, and me with a startled look on my face. I stared and waited to feel my legs be ground up like sausage and spread like strawberry jam.

But the wheel stopped. It groaned and squeaked to a halt with my buttocks inches from the grate. I let go of the cart and fell unceremoniously backwards those few inches. Nara leapt down and leaned down to help me to my feet. She turned to Isadore, who was still trapped in the cart bent over and hauled on the bar until it gave. He awkwardly hobbled out.

The wheel stopped because of rusty gears and hinges, metal grinding on metal. Had the wheel people been more diligent with their cans of Water Displacer-40—an oft-used lubricant—Nara, Isadore and myself would have most definitely perished. So it was that most ubiquitous and prevalent of human traits, negligence, which ended up saving us in the end.

"So what now?" Nara said, looking down at the prone forms of Lloyd and Lil Lloyd crumpled at the top of the stairs like a pair of discarded marionettes.

CHAPTER TWENTY-ONE

Mr. Moustache's Wild Ride
and the
Hapless Cotton Candy Cart

Everywhere around us people are talking. Some are clapping and cheering because we are alive, which is nice. Others are irritated that the Ferris wheel is busted because they just spent close to twenty minutes in line. And some, like those afraid of policemen because of their illegal homegrown marijuana operations, are freaked right out and staying awfully quiet.

Bubba the Satiated Bear has finished his hotdog, as well as some bawling kid's blue swab of cotton candy, and now feels restless. He notices that the carnival seems strangely empty, and can hear a great deal of commotion coming from the other side of the tent, so he staggers over, all the while ignoring the frequent frightened stares of the people he passes. Bubba can't help but love a crowd: he is a show bear.

Lloyd clutches his injured head with his left hand and lets out a low moan as he shakily rises, and the moment that he is at eye-level, the police are on him. Apparently they could see all that was going on at the top of the wheel and are reading him his rights.

The cops are also moving towards Isadore.

Nara leaves my side and steps up in front of them. This is not an act of free will, she was raised to protect and care for other less fortunate humans. I stand up and back towards Nara. It is in my nature to be afraid and want to be protected.

Officer Cohen steps proudly out of the throng of blue uniforms clogging the small platform. "Isadore Abella, come with us please," he says civilly. It was not in Brent Cohen's nature to be polite, he was programmed by the law enforcement folk to say that.

But Isadore has a few dumb and misguided surprises left in him. He turns and leaps off the platform as the cops draw their guns on me and Nara. I cover my head with my hands, hoping, I guess, that this will at least slow down a hail of gunfire, which it will, slightly. Nara spins to see if Isadore is making good on his escape.

He's not. He landed on the bunged-up foot that was pinned in the cart, and has folded like a lawn chair into a mass of limbs on the grass beside the stairs. The undercover cop in the peach sweater is on him in seconds.

"Freeeeeeeeze!" she bellows. We all freeze, even some of the cops.

Isadore isn't really going anywhere, but he does manage to pull himself up so that he's hopping on one foot. The cops lead Lloyd off the platform and onto the grass, and we follow. Nara is preparing her speech in defense of Isadore, mulling over whether idiocy is grounds for innocence. Armed robbery was a serious offense then, so he faced a good fifteen years in prison. Alas and alack, she never got to deliver that speech, but I can imagine it would have melted the hearts of all that heard it, even the funless couple.

Jumping into her head now, some key poetic phrases leap out. "Helping those who can't help themselves" and "Unconditional empathy given in a non-judgmental way," but also "hapless moron" and "nerd with a death wish."

Just as Nara was clearing her throat to get the cop's attention, Bubba French the Dancing Bear spotted Lloyd being led away in handcuffs by the cops. He let loose a gin-soaked roar which drew the attention of all the humans within twenty feet of him.

"Bubba?" said Lloyd, turning to see the ponderous figure raise himself up over the people's heads.

The cops rushed on Bubba, which was a bad idea. He swatted at them like they were 185-pound mosquitoes. One uniformed enforcer of the law dodged to the side of the hulking beast, but received a furry hip-check and sailed past us. Lloyd rushed forward to try and placate Bubba, who was quite clearly enjoying himself. He didn't stop until he was facing a dozen or so pointed pistols, which begat a sudden cessation in his thrashing and he acted like nothing had happened, swaggering up to Lloyd's side and nudging his hand with his big black nose.

Nara looked at the cops with all their guns drawn, then at Isadore's stupid, sweaty face. He looks at her and his mouth opens slowly to speak, but no words come out.

Nara was aware of the fifteen or more years of jail time Isadore faced, having had several short, sporadic relationships with criminals. She also knew that Isadore would be easy prey to the other inmates. Looking down at the ground for a moment, she shook her head to herself, and then grabbed my sweat-shirted sleeve and started to pull me with her towards Isadore. We moved in small, staggered steps until we were at his side. I was very anxious to escape the rampaging grizzly bear and was relieved that we seemed to be moving away from the animal.

Once we were finally on either side of the hobbled hostage-taker, we used the distraction of the massive bear to bolt. Grabbing one side of Isadore, Nara took off as fast as we collectively could, melting into the crowd before anyone could say "Holy fuck! It's a rampaging grizzly bear!"

Nara had one arm tucked tight under his armpit, her gaze fixed ahead, and was propelling him forward at a fair clip, with me panting behind. I hadn't yet recovered from the trauma of the wheel, and was having difficulty getting my shaky legs to work. As a result, I stumbled and fell, landing on some soft popcorn and empty paper cups. Soon Nara and Isadore were far ahead, three-legged racing their way behind the porta-potties.

Officer Brent Cohen looked past Lloyd's shoulder and saw me hit the ground. "Hey!" he shouted.

In moments a small battalion of police were huffing and puffing after me as I scrambled to my feet and took off like a chubby bat out of hell.

Nara and Isadore rounded the corner to find themselves next to the potent-smelling home of Mr. Giggles the pony. Mr. Giggles stared back at them with only a mild purveyance of interest on his pony-face.

"This way. . ." Nara said, leading them past the pen. She looked over her shoulder. "Hank! Keep up, okay?" she called, but I was way behind.

Knowledge isn't always a horrific burden. I am here, the very atoms and molecules of this splendid summer night. I know the particular ions in the air, how the barometric pressure of the valley the fairground lay nestled in provides a shelter and haven from the cold ocean air. This, coupled with the miraculous harnessing of electricity in the carnival lights, the sweet scent molecules of cotton candy in the gentle breeze, all of these ingredients moving to concoct a truly beautiful night. As I run, I am alive at that moment like I have not been in a long time. I am buffeting those atoms with a force borne of true urgency. I am emblazoned with purpose. Away, away. That is my purpose.

Then it hits me. I feel the sweep of acid and panic in my stomach and the sudden onset of the lost-in-the-mall feeling again. I am getting left behind. My jog turns into a flat-out sprinting surge. Thoom! Thoom! My sneakers slam against the trampled grass. I round the porta-potties but Nara and Isadore are long gone, so I keep on trucking towards the carousel. Purpose has been trampled into wild panic. I am fast approaching an old lady and her scrawny, pig-tailed granddaughter. At the speed I am moving, there is no option of turning—it is painfully clear that I am going to fly right into them much like Isadore and that poor child with the blue cotton candy earlier. We are a clumsy, hasty bunch.

"Why-why are you helping me?" Isadore said as they limped along.

"Because you're too stupid to help yourself, okay?" Nara answered, not looking at him. Isadore seemed to accept this. Soon they were at the Puppetmobile. She leaned him up against the side. "Stay here and stay down, I'm going to find Hank."

"But. . ." Isadore said.

Nara ignored him and ran off. He looked after her as she rounded the garbage cans and then something caught the corner of his eye. He looked up to see the giant grinning face of Lil Lloyd, holding an accordion.

"Wahhh!" he yelled. He regained his composure and shot the mural a dirty look, before hobbling his way into the cab of the truck and hunkering down so that no one could see him.

I sent the scrawny kid in pigtails flying, but managed to avoid the grandmother. She drew back her ringed, sinewy claw to strike, but I was faster. I hip-checked her as I burst past, making a wild dash to the left in the hopes of shaking the cops. "Nara!" I called, stumbling through the forest of people and trying my best to dodge the two policemen directly behind me.

"Hank!" Nara called.

I spun around and saw her. She had one hand up to her mouth, her slender legs poised and her hair dramatically tousled. She saw me too, and smiled a slight smile. I smiled a big dopey grin back at her. And then the cops were on me, wrestling my dopey face down into the ground. When I looked up again, Nara was gone.

Not gone exactly. She had actually ran around the corner of a booth to find the Puppetmobile idling noisily and Isadore sitting in the front seat. He had found the keys in the ignition, where Lloyd had left them, and had wasted no time in starting it up.

"Get in!" he yelled at Nara.

"Just go! Drive!"

"They'll shoot me without you!"

Nara hesitated and thought back to her stupid life at the gas station for a moment, "Fine. I'll get you out of here, but then you're on your own." She hopped into the cab and almost immediately regretted her decision. Just as she closed the door, a parade of blue uniforms and one peach-colored sweater came swarming from behind the stinking pony pen. Isadore slammed the pedal to the floor, sending muck and mud flying back in their direction. The truck dug a deep groove in the soft earth before at last bounding forward.

"There!" Nara exclaimed, pointing for Isadore to make a sharp turn. As the truck wheeled around the corner they could hear things falling over and crashing in the back. The back door was still open, so as soon as they rounded the corner a life-size wooden puppet that looked like an orange ostrich came crashing out, its long neck and legs in disarray.

Isadore had to slow down considerably once he pulled out of the turn, as there were families and couples grazing in tiny clusters everywhere.

"Get out of the way!" Nara hollered out the window. Isadore honked the horn at a particularly bovine couple directly in front of them.

"I don't see Hank anywhere. . ." Nara muttered to Isadore. "He was just here." They bounced, crashed and honked their way through the grounds, sending people scurrying out of their path.

Meanwhile, I was not having much luck with the police. After helping me up to my feet, most of them didn't know what to do with me. I was not resisting arrest, even though I had been running from them. I had committed no crime, so they couldn't put me in handcuffs. I was under the impression that they should wrap me up in a blanket and sit me down somewhere with a small cup of apple juice or coffee, as that was what happened to all the hostages I had seen on TV.

Instead, they were angrily grilling me for information that I did not have. One of them pulled out a flashlight—even though there were plenty of other flashing lights around—and aimed it at my eyes. I squinted into the white light and stammered my usual babble, which went like this:

"No, muh—maybe a ghost puppet."

To which there was no response. Finally, Officer Cohen strode up to join the semi-circle of uniforms. He tried to be all buddy-buddy with me. He put one hand on my shoulder and gave it a congenial squeeze. This bothered me greatly, as I liked to avoid human contact unless absolutely necessary.

"Hey, I know you've been through a lot, uh. . ." he looked down at my name-tag and I followed his gaze, ". . .Hank. But we just need you to answer some questions. Where's the kid?"

I took this to mean Isadore. "Don't know," I mumbled dejectedly.

And, wouldn't you know it, just then the Puppetmobile came thundering towards us amidst a chorus of screams and shouts. The majority of the cops scattered. I stood there frozen in place, while Cohen took a step away from me and swept his gun from its holster in one quick motion, like a real cowboy, aiming it at the advancing truck.

Westerns, which are tales of violence from a decidedly unpleasant period of North American history, played often in the home of Officer Brent Cohen, back when he was just little boy Brent Cohen. He had practiced this move over, and over, and over, and then a few more times in the backyard of his mother's house. Drawing beads on the household cat as it lay lazily on the wicker chair in front of him.

Only this time, it was a real gun, with real bullets and a real trigger, which he fired twice, the bullets hitting the bumper of the bouncing truck. Officer Cohen was aiming for the tires, not shooting to kill, not yet. Isadore took evasive action, banking hard to the left and knocking over the cotton candy stand. It's not a good car chase—in a motion picture or otherwise—unless some sort of stand gets knocked over.

The jogging parade of cops, most with their guns drawn, followed close behind surveying the decimated stand. The girl, Mandy, who had been dipping the paper cones into the magical whirring machine, just stood there aghast, gripping an unused paper cone tight and useless in her right hand as the Puppetmobile bounced and crashed away out of sight.

"You're coming with me," Officer Cohen said, dragging me by my arm. I did not resist. I did not know how to resist. I might know how to flail with the best of them, but my diligence in watching cartoons had not filled my head with a vast array of fighting techniques. Besides, he was a cop and I couldn't help but be afraid of cops, largely because of their moustaches.

"Okay," I replied compliantly.

Officer Cohen was very determined to solve this case single-handedly. He felt cheated that the robbery had started during his patrol, and guilt that he was jerking off when if he had been at the gas station moments earlier he could have caught Isadore in the act. Nothing ever happened in this quiet seaside town and now there was high profile manhunt happening right on his beat. He marched me quickly, almost greedily away from the other cops and towards his patrol car. No one stopped him.

I avoided looking at his big bushy brown mustache by staring fixedly at my large white sneakers as they plodded and stumbled forward. He led me towards his car, which was parked illegally, blocking the only exit from the fairgrounds.

"No funny stuff, you're going to tell me everything you know," he said, pushing me into the passenger side of his car and slamming the door. I had time to consider what he meant by this as he ran around to the driver's side of the car. I didn't know how to be funny. I tried to remember one single solitary joke I had heard in my thirty-seven years, but none came to me. Well, I thought, nothing to worry about there, Mr. Moustache.

I know a billion jokes now, but I will spare you from an onslaught. One thing's for sure, it's all in the delivery. Here's one:

Did you hear about the zoo with only one animal?
It was a shih tzu.
Badoomshhhhhh!

Cohen hopped in, leaning in my direction to fiddle with his radio, so that I cowered and pressed myself up against the window, away from his bristly horror. My sweaty face made a small greasy stain on the glass.

"All units, suspect is escaping in a large, brightly painted truck, headed west. Is considered armed and dangerous, this is Unit-14 engaging pursuit." His voice was proud and cocky, as he was the closest to Isadore, and desperately wanted, needed, to be the one that caught him after spending a whole day looking for him. I wanted to tell him then that Isadore was in fact, unarmed, but as I saw that big brown caterpillar bristling into the radio right next to my face, my voice clogged up in my throat and wouldn't come out. It was also then that I noticed a crusty stain on his trousers, which was semen, though I didn't know that then.

"Um. . ." I said.

Officer Brent Cohen was too busy to notice my meager spit bubble of a comment, as just then, the Puppetmobile came bouncing, thrashing and honking right in front of us towards the exit. I could see Isadore, his eyes wild and his hair disheveled, and Nara, looking irritated and worried, beside him. Then they were gone. Cohen revved up the engine, switched the car into drive, and did a nice peel-out in the mud before we went roaring after them.

The car we were in ripped right through one of those creepy Suth things, the things that just watch our reality with the one big red eye and tentacles of matter, but because it exists on a different plane than our physical realm, we passed right through it unscathed. My left eye did tremor, as did Officer Cohen's, but we were too busy to notice.

As we bounced along the grass with the Puppetmobile in front of us, he picked up his radio and started rattling off the details of our hot pursuit, but he neglected to mention his shanghaied passenger, the rescued hostage: me.

Just ahead, the Puppetmobile went into a large dip on the grass, soaring downwards, and when they came up, I saw the purple octopus come flying out of the back of the truck towards us. We were close behind them now, so it crashed into the hood of the car with a heavy tentacled fury.

Cohen halted in mid-sentence, and I screamed my loud, high and piercing scream. I didn't stop screaming until 4.6752 seconds later, when the thing with its googly, sparkling eyes slid off the hood and was mashed to splinters under our wheels. Officer Cohen looked sideways at me, put down the radio and grabbed the wheel with both hands.

"Put on your seatbelt," he said. I did not. I was afraid of seatbelts. I was afraid that if we did get in a car crash, the seat belt would cut into my neck and I would be decapitated—kefalitemnozonophobia (kefalitemnophobia: fear of decapitation. Zonophobia: fear of belts).

A flurry of blue and red lights appeared behind us, bobbing and coruscating across the grass. The rest of the cops had joined the chase.

"Subject is leaving the fairground. . ." Cohen said with pride into the radio, "and east-bound. Headed towards Interstate 12-A."

CHAPTER TWENTY-TWO

The Anti-Astronaut Pill
and the
Flying Fairy Princess

I used to sit when I was a child and watch the night sky. I'd sneak out of my window, wriggling through the small opening and onto the gravel coated roof of our garage. Sometimes I would bring a blanket, but mostly I would just sit there huddled and shivering, my legs up by my chest. It was easier to rush back to bed and act innocent if wasn't trying to yank the bulky blanket behind me. I'm not sure exactly why I was so careful and covert, as looking back it seems a fairly benign and wholesome activity. My only guess is that it was all in an effort to escape the wrath of my mother, who would be livid to find me awake and sitting on the garage in plain view of our neighbors had they decided to go for a stroll at three thirty in the morning.

Even from my suburban wasteland of cul-de-sacs and ample parking, we had a pretty good view of the stars. The brownish-orange glow of the streetlights couldn't quite diminish the thick band of the Milky Way as it glimmered and beckoned above me on a clear night. I would sit and look at the countless dazzling points of light, and see myself racing between them, rapt with the idea of my future life as a fearless and intrepid astronaut.

I pictured all the amazing things I could and would do in my spaceship, which was the kind with gravity machines, with none of that archaic floating or bumping of heads into the instruments nonsense. This would be a spaceship like the ones on TV, except with more windows. I would have windows below me, windows above, all sides, windows. This way I could see the stars from every direction and not just when I looked up. Alas, three things kept me from my life as an astronaut.

The first was my complete lack of comprehension, and thus, unbridled adversity towards mathematics. From Grade 4 onwards I had displayed a remarkable incompetence towards simple equations, which frequently resulted in me spending extra time after school with the stern and fur-lipped Miss Gail.

The second was the sudden onset of my apeirophobia, a fear which would spread like a cancer through my idyllic childhood, leading to all the fears I have mentioned so far. But this was the first one, this is the biggest, the grandaddy.

My fear of the infinite came about during another one of my favorite childhood activities: staring into the mirror with the lights off. I would watch my face twist and shift with unadulterated glee at any hour of the day, though most often before bedtime, when I could be sure I wouldn't be disturbed. Although if I saw sufficient opportunity I could and would do it pretty much anywhere I could find a moment alone.

The idea was to position your face close up by the mirror and let your eyes relax, so that your own face becomes distorted and unrecognizable. I would do this for hours, fearless and with a determination I would later turn towards avoiding things that scared me.

This continued until the fateful day I was in my parent's bathroom, which had two mirrors on each side that you could tilt in such a way to create reflections of yourself that stretched infinitely inwards. A countless number of me stretching down a long tunnel with no end. It was the "no end" part that slowly started to unhinge me. I stared alone in that bathroom for what must have been hours, and no matter how long I stared, or how hard, the tunnel just curved and stretched and I began to understand that it went on forever.

Forever was to become my least favorite word. Every second that I looked down that hallucinatory tunnel did me weeks-and-months-worth of harm. I was so horrified by the idea that something could not end, that I ran as fast as I could from the bathroom in an effort to regain my ignorance. But by the time I had groped my way out of there and into the carpeted hallway, it was too late. It suddenly hit me in a tangible way that there were an infinite number of things out there with no beginning and no end.

Which led to a series of drool-inducing questions: Where did I fit in? How could I possibly matter? And my penultimate horror: What if they were wrong? What if I was infinite too? What if I somehow went on living forever and ever? It's hard to imagine oneself dying, but it is even harder to imagine living eternally.

It all slowly ramped up into a peak of hysterics during my fragile junior-high years, until the very idea of the stars and infinite space was enough to send me and my mom straight to K-mart to buy a set of new industrial-strength heavy curtains to block out their twinkling horror. Later that week, when I lost my cool in math class over a pair of parallel lines drawn on the chalkboard, mom was called in about my outbursts.

She and Ms. Gail had a long talk about my uncomfortable new affliction. I had refused to join the class project in which we converted the classroom into a mock-up of our solar system, and had simply bolted to the playground when the other students started busily applying glow-in-the dark stars to every wall and surface available.

Ms. Gail taught arithmetic, not metaphysics. She liked punctuality, the Dewey Decimal System, and the Periodic Table of Elements. She found plutonium and tattoos offensive for their non-conformity, and thus my disturbances needed to be dealt with promptly and severely.

And mother was busy trying to mold our life into the box that reflected the lives we saw on the square TV screen; one surrounded by bright green lawns and tall brown fences. A predictable and concrete existence with a beginning, a middle, and a most definite end. My habit of constantly bringing up the specter of endlessness was uncomfortable for my mother and Miss Gail for the simple reason that all humanity has a problem with infinity. Nothing on Earth is truly infinite, so, besides the occasional convoluted story about an eternal afterlife, we try to avoid the topic whenever possible. We may use the word infinity often, but that is where the notion ends. We actually avoid pondering its meaning as much as possible. So you can shut up about it already, awkward teenage Hank.

When I was trying to relate to the rest of humanity and its avoidant tendencies, I would return to my mantra.

"Infinity Schminity" I would say. Over and over, with mixed results.

This was the beginning of The Fear. In the next few years, the very notion of sitting in a spaceship with windows on all sides would seem more like hell than heaven. It was after this point that I started avoiding mirrors entirely, which led to a great many unsettling things, including my new-found taste for wearing airbrushed wolf sweatshirts. I also stopped combing my hair but started again in later years due to a fear of ticks and lice. My mother watched me closely after this, and couldn't help but notice my continued erratic behavior.

I'm sorry, Mom. Sorry for the hollering in the night, the violence of my many outbursts, the period where I did lots of illicit drugs in order to self-medicate myself into numbness, and the weird things I would say to your friends when you would have them over to play cards.

I'm not sorry Ms. Gail. You could've been nicer.

And now you know the story of my short, yet fierce dissent into madness. It grew to be too much for my poor mother to handle, and two days after my seventeenth birthday, on New Year's Day, I found myself committed by my friends and family to the Aaron Martin Institute of Mental Health. And it was during that first tenure in the loony bin that my astronaut dreams met their final deathblow in the form of a fellow patient—Mr. Anthony Hepburn.

Anthony, like me, was a young man who'd suddenly found his family and friends announcing one night that they were fairly certain he was a few bricks shy of a load. It wasn't so bad. We watched a lot of TV during those first months. And when we weren't doing that, we managed a complicated barter system with the other patients in which we acquired better and better meds. It was during one of our more sedated conversations that Anthony first unloaded his cultivated knowledge of the astronaut pill.

According to Anthony—who coupled with the onslaught of codeine could be very convincing—certain government agencies were busily pumping their "astronaut pill" into all the major cities' water supplies. The effect of the astronaut pill was fairly simple.

It made you want to be an astronaut so badly you could taste it: dreams of aliens, cravings for freeze-dried foods, a tendency to wear white and watch the National Aeronautics and Space Administration channel all day long with the sound turned off, fed by a continuous longing for space and its cold, vacant depths.

The problem with the pill, said Anthony, was that it wore off as soon as you found yourself anywhere near zero-gravity. You would all of a sudden realize that you didn't want to be in space at all, had in fact never wanted to be an astronaut in the first place.

You would then scream and howl like a displaced chimp until you died up there, sealed up in your tiny tomb and spinning around and around and around through the void.

At the moment that I was crammed into a cop car with officer Cohen, Anthony Hepburn had just blown the front half of his friend's house into the street. A result of his life's work perfecting the anti-astronaut pill.

Now that I can watch Anthony and NASA a little closer, I see that his theories are a bit off. There is no astronaut pill. I have no idea what prompts humans to desire space-travel, other than a supreme dissatisfaction with other humans and the world they live in. And of course, that most beautiful of cognizant characteristics: curiosity.

There are beings out there who get along with each other quite nicely. Those suicidal robots I told you about, and one other race. It is a race of all females that only become male once in their life to procreate, but that's not why they get along. It's because these creatures all have a large, rubbery tube-appendage coming from the tops of their heads, which gives them the power to immediately kill anyone they so desire. Seeing as how everyone has this power, no one uses it, because they know the retribution would be swift and merciless.

Almost no one I should say, as there was a young couple that could never be together, due to the elaborate caste system of these females. So one of them killed the other, and then the deceased's mother killed that murderer, which led to this mother being killed by the aunt on the other side. Centuries of peace were restored soon after.

And back on that ugly, demented, fragmented little world that we have come to know and love as our own, two motorized vehicles are speeding down a highway, one following after the other. Behind them floods a whole fleet of motorized vehicles with flashing lights. Looking at them now from way up above, it's hard to believe there are tiny endoskeletal pink and brown creatures inside, presumably controlling which way they go and how fast. They are going incredibly fast.

And, further down this highway, and travelling much slower, weaves a shit-filled motorized vehicle manipulated by an endoskeletal pink creature named Philip Coover. His vehicle, like a mirror of himself, appears drunk from up here as it meanders across double yellow lines and squeals and spurts unnecessarily.

Together with the air above, I also lie stretched out in the soil, reaching upwards to myself as the slender blades of grass that caress each other in the billowing evening breeze. Suddenly the ground starts to shake. It shakes in such a way that a human would not notice, especially one in a speeding car. To me in the grass it feels like a Mack truck thundering down my spine.

Hundreds upon thousands of crickets are moving all as one. Some are flying, others are hopping, more are crawling, but all are headed in one chaotic straight line. They take over the blades of grass one at a time at first, but within seconds they are in plague-like proportions, their antennas whirring and whipping in a frenzy to communicate.

The first ever United Cricket and Insect Coalition to Protect the Planet meeting had been a resounding success. In their chirping and scratchy song language, they had decided the best way to deal with the biped menace was to speak to the humans in their own language, as all the more subtle approaches at communication had failed horribly.

The plan was as follows: The crickets would find fields throughout the world, and eat one simple message into the field, and then sit there and sing and dance until the humans couldn't help but notice the shimmering, buzzing letters. The message was this: "You Must Change Everything You Are Doing." These crickets were on their way to eat the word "Must" into a huge field on the other side of Interstate 12-A.

Alas, the crickets made the fatal mistake of choosing what they thought to be the most eloquent of all the human languages, ancient Etruscan. And indeed, in many ways it was so beautiful that long ago the crickets had learnt it as a hobby, teaching it to their kids. These particular crickets had been schooled in it since birth, and most crickets have a basic knowledge of its key phrases. Humans, not so much.

The crickets oozed purposefully onto the highway like a great sparkling sea of shimmering bodies in the starlight.

Headed towards them at a speed which would most certainly decimate their numbers, were Nara and Isadore in the Puppetmobile, engaged in one of their customary four-lettered arguments. Nara had one hand on the dashboard to steady herself as Isadore whipped the truck around a curve in the highway.

"You don't really think you can outrun them in this piece of shit, do you?" Nara said.

"Shityes, I fucking damn well do!" Isadore snapped in his most irritated poodle voice.

"Listen! We have to get off the highway like last time. They'll just set up a roadblock."

Isadore was happy that at least she was being helpful, but he still wanted to feel in control of the situation—and possibly, though this seemed less and less likely, impress her.

"Do you see anywhere to pull off? Huh? Cause I fucking don't!"

Nara had no response to this. She scanned ahead and saw no place to turn.

Looking in the side mirror at the whirring lights and wailing sirens not far behind them she said, "I have an idea," and pulled open the small sliding window in the back of the cab. She pushed a box blocking the window out of the way, so that it landed with a crash, and proceeded to crawl her way into the back of the truck.

"What the fuck are you doing?" Isadore said in a panic.

"Just don't crash, okay?" she said eyeing his sweaty, nervous grip on the wheel, "I'm going to slow them down."

Once she had eased her way into the back, Nara saw the clutter of the Puppetmobile painted in the kaleidoscope blue and red flashes of the police lights. Looking past the various puppets and props she saw one cop car right up close, and more in the distance. She quickly hunched down behind a small wooden two-dimensional castle, knowing that if the cops saw her hurling things out of the back of the truck it could do damage to her claim as a frightened hostage. She eyed a human-sized wooden puppet of a princess and reached up to unhook it.

"Pull over the vehicle!" Officer Cohen ordered over the loudspeaker mounted on the roof of his car. His voice was barely audible over the wailing sirens and didn't actually expect Isadore to pull the truck to the side of the road, he was programmed to say that. "Godamnit!" he said, angrily hooking the microphone back onto the dashboard. Part of his irritation was his urge to rebel against his programming. He was looking down, fiddling with the radio, but looked up in time to see the fairy princess come flying towards us and straight into our windshield.

"Look out," I said. But there had been a good full second of pondering what I was looking at, so I spoke late and flat, a moment before the big wooden head with the pink pointed hat came bursting through the glass right between us. Its painted face was now scratched and disfigured, but its big vacant eyes and massive pink lips stared up at me and Officer Cohen amongst the shattered shards.

Our car swerved and careened into the other lane as Cohen tried to regain control of the vehicle. As we swerved back into our lane, I saw a bridge ahead. I immediately started to freak out, muttering and pounding on the dash. Not because I knew that I was going to die on that bridge, because how could I have known that for certain? I just happened to be horribly afraid of bridges. My gephydrophobia was in no way related to a fear of heights, as I wasn't afraid of heights until that Ferris wheel.

I was afraid of bridges because when I was seven years old, I thought I had seen a troll, and the image hovered in the back of my mind until the day my fear floodgates opened. It was a homeless woman, she was not a former university professor like the old man in high heels; she was a former bank teller, someone's daughter, sister and aunt.

Officer Cohen did not have time to deal with, or even notice my supremely agitated state. The problem being that the long flowing dress of the princess puppet on the hood was whipping up in the wind, slapping him in the face and making it impossible to see out the windshield. He had his head out the window, trying to keep us from crashing while pulling out his gun and trying to shoot out the tires of the truck. He gripped the wheel with one hand, and had one good shot, but it was immediately foiled by a sudden flapping of the princess dress into his determined cop face.

Meanwhile, Zulaikha and her herd of tokay geckos had barked, hopped and scurried all the way from where we had last seen them by the van, taking a shortcut past the fairgrounds, to the ditches on either side of Interstate 12-A, near the other side of the bridge. They had been following the masses of crickets and were awaiting Zulaikha's orders to leap from their hiding place and devour every last one of them. Tough times for crickets.

Before the sirens of the police cars could penetrate the buzzing of the crickets, Zulaikha gave the order, and the tokays leapt onto the road headed straight for the massive shimmering shield of insect mass. The crickets, though experts at communication, could not escape the bigger blue lizards. Zulaikha was a cunning strategist, so she had them trapped on all sides. *Retreat!* their little antennas signaled, but there was nowhere to retreat to.

Philip Coover rounded the corner just before the bridge and noticed a little blue lizard in the middle of his path. He swerved to miss it, saw another one just a bit farther, and swerved to miss that one too. And then the entire road was coated in them. He cranked the wheel and hit his brakes, exclaiming "Holy Toledo!" as the truck's ancient brake pads—never replaced—wailed in protest.

The poop truck made a nasty paste out of a couple of blue lizards and their captive crickets, a slippery paste on an already slippery road which caused the tires to slide sideways and the truck to go bouncing off the railing of the bridge. Had Philip been less drunk, he might have corrected the turn—instead the truck bounced from one side of the bridge to the other, the back tires slid out, and the truck came to a rest across the road amidst a slew of tiny crushed lizard and cricket bodies with Philip slumped over the wheel.

Isadore, Nara, and the truck filled with puppet paraphernalia bounded onto the bridge soon after. The first thing Isadore noticed was that the ground was nothing more than a shimmering black mass, and then he saw that there was a truck with a large tank blocking his path. He went to hit the brakes, but his injured foot made the first attempt, and he yanked it back sharply. Using his other foot, he slammed the pedal down and the tires stopped spinning, but the Puppetmobile continued to fly forward on a slick paste of cricket carnage as Isadore looked on in wonder at the mass of familiar blue bodies before him.

"Fuckshitfuck!" he said.

The crickets saw their death from all sides. The mothers gathered their tiny cricket children to their sides as the tires came down. They whirred calming messages with their antennae to the children, even though they knew their situation was hopeless. Such is the beauty of the creatures of Earth. A few of the heartier crickets had attempted to fight back at the geckos, and taken to the air. These ones were mashed into the grill of the Puppetmobile as it came sailing forward. Many brave crickets were slain by the four massive tires as they slid forward; many more drowned in the coming tsunami of fecal matter.

The Puppetmobile cruised straight for the septic tank truck, Isadore hauling on the wheel to try and limit the impact to one side, but it was moving way too fast. It hit the ass-end of the truck with a hearty slam and crashed over the cement barrier of the bridge next to it. Shit, chemicals, and chunks of cement exploded into the air, as the Puppetmobile ground its bottom along the broken edge until it finally stopped, its front end dangling precariously over the edge, front tires still spinning. Huge pieces of concrete went tumbling and turning over the edge, hitting the dark water below with a deep splash. The truck bobbed up and down slightly, making an awful metal-wrenching noise.

Officer Cohen, not being drunk or injured, hit the brakes just as we got to the bridge and we squealed to a relatively well-executed stop. I used both hands to brace myself, saving my bulky blundering body from yet another head injury. The wooden princess went sliding out the hole in the windshield and fell onto the ground in front of the car. Cohen burst from the driver's side, holding his gun, but then stood in shock looking at the sea of crickets and blue lizards before him, two thin paths of corpses leading to the bubbling shit truck and the dangling Puppetmobile.

A tokay lizard hopped up onto his foot. "Tok! Tok!" it said.

I got out the other side and watched the dangling truck with a sick feeling in my stomach. I looked at the bridge, and then the truck, then the crickets, then the lizards, and then the gaping open septic tank and blurping piles of feces oozing steadily out of its ominous hole.

"Nara. . ." I whispered, but I did not move.

Nara was tangled up in a jumble of puppet strings, limbs, and wires. She had a cut on her forehead, one on her cheek, and a new bruise on her side, but was basically intact. She could see the night sky out the back of the truck as it bobbed up and down. With a grunt she pushed a wooden castle off of her and tried to pull herself free of the strings coiled and twisted around her waist. As she did this, she could hear Isadore yelping and screaming in the front seat behind her head.

"Isadore! What the fuck did I tell you!" Nara yelled, but then turned her attention back to her own situation. "Don't crash! Ow. Mother*fucker*," she muttered to herself, yanking at the wires.

"Nara. . ." Isadore said. His voice was even and steady, but only in an effort to express the gravity of the situation. No pun intended, as gravity *was* the situation.

"What?"

"Don't . . . Move," Isadore replied.

Nara stopped thrashing with the wires and pushed up with her legs, straining against the cords at her waist to look through the window into the cab. She could see Isadore, the windshield with one large crack in it, and below that, way below that, dark black water. There were crickets skidding along on the mangled hood of the truck, and when one of them fell, it fell for a long, long time.

"Fuck," she said. "Crawl back here and help me, right fuckin now. I'm stuck."

Isadore stared for a second longer, then gingerly eased out of his seat. Gripping the window behind him, he slowly pulled himself out from behind the wheel, painfully aware that every movement made the truck dip farther down. He hauled himself through the small window and wriggled out of the cab and onto the floor in the back of the truck. Once he was out and squatted next to her, he looked at Nara, saw that she was coiled over and over with puppet strings, and started pulling at them.

"Hurry," she said.

Uhg. I don't know if I can do this. It was all fun and games until now. Maybe we should go look at something else. There are so many wonderful times to discover across the universe. Or dinosaurs! I bet you always wanted to know more about them and what they were actually like; their bizarre social structure etc. Hint: Very similar to birds.

Besides I think I have a very strong idea of how I ended up trapped alone in the universe, and perhaps you have the same inkling. It was the drugs. That bizarre and largely unprecedented chemical cocktail was jamming the signal on my brain radio in such a way that it could not transmit me into the cosmos. This is my theory, made ever more clear with my attunement to my actions on this day. Sigh.

We might as well continue, as there's only one way to be sure.

Philip Coover was unconscious. The impact of the Puppetmobile had smacked his drunken head against his driver's-side window, and he now lay in a lump over the seat with one limp hand twitching slightly. This made him neglectful in his shit-management duties and the poop that had sat so long in his truck continued to leak out onto the pavement unchecked.

On that bridge an epic battle raged as the crickets attempted to assemble themselves amidst the waves of muck-covered barking lizards. The crickets were having a hard time escaping, as a large number of them had been soaked in the feces. For their part, the lizards were having a hard time staying focused on eating, as there was shit in most of their mouths.

I took a step past Officer Cohen, who was still processing the sight of all those lizards. I put my left hand over my anus to prevent any lizards from crawling in there unchecked. Then another step. One step at a time towards the Not-So-Great Beyond.

CHAPTER TWENTY-THREE

The Bridge on Interstate 12-A

I inched forward, my eyes going from the mass of bugs at my feet to the headlights of the Puppetmobile shooting down at a forty-five-degree angle towards the water. I tried desperately not to picture a troll rising up, one clawed hand at a time, and hauling the truck over the edge and under the bridge. The smell of feces from the septic truck hit me hard in the face like a dirty slap. I recoiled instantly, but there was no way to escape it.

"Not now, Gladys," I said to myself. At first I diligently flicked the crickets out of my way with the toe of my sneakers, but soon that became impossible. When a large blue lizard scurried between my legs I stopped moving completely. For a second I considered turning back, even going as far as to spin around and face the other way.

The other cops had arrived at the scene and were piling up at the end of the bridge, surrounding Officer Cohen and staring stupefied at the scene before them.

Inside the Puppetmobile, Isadore was searching around for something to cut the wires with. Finding nothing, he grabbed Nara under the arms and tried to yank her loose by bracing his feet against the side and pulling with all his strength.

"Ow," Nara said.

Isadore let go, and was looking at her helplessly when a long black lizard-head-shadow spread across her face. It was caused by the reflection of the septic truck's headlights off the metal barrier on the other side of the bridge, creating a Godzilla-sized shadow that fell over both of them.

"Tok! Tok!" came the call of a tiny blue gecko as it stood on the metal floor of the truck. Isadore spun around at the sound. They looked at it with horror.
"Now," Nara said, "Get me the out of here, NOW!"
The lizard cocked its head to the side and looked at them, then it started to pad with its tiny lizard feet in their direction. As it did, the whole truck made a shuddering noise as it slid forward and dipped down. Nara and Isadore froze, bracing themselves for the fall. The lizard stopped too, seemingly unsure of its new home.
"Tok?" it said.
I saw that the clearest path to the suspended truck was on the sides, but there was no way I could go that close to the edge of the bridge without falling to my knees and crawling. I tried looking up, but now that we were far from the carnival lights, the stars shone and twinkled with sickening limitlessness. The only way was straight through. I cautiously made my way around the lizards, until one of them crawled up my leg and I had to bat it off, which prompted a fit of spasms that effectively halted my progress.
Isadore managed to get most of the strings off of Nara, except for the ones around her waist, which were pinned under a heavy trunk that had slid beside her. Every time he tried to lift the trunk, the balance of the truck was thrown forward so that they dipped down. He would quickly put the trunk back down and back away, then try again. His selfish gene was kicking in full force now, and despite his saving Lloyd on the Ferris wheel, he was still essentially Isadore and wanted to leave Nara behind and

save himself. This thought pounded on him until finally he turned away from Nara to face the open back of the truck, and freedom.

"Don't . . . you . . . dare," Nara warned.

"I'll go get help," he said.

Zulaikha barked twice over the chaos, but not even her formidable presence could capture the attention of the crazed geckos. Those nearest to her were gathered in a small semi-circle awaiting her orders. With three long whips of her tail, she ushered them out of the poop and onto the bumper of the truck to give them a good viewpoint and tactical advantage.

"Shit!" Nara cried.

Isadore spun again, this time to see the solitary lizard joined by five, then ten, then fifteen other tokay geckos. They barked and hopped over each other, staring at the two humans with their bright yellow eyes. Every few seconds, a new lizard head popped up. The noise of their barking in the cavernous truck echoed and rang as it was amplified by the metal, and their sudden weight counter-balanced the truck, causing the fender to dip down towards the surface of the bridge, away from peril.

But, as they started to clamber forward, the truck went with them, tilting up so that the back lifted up into the air and the whole thing crunched forward. Nara screamed, but this time it was not the short, alarmed scream of surprise she was known for. This was a long, terrified scream, similar to the one I had wailed when the octopus landed on the hood of the cop car. Isadore screamed too—an angry, frustrated sound.

And then, suddenly, all the lizards froze, but not because of the screaming, they stopped exactly as they had earlier, with their small, reptilian necks craning upwards. The truck halted its descent, with most of it dangling over the side. Isadore and Nara had stopped screaming. They looked at each other, and then back at the lizards.

And with my panoramic view of the invisible strings that bind us, I can see the lizards of Earth staring at the fabric of the

Omniverse as it bubbles and curls outwards in small shimmering waves, like ripples on a pond, because millions of light years away, so far as to boggle their tiny lizard minds, Hord the World Eater had belched, thus sending pulses of undulating matter in all directions. I can these ripples now, and the way they affect us. I can see it all in my state of panoramica.

Across the Earth as the wave hit, old ladies fell off of stepladders; old men fell against bathtubs; most kids on roller skates tumbled to the sidewalk; deep-sea serpents in the darkest chasms of the Atlantic smacked into each other; rhesus monkeys paused in their orgies; Ryan Totten ceased his nonsensical chanting as the candles around him were suddenly extinguished all at once; Penny from the ice cream counter dropped a cup of water she had brought to her bed from the bathroom; Murray MacDonald awoke from a dream involving his nurse to find his son Julian stealing tongue depressors; Bubba French the Dancing Bear fell off the ball he was balancing on beside Lloyd, the peach-sweatered lady cop from the funless couple lost her balance and fell against the male cop, who then caught her tenderly in his arms; Mrs. Emilia Knudson woke suddenly from a dream of talking nasturtiums and snails and reached for her husband who was not there; New Elvis stubbed his toe on that alien planet and said "Dangit!" so loud they could hear it in the next sphericle; Tammy, who was next to Chuck on the Tilt-a-Whirl, vomited cotton candy onto his lap; my imprisoned father pooped into his yellow pajamas; the door of that haunted house of Lloyd's swung open and creaked loudly; one of those invisible Suth watching things with its tentacles of matter and its giant eye blinked; Gladys the noseless wonder one universe away tripped, smacking where her nose should be against a window; one of the robots from the solar system composed entirely of other robots had a glitch in its monotonous over-played singing and accidentally invented robot jazz; that beaver near Philip the Septic Guy's trailer choked on a stick he was gnawing on and decided to move to new creek with softer wood; a droplet of spittle fell from Phil the Septic Guy's unconscious mouth and made a wet spot on his coveralls; all the crickets antennae flattened against their backs swiftly,

... And the Puppetmobile, poised on the edge of the bridge on Interstate 12-A, came loose and slid off, plummeting downwards into the icy black water below.

I had been mere feet from the truck when it fell, running to the side in time to see it fall and hit the water with a crunch and a splash, a trail of tiny blue lizards following after it. I rushed over to the point where it had gone over, crunching crickets, geckos, and one ant in my path. Below me it bobbed upwards for a moment, as the air inside kept it afloat. I could not see Nara and Isadore in the shadows. It rose to one side and then started to sink, water pouring over the back. And then they were gone, leaving only a steady stream of bubbles and some floating puppet parts.

"No," I said.

Officer Cohen had already recovered from his state of narcosis and had been running after me towards the truck when it had gone over. He stopped now, and stood dumbfounded again. "Call an ambulance," he said to the insects at his feet.

"Oh my god," whispered the rookie policeman. This was his second crime scene, the first having been earlier today when they found the abandoned van with the safe full of porn inside. He had been a part of the force combing the carnival with pictures of Nara, and dearly hoped he would rescue her from the evil clutches of her nefarious captor.

"My god. . ." Cohen muttered as he arrived at the edge of the bridge to my left.

"Ohmygodohmygodohmygod," Isadore wailed as the truck filled with water.

A word about God: He is not a he. He is not a she. He's actually only one of many beings that are much larger than us. To hold this being responsible for our creation and survival and also consider them the extent of *everything* is to confuse the issue a bit. It's too small. There are lots of planes of existence—if you want to call them that—in this big ole Omniverse. To help you understand this, it is best if you try and see the world exponentially, that is increasing and decreasing by exponents, like two to the power of . . . ahh forget it, the math we're using is wrong anyway. The numbers are too simple, too limiting, but kudos to all those mathematicians for trying. Reality is nothing like that. Let me just say that God's level is more than ours, but includes our Chia Pet of a universe as part of the fabric that makes up their being.

So, why does God keep us in that water filled bowl with our thin green paste spread on our beige porcelain lamb shape? Why do they keep us at all?

Because they need us. We are essential to keeping God's reality intact. Our physical working of this planet, this solar system, the rapid growths and deaths, all kinetic motion in general, we keep them trucking. Our whole universe, from tip to tip, *is* God. When we feel bad, God feels bad too. War and strife and doubtfulness of their very existence keep God up at night like a root beer float right before bedtime.

A root beer float is made of ice cream, usually vanilla, and root beer. Two things that taste great alone, but spell indigestion when consumed together.

Why can't we live in peace? Why would God let all this happen? Well, the truth is, we can. But war generates a whole lot of energy, and until that energy comes from somewhere else, specifically, our balancing point in the Omniverse, then we will continue to kill each other for inane reasons.

As for what God looks like, well, the shape you most likely wouldn't recognize, so it's almost pointless for me to describe it. I can tell what they *don't* look like. They don't look like a human, and they don't look like a football. It might help you to know that ours is a pretty happy god; not socially awkward with the other gods, has lots of hobbies, and is one hell of a lover. They've got a great sense of humor too, but I'll get to that later. And when we die, just as our physical mass gets recycled by the planet, normally, our consciousness gets recycled through God so that we can continue on.

I say normally, but that's not what happened to me. I started leaking out of God from all sides, like sweat and smell, essentially free and hopelessly lost. And now, here I am, watching God watch the neighboring gods discuss whether or not there is anything greater than themselves, watching that which is greater watch them.

The wind is whipping about me, a lone cricket is crawling over a piece of broken concrete, and I am looking down at the black depths. I look forward for one long second at the stars blazing above the dark trees in the distance.

Nara, I think. But my lips don't move.

I cannot bear the thought of her dying and me being left alone up here on this shit-soaked bridge. I see the rest of my days stretch out along either side of me. They are long, lonely, fearful days, full of regret and sadness. Full of crying jags in the shower, leading ultimately to my terminal hospitalization where they pump me full of even more medication, if that is even possible. Oh, the lonely. To have seen a shaft of light from under the gas station bathroom door, to have seen an escape, a way to be a different person, a new person, reborn through the understanding and willing of someone else. And now to see it gone again, so quickly as to leave me static and frozen in time.

I inch my white sneakers towards the edge. I have to do something. Just this once, I have to do something about all the evils that surround me. I could save her, that would be good.

"Hey! Stop!" Officer Cohen calls, but I don't hear him.

And under the water, Isadore is kicking away, pulling himself to the surface. He feels a strong current pulling him down the river. His entire body is bruised, so he can't swim very well. He bursts to the surface, but is carried downstream and into the darkness.

"Somebody help me!" he croaks.

I do a couple quick dashes back and forth, trying to imagine throwing myself over. Crikey, this is even harder to watch this time. I want to yell "JUST DO IT!" at myself, but in truth, I don't want me to jump at all. I should yell "THINK OF SOMETHING ELSE DUM DUM!" at myself, but it wouldn't do any good. What has happened, what will happen, is what always happened at this moment.

I leap headfirst over the edge, my wolf sweatshirt rising up to expose my soft white belly. My arms stretch out in front of me, like a superhero on his way to the rescue of the needy. I am on a rescue mission yes, but I am not flying.

Clearly, I am falling, and with increasing speed.

CHAPTER TWENTY-FOUR

A Part of Everything
or
Infinity Schminity

We often wonder why we do anything. Why do we get up in the morning to work some job to earn money to wake up in a house that is close to our job, so that we can work it more? Or why we shave every day knowing that it will just grow back the next day. Why we bother reading anything at all, when we know that any knowledge gained will most likely be taken with us to the grave. Why have children when we know that they're just going to grow up to hate us? Why jump off of a bridge to save someone we just met earlier that day? Why bother doing anything really. Why does anyone bother doing anything when death is the only reward?

Well, that I can answer for you.

We have to keep God going, don't we? So God is very careful to give us some beautiful things that let us see, just for a minute, how good we got it. And why do we have to keep God going? Why does God exist besides being a nice home for us, and giving us something to look up to?

Near as I can tell, the gods are very busy doing *something*. They are constantly moving, and I get the feeling that if they stopped, something very, very, very bad would happen. So God's function, if you will, is to keep moving. Is function the same as purpose? For now, I will just say, yes. One less tummy ache caused by doubt for God.

I have gathered through my observations that God's true purpose has something to do with their impenetrable black holes. If I could just figure out how to get through one of them. I probably just have to focus and wait. Let everything slow down to an imperceptible crawl. That's a lot of focus. Which, as you surely know by now, is not one of my strong suits.

God generally doesn't have time to focus on us much, can you imagine trying to pinpoint one cell in your body and think about it? But right now they are looking at one human. Which to them, is similar to looking at something smaller than a sub-atomic particle.

At this point in the whirling fragments of time, they are watching Nara with great curiosity and apprehension.

Nara saw the bridge disappear above her, and then the water come flooding in from all sides. She had seen Isadore smack against the back of the truck beside her when they hit the water, felt the intense pain all through her ribs and lower back on impact, which must be broken, and then Isadore's wide-eyed horror as the truck filled with water and began to sink. The water soon covered her body, with just her head exposed. It was then that the panic had set in, that she had decided she *was* actually quite used to being Jahanara and would very much like to continue being her. It's surprising the perspective death brings. The water was up to her chin. With her last breath, she closed her eyes and yelled "Fuuuuuuuuck!" as loud as she could, and for a very long time. And then the water rushed over her head and all was dark and blackness.

Isadore had floated before her for a moment, hovering in a swath of cold dark water, and then started kicking his way out of the truck, past the ghostly waving limbs of the puppets as the truck rolled and twisted in the current.

Now she was alone.

She could see a dim light from above, casting shadows that spun slowly over her. "Everyone dies alone," she thought. And then idly, "I wonder how long I can hold my breath? I remember someone said once that you never actually run out of oxygen, it's the build-up of carbon dioxide that kills you. Not helpful, Brain, think of something!" Then, as her lungs started to burn, only one thought came to her, "Oh please God, don't let me die." She couldn't help it. She can't help it.

I would love to tell her that dying ain't so bad. But I don't really know having never died in the more traditional manner. I know that soon there will be a chemical released from her brain that will replay all of her favorite memories and give her a pleasant feeling of oneness, a nice farewell on God's part. But after that... I imagine being recycled *could* be nice, but oh Nara...

While above, I fall and it is like I am falling into the sun.

I see that point where I died shining before me like a hundred stars. I haven't ever made it past this point. I have stumbled in my ethereal form into the future, but it was not my future. So there is an axis here, a moment that I am chained to, despite my being a part of *the All*. My being was supposed to be recycled and redistributed—instead I oozed out, and got lost. And this point blazing below me was the bad directions that led me to the nowhere I am now.

I have slowed everything down. But not to relish in its euphorics.

This is some kind of masochistic torture, this moment with me falling from above and her running out of air below. If only I had taken those swimming lessons at the recreation center my mother had tried so hard to get me to attend, I might have pulled off an expert swan dive and swum down to her and avoided all of this. Even a cannonball! What if I had landed nice and tight, and then swam over and pulled her broken body free, or at least died with her. There an infinite number of "what-ifs."

I swing my imagined hands through the submerged Puppetmobile like a tennis racket through smoke, but with less effect. I let out my mute ghost moan for no one to hear. A silent scream to shake the world—still the water rises around her, and still she is stuck there.

I can see only one way out of this. I have to fill Nara with as much of me as I can, and use our combined strength to get her out of that truck. I have to try, even though all day, for countless days, I have observed and done nothing. I have to try and change the Omniverse to work in my favor, not because it owes me, but because I owe it to her to try.

Having never meditated before, I find it hard to focus on one single thing or person. Ah, but she does make it so easy. Her fingernails, her memories, the last precious bits of oxygen coursing through her blood. I feel myself as each strand of hair weaving in the water around her silent beautiful face. The tiny mites in her eyebrows, more, I need more, her heart, pumping fiercely, the blood cells, rushing through.

I am the ratdog in her stomach.

How is that for romanti—

Agh!

This is new. Something is wrong!

Something is really, really wrong! Everything is happening at once!

It's like I'm being pulled in, it was never like this before . . . like a vacuum tube . . . but strong and . . . I feel every atom I leave behind ripping from me like a thousand needles through my flesh.

What the hell is happening?

Oh no . . .

She's dying.

The last bubble of life rises towards the surface from her terrified mouth. My world is getting smaller and smaller and I am getting trapped in her. Like a black hole, like a Tilt-A-Whirl, like . . .

No! I don't want to die again.

I think I made a mistake here, I need to go back, pull myself out of her and rethink this one through. Try it again, like before. But I can't. It won't let go and I can't stop it from pulling me in! I can feel my being pulled away from all those alien creatures, those gaseous planets. I am shrinking fast, already at the edge of our universe, and now, I'm getting sucked back into God like a toilet flushing . . .

Somebody help me!

The farewell chemicals from her brain are releasing. I feel them shooting through and the memories flooding over me, over us. If it weren't for the intense pain and awareness of being dragged across the universe by my intangible rectum I would sit back and enjoy them.

Here's Nara's brother, sitting with a bleeding knee and looking up at me and smiling. Her long legs in the back of a pickup truck as it bumps down a logging road, watching the stars vibrate. And the moon, the big red moon as her father's hand squeezes our shoulder, stern and proud. The swingset, the potty, the first pack of cigarettes, all of it. Like fireworks coming from every direction.

I am at the edge of the Milky Way, with its long spiral arms, and now I am inside it. I try to kick my way out, but the pull is relentless and stronger than anything I have seen. Stronger than gravity, than magnetism, than the as yet undiscovered jellfluism.

Oh Nara. What have I done? I failed us again. And this time, for good.

I'm at the galaxies surrounding ours, and there's no time for a goodbye to all the creatures I have been there, I'm already in our solar system, compressed towards Earth. God! Help me! I don't want to be recycled!

Okay, now I'm afraid.

I'm afraid.

Oh, how I'm afraid.

Help!

Everything is light.

Hi.

It's Nara here.

I know what you're thinking. Oh sweet Christ, not again.

But don't worry, I'm not gonna make either of us live through that day I died in a van full of puppets more than once. I gotta say, the way I'd have told it, there'd be a lot less useless trivia.

As for how I got to be here, talking to you in the first place . . . Well, Hank's big plan backfired.

What I mean is, thanks to Hank's efforts, cramming himself and the entire cosmos into me at the moment I croaked, I took a part of everything with me. He glued us together and for a split second, it was Hank and his awareness of everything, and then me, all trapped in my little body. It was a lot.

And as you can imagine, the awareness of everything that ever existed can't just pass easily through one point, in this case one of the black holes of our God, so Hank and I and all the rest of it got barfed, or like, shit out real fast. Imagine trying to eat an entire ocean of that gas station nacho cheese all in one sitting. Gnarly.

I think we might have caused God some damage, sorry God. Don't worry, she seems okay. Though you might notice things are sort of fucked up for a while. Our bad.

Maybe all that fusing together of Hank and me is why I can talk to you now, I dunno. What's more important is that I wanted to tell you where all the souls go, where I am now. I wish I could draw you a picture, but this is what we got, so bear with me . . .

It looks like this, our God and everything inside her, well, she's just one of many gods, a whole lot of them. Lots. So our God follows this one track, like a subway train, pretty much indefinitely, round and round, over and over, looping up and then down. Meaning that the whole shebang, *The All* looks a little like a figure of eight on its side. Infinity. Which is a nice idea. I always liked that symbol. Not enough to get it tattooed on my lower back or anything, but it's pretty.

So when things die, the gods shit a small part of them out into the middle of the track through their black holes.

The problem was that when Hank died, he ended up on the wrong side of the track. A part of the whole thing, except on the outside, looking in. In order to get through, you have to die for real. What happened to him is pretty fucked up, but I'll give it a shot...

You're not going to be shat by God until you are whole. Hank was a lot of things when he died, but he definitely wasn't whole. He had to get over being afraid all the time first. I know he thought it was the medication that was preventing him from joining the rest of us, but that was bullshit by the way. He was so sure of it too. People can believe almost anything. From where I sit now, it's clear that reality is very subjective. Just because you believe something, it doesn't mean that's the way it is.

I wasn't whole either, not even close. I had to learn not to be bored all the time. But when Hank and I fused, we created a whole being. That doesn't mean we're soulmates, or any of that nonsense, any two souls probably would've worked. I guess we cheated in a way, but apparently existence likes cheaters.

As for what's inside this weird-matrix-infinity thing, I guess you could call this middle part heaven, because when we first saw it, we were pretty blown away. So all these things, these little beings, us and all other creatures, animate and inanimate, hang out here. And when you're in here, you remember everything you've been and you can talk about it to all your friends. And then a God comes and asks you if you want to venture into himself and your energy gets used to make something, which is pretty fun.

And this part I love, when you've been *everything* inside one God, then you know everything, so you *become* that God. And that God goes back into the mix to become something else. Seriously. It happened to this guy I knew from high school. He died when he was only fifteen. I guess he was pretty eager to skip being human, as he had a lot invested in the afterlife.

Which means that every little piece of everything is vitally important. You matter.

If something was missing or went wrong, then the whole system wouldn't work, and it would start to turn itself inside out, which is bad. We'd all be like Hank, on the outside looking in.

And what's on the outside?

Good question.

The answer is nothing.

Then what is nothing?

Nothing is what happens if it ever fell apart. If the works clogged and everything just stopped. See, gods are pretty smart. They would immediately start rebuilding, but it wouldn't be near as cool. It'd be a whole lot smaller for one. Nothing is whatever happens while everything gets put back together.

Hey man, don't blame me, it's the English language that's lacking.

Oh yeah, in case you're curious, Isadore, that little shit-for-brains, he died too. He drowned. But lucky for him, he *was* whole.

Now I know what you're thinking . . . Isadore? How the fuck was that little twerp whole and we weren't? Well, it all comes down to the moment when he shoved the puppet-guy, Lloyd, off the Ferris wheel as it was going down. Ya see, Isadore needed to learn to do something on his own, and for someone else. Which he did right there in that moment. Lucky little shit. So lil Isadore went through, where he is quite happy and looking forward to becoming a Sadeekinian alien manta ray thing.

Anyway . . .

I just wanted to say that everything will work out in the end.

I would say more than that, but I know that being curious is what holds this whole thing together, we need that energy to keep things moving. Without that, it'd be a pretty dull place, let me tell you. Everywhere, on all the planets besides Earth, things are wandering around wondering. Of course, sometimes this makes them do some totally bonkers shit, but it definitely keeps things movin'.

And I guess, like, while I am here doling out the life lessons . . .

People have a lot of things they think about other people . . . as in, *I am never going to talk to them again, because they said that thing that one time* . . . But know that most things people say are about themselves and ego isn't everything, so just let it go. Just forgive them and move on because you will be so much happier and you're actually a part of them anyway. I was a very angry human, and I see now that was just me being angry at myself.

Oh, another thing . . . once you get on a roll it's hard to stop . . . Maybe I see why Hank was so chatty now.

When I was alive I was so bored all the time. I'm not bored now. In fact, I'd say what I feel is the opposite of boredom. I thought of myself as a pretty imaginative girl, but what I found after we got shat out is more than I could possibly imagine and then some. So at least know that you have something to look forward to. It won't being boring forever.

I'm still getting used to this being able to jump to a bunch of places all at once, but Hank is here with everyone and everything else coaching me through it.

Right now, we're watching these alien snail-things the size of Manhattan Island mate in mid-air. It's pretty cool.

"They look like Zeppelins."

Yeah, sorta. I think they look more like creepy crystalized turds, myself.

"Hey Nara."

Yes, Hank,

"I—I don't think they're creepy."

Seriously? I mean, look at them! That one has sixteen eyes, and each one is moving in a different direction! Ick!

"Naw, what I mean is—"

Uhg! And the pink one just puked on the blue one's face! I know it's a mating ritual and all, but *look* at that!

"I'm not afraid anymore. Of anything."

That's good, Hank. Happy to hear it.

Gimme one sec . . .

Well, I guess this is goodbye, for now.

Don't you be afraid either, okay?

(not) The End.